AUGUST REUNION

JULIET MADISON

BLOODHOUND BOOKS

Print ISBN: 978-1-917705-13-4

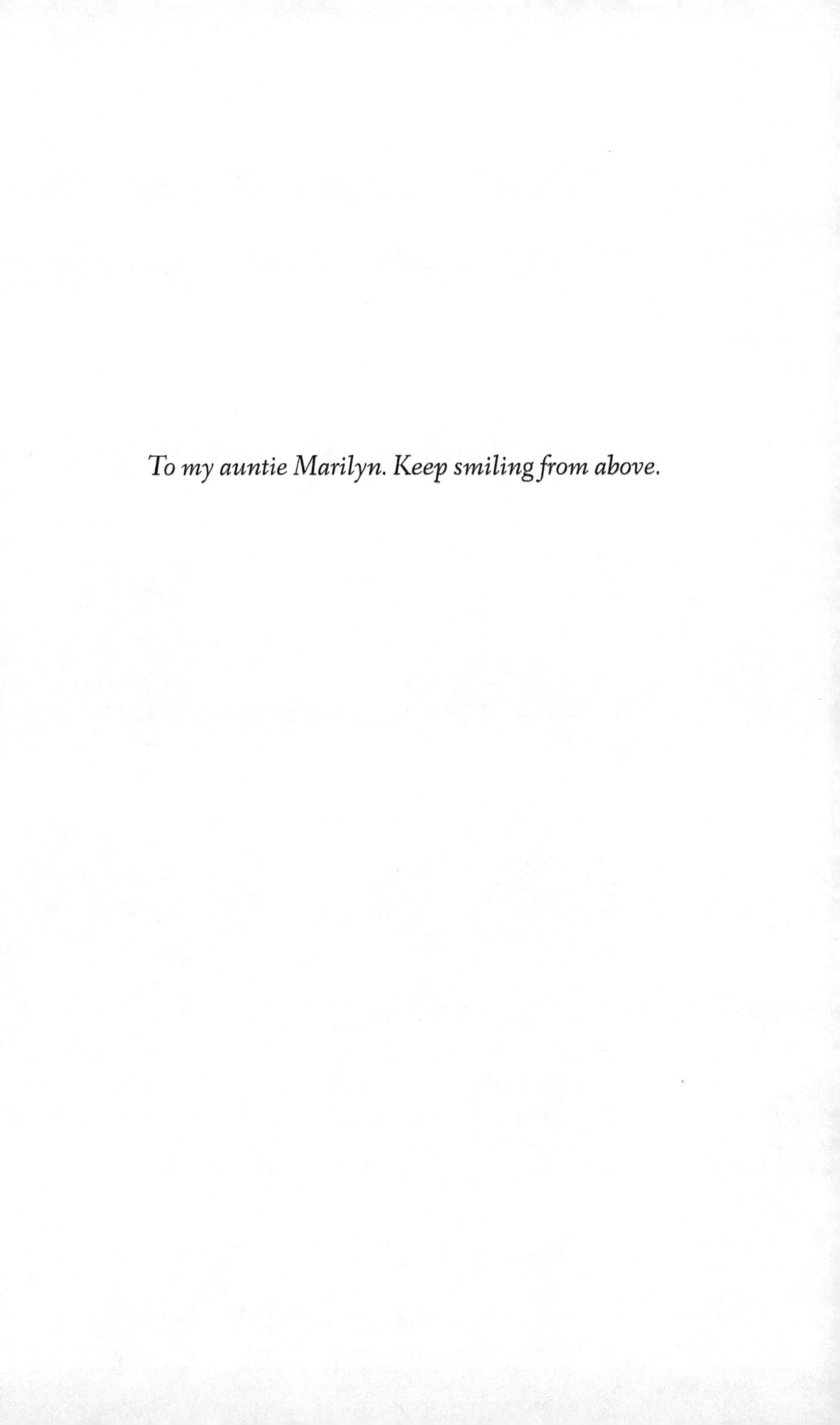

To my auntie Marilyn. Keep smiling from above.

CHAPTER ONE

When Katy McKenzie opened the door for her internet date, she had no idea she'd also be opening the door for an unexpected visitor, making it a night to remember for all the wrong reasons. After years of looking after the needs of others, both personally and professionally, she was finally taking steps to take care of her own. Starting with her first foray into dating since her divorce nine months ago.

'Nice place you've got here,' Jon – or Jonno as he'd mentioned his friends liked to call him – said, as he wandered around the entry hall of the double-storey home with ocean views, after they'd enjoyed dinner at a fancy restaurant. 'You sure you don't have an abundant side hustle as well as being a nurse?' He eyed her with eager curiosity.

Katy shook her head and hung her handbag on the wall hook. 'My inheritance helped me out a bit.'

'Oh, of course, you mentioned about your parents. Sorry. Again.' He came close and touched his hand to her forearm, making her skin warm.

She shrugged. 'Thanks. All good. Over a decade ago now.'

'Still, I'm sure the grief never goes away.'

No, it never did.

'Can I get you a drink? Non-alcoholic of course.' She winked. Jon, a personal trainer, was a self-confessed health-nut. No sugar, alcohol, or what he called 'empty calories'. She'd checked out his staff profile on the website of the gym he worked at, to suss him out and make sure he seemed genuine before accepting his offer of a date.

'No thanks, I'm happy to just hang out with you and chat, or...' He ran his hand up her arm and brought it to her hair, sliding a finger between the silky brown strands.

Katy cleared her throat and her belly fluttered. She was happy to just 'chat, or...' also. It was about time. She smiled and instead of giving him the grand tour as she'd planned (minus the walk-in pantry filled with salty snacks and sugary treats), she allowed her hand to drift to his spare one, entwining their fingers together. As though his gentle caress of her hair followed by her cheek was an invitation, she responded with a caress of her own, trailing her other hand over his sculpted shoulder and around the back of his neck, drawing him closer. She liked how, although keen, he hadn't launched himself at her, instead waiting for her to make the next move.

He returned her smile, and slowly, she leaned closer to his face, as he did the same with hers. The thrill of the kiss reached her nerves before their lips even touched... a tingling on her skin, an expectant energy buzzing in the air between them, until everything intensified as she welcomed his lips to hers. It was like being a teenager all over again. After being married for so long, her now ex-husband's kisses had become more like obligatory pecks, and she'd forgotten what it felt like to be fully immersed in the moment, of *really* being kissed.

Without separating their hands and lips from each other, they shuffled backwards, towards the living room, Katy's heart racing with each new sensation and the anticipation of what might unfold next. The logical part of her brain didn't want to have a hasty first date and make any mistakes, but somehow it felt right, and she'd been chatting online and over the phone to him for two months and they got on well. She was a grown woman and deserved to enjoy herself and live in the moment.

When they reached the couch that overlooked the beach through the floor-to-ceiling windows, a view of Serendipity retreat in the distance, they leaned back against the soft cushions and Katy inhaled deeply before kissing him again. A ringing sound distracted her momentarily and she thought it might've been Jon's phone, but realised it was the doorbell when it was followed by firm knocks that became louder and more urgent. She broke away from him and straightened up.

Disoriented, she glanced towards the entry hall. 'It's late, I don't know who that could be.' She stood. 'Maybe kids playing knock and run.' She shook her head. 'Sorry. I'll just check.'

Jon followed her to the door where she looked through the peephole.

'Oh my God. Kane.' She glanced briefly at Jon. 'My brother.'

She unlocked the door and opened it, a gush of cool night air rushing in just before her brother did. His face was red and puffy, his eyes filled with despair.

He flung his arms around her and then pulled back, holding on to her arms. 'I've been trying to text and call, but I didn't hear back!' he said with urgent frustration.

'I've had my phone on silent for a few hours while we were out,' she explained, gesturing to her date.

Kane's eyes widened on seeing Jon, and he exhaled as he dropped his head. 'Oh man, sorry.'

'It's fine,' Katy said. 'Are you okay?'

Kane paced back and forth and ran a hand through his greasy hair. 'I just... had an issue. And needed... something.'

Katy's heart plummeted. 'You didn't, did you?'

He shook his head vehemently, like a child adamant that he hadn't raided the cookie jar. 'Like we agreed, I called you first.' He glanced awkwardly at Jon and Katy turned to him also, her date scratching his head as though unsure what to do.

Sorry, she mouthed.

Jon grabbed his keys from the hall table and gestured to the door. 'I should get going and leave you two to, ah, discuss whatever needs to be discussed.' He gave a nod.

Katy approached him. 'No, it's okay, you don't have to leave.'

'Yeah, sorry, man, I didn't mean to interrupt.' Kane did his best to offer an apology but his voice was still high-pitched, which always meant he was near breaking point.

Jon offered an accepting smile to Kane. 'It's okay. Katy, I had an amazing night, thank you. We can catch up again another time,' he suggested, turning to the still-open door.

Katy's heart plummeted again. Concern for her brother, but also frustration and disappointment that the one night she decided to move forward with her personal life it was interrupted. It was a sign. She should've stuck to her original plan: no dates, no men, no relationships until her one-year 'divorce-a-versary', which was only three months away anyway. That way she could feel a more certain sense of closure, have time to rediscover herself as an individual, and hopefully avoid repeating her history.

'Okay. I'm sorry,' she said softly. Jon nodded and closed the door behind him, and she turned to face Kane.

Her twin brother burst into tears and she held him close. 'Come on, tell me all about it,' she said as she ushered him to the couch, cushions haphazard from the passion of moments ago. It was probably a good thing he'd interrupted them now and not in half an hour's time.

Katy had thought her brother had turned a corner with his drug addiction after his latest stint in a new rehab program had been wonderful for him. But clearly, he still needed help, and he still needed her. Many addicts didn't have family support, and with their parents gone and no cousins or close relatives, she was all he had. He was all *she* had. She had to keep helping him. She couldn't lose her brother too.

CHAPTER TWO

Katy tripped on the step as she entered through the back door of Tarrin's Bay Medical Clinic. Her phone flew from her grasp and landed on the floor, the screen cracking like a lightning bolt.

'Crap!' She bent and picked it up. She'd have to see if she'd have time to take it to a repair place on her lunch break.

'It's only Monday morning and already the swear words are let loose?' said Joyce, one of the receptionists, pouring herself a cup of tea.

'Hopefully it won't progress to other swear words by the end of the day,' Katy said with a sigh.

'Take a breath and start again,' Joyce said. 'Do it with me... in...' she gestured to Katy and made a show of inhaling deeply, '...and out.'

Katy obliged. It wouldn't fix her screen or her other problems but it did help to calm her nerves, if only slightly. Joyce, with her years of experience dealing with patients, some who could be difficult, was a pro at making people feel at ease.

'Tea, coffee?' Joyce offered.

'I'll have whatever you're having, please, Joyce.' Katy smiled. 'How was your weekend?'

'Tiring but happy. Those young grandkids of mine sure know how to give my ageing body a workout.'

'I bet. Thanks,' she said as Joyce handed her a cup of herbal tea.

'And your weekend?'

Katy glanced upwards. 'Umm, let's just say, it was... eventful. I need another weekend to recover from the weekend!'

'Well, make sure you take some time out at lunch today.'

She held up her phone. 'Depends how long this takes.'

'Can it wait till tomorrow? If you can still read the screen through the cracks, for now?' Joyce suggested.

Katy shrugged, looking at the half-written text message she'd been typing to Kane. 'Guess so. I'll see how the day goes. Thanks, Joyce.' She left the staff kitchen and walked into the extension that had been built two years ago to house a nurses clinic with three patient beds, two private consultation rooms, a quiet room, and a waiting room that doubled as a workshop space when they held health education sessions.

> You sure you'll be ok on your own? Let me know if you need anything, or come visit me at work.

She finished her text to Kane. He replied:

> I'll be fine. Please don't worry.

She was still looking at the cracked screen as she placed her tea on the desk and put her bag in her locker in the medication and storage area.

'Good morning to you too, my dear.'

Katy's gaze shot up. 'Oh, I didn't see you there behind the desk! Sorry. Good morning. How are you?'

Her colleague, Jenna, nurses' receptionist and all-round helping hand, smiled, her round face lighting up. Her frizzy blonde curls poking out in all directions like she was the sun itself shining. 'Just had my coffee so I'm feeling great! Ask me again in a few hours though.' She chuckled. 'You seem distracted, is everything okay?'

Katy held up her phone. 'First world problems. But, um, Kane showed up on Saturday night in distress.'

Jenna closed some files and placed them in the document tray. 'Is he okay? Weren't you meeting that new guy on Saturday?'

'I'm not sure. And yes. It all happened at once.'

'Oh dear.' Jenna eyed her with concern, as though waiting to see if she wanted to mention anything more. Working with her best friend from school meant they always made time for personal chit-chat as well as professional, but Jenna had the knack of being caring and curious without being nosy.

Katy glanced back to make sure no patients were arriving early, then leaned closer to Jenna. 'He almost had a relapse,' she whispered. 'Tried to call me but I was on my date, so he turned up later that night, just when things were...'

'Getting good?' Jenna assumed, and Katy nodded.

'Damn, girl.' Jenna shook her head. 'And so soon after his time in rehab.'

'Yeah. We talked a lot yesterday after he'd had a good night's sleep, though I tossed and turned most of the night. I've helped him make a simple plan of activities for today while I'm at work, and he's set up an urgent Zoom call with his rehab counsellor.'

'That's good. That's all you can do. Keep guiding him in the right direction.' Jenna placed a hand on Katy's arm.

An uncomfortable fullness rose up in her chest; unspent

emotion wanting to overflow and release itself, but now was not the time nor place. Her eyes stinging, she blinked hard. 'What's on today?'

'A few iron infusions, the usual vaccinations, injectables instruction session, and probably the usual walk-ins. Will you be okay for the teen health workshop tomorrow afternoon?'

Katy nodded. 'It'll only make me two hours late home, I'll let Kane know.' Katy loved her job and the lifestyle friendly hours. No more long hours or night shifts working in the hospital. When the opening for a Monday to Friday, nine to four job (with occasional overtime) had come up at the perfect time, right when she and Erik had decided to separate, she'd jumped at the chance to start afresh in the town she'd grown up in. She'd waited for her tenants' lease to be up then moved into her investment property that had been bringing in income to pay the remaining mortgage after her inheritance had paid a hefty deposit. It was time for her to live life the way she wanted, instead of fitting in with her ex-husband's goals.

'And more importantly.' Jenna rubbed her hands together. 'Will you also be okay for this weekend's reunion?'

In the haze of her new dramas, she'd forgotten all about it until now. 'Is it really this weekend?'

Jenna nodded. 'Lexi is spending the night at a friend's house, so I'm looking forward to a night out. Even if it is with the old school crowd.'

Katy gave a vague nod, but her sense of overwhelm increased. It would be a busy week and she was worried how Kane would cope. He already knew about the school reunion but was refusing to attend, not being proud of how his life had turned out so far. 'I hope so. Let me see how things are with Kane by then.'

'Who knows, maybe he'll decide to come after all.' Jenna

held up her palms. 'Besides, don't leave the only other single woman on her own in a crowded high school hall!'

'Are we really the only single ones left?'

'Think so, from what my research tells me. Not that it matters, but still. I bet the old gang will be showing off their partners with a smug smile on their faces... "Look who I nabbed!" and "Yes, fifteen years together and still going strong!"' Jenna huffed. 'Idiots.'

Katy chuckled. Her phone chimed. She normally kept it in her bag at work, but had it in her pocket today in case Kane needed her.

> Where do you keep the paracetamol? Got a headache.

Katy sighed.

> Cupboard above the fridge. Let me know if it doesn't help.

Oh boy. This was going to be a long, mentally draining day, she could tell. She just hoped she could help Kane get sorted and back to his usual routine in Sydney sooner rather than later, not only for his well-being, but for hers too.

CHAPTER THREE

—————

'The sleeves are too frilly, aren't they.' It wasn't a question. Jenna stood in front of the mirror in Katy's bedroom, her lips twisting, turning side to side as though doing so would change the appearance of her kaftan-type tunic that she wore over black slimline pants that tightly hugged her curvy hips.

'They're fine, and it suits you,' Katy reassured.

'Probably too much chiffon. And too patterned, like it's too busy. And frills. Did I mention frills?'

Katy held on to her friend at arm's length. 'Honestly, you always look lovely. There's nothing to worry about. It's just a school reunion.' Katy was comfortable in a simple black slinky dress with her hair tied back in a claw clip. But Jenna wasn't Jenna without bright colours, patterns, and... frills.

'If you say so. And it does go with my frizzy hair.' Jenna sighed. 'Has it really been twenty years?' She shook her head in disbelief.

'Apparently so. Crazy, huh?'

'Yep. Feels like only yesterday we were riding our skateboards at deathly speed down the hills, before skate ramps even existed. Or more accurately, *you* were, and I was sitting on mine holding on for dear life trying not to fall off.'

Katy laughed. 'Those were the days. I miss my skateboard. I really should get back into it. Might help me arrive at work more quickly.'

'Ha. I dare you. Skateboarding nurse arrives to work with grazed knees requiring expert band-aiding.' Jenna chuckled. 'Plus, it's in the Olympics now. So you never know, you could even get a gold medal one day.' She winked.

'I think any Olympic aspirations I may have had are long gone. A simple, enjoyable life is all I'm after now.'

'Me too,' Jenna said softly. 'Me too.'

She'd noticed her friend had been looking sad sometimes. Nothing major, just a slight hint of... something... underneath all the smiles and laughter. 'You okay?' Katy asked. 'You really do look great, you know.'

Jenna shrugged. 'Thanks. I don't know, it's just...' Her eyes held a sheen and her gaze rose to the ceiling for a moment, which Katy had noticed often happened with patients when they were trying to process information or find words to describe how they were feeling. Jenna sat on the bed and it bounced a little. 'I feel like a remnant of who I used to be. Like a shell or a... fossil. Yes.' She stood. 'I'm a fossil, Katy. A frumpy, frizzy, frilly fossil!' She gave a firm nod.

Katy didn't know whether to laugh, commiserate, or defy her declaration. She bit her lip and slung an arm around her friend. 'Oh, don't be silly. Anyway, I happen to like fossils. They're fascinating.'

'So, I'm a fascinating fossil?'

'Indeed. Shall we excavate this fossil and show her off to the alumni of Tarrin's Bay High School?' Katy held out her elbow and Jenna hooked her (frilly) arm through.

'Let's do this.' She nodded, this time with a big smile. 'I for one am proud to tell everyone that after twenty years I not only work in healthcare administration but am the proud mother of a sixteen-year-old daughter I raised on my own, thank you very much.'

'And so you should be. You're an amazing mother and the best co-worker I could ask for.'

Jenna leaned in and squished her voluptuous side into Katy's skinny one, and they walked out into the hall and down the stairs, stopping by the living room where Kane sat in front of the television.

'You sure you don't want to come?' Katy asked her brother. 'There's still time, we can wait for you to get ready.'

Kane paused the TV show and turned his head to face them. 'You two look great. And no. Thanks anyway. I'm all set to binge watch this new show.' He gestured to the TV with the remote.

Part of her hoped he'd reconsider and join them, remember the good old days, but part of her was glad he was staying at home. Less risk of beating himself up with comparisons and feeling triggered and in need of... something. He'd been reasonably stable since arriving a week ago, and she didn't want to rock the boat. 'Okay. Enjoy, and remember...'

'You're only a phone call away, yep, got it.' He gave a thumbs up and returned his focus to the TV, pressing play and putting an end to any more discussion.

When Katy parked in the high school car park, jittery butterflies danced around her belly. She hadn't realised until now that she was just as nervous as Jenna. A few people from school still lived in the area and she often saw them around, but many didn't, and although they'd be wearing name tags, she hoped she'd be able to recognise everyone. It was like the first day of school all over again, only with the baggage of memories instead of a backpack of future dreams.

They were about to walk up the steps to the main hall when a car approached the school entrance. When it stopped, the engine still humming, a man wearing a classy tailored suit of navy-blue with a faint shimmer to it stepped out. Katy's mouth hung open. It was someone she thought would definitely *not* be attending the reunion because he was overseas and had better things to do. But somehow he was here, in that amazing suit, stepping out of a classy Uber, and looking right at her for the first time in almost two decades.

CHAPTER FOUR

Dan Dexter was only going to his school reunion because he was in the country for two other more important reasons. At least that's what he told himself. A work commitment and a family issue. They were top priority, this wasn't. Might as well attend while he was in the area, though. It had nothing to do with the fact Katy McKenzie might be there, although it would be *nice* to see her again, say 'Hi, how've you been these past twenty years?' while trying not to remember the Awkward Incident when they were sixteen years old. He was pretty sure she was married anyway, so it wasn't like he was looking for one last shot with the first girl he'd ever had strong feelings for. Not at all. Too much time had passed. He'd moved on. Very much moved on. And all his past classmates surely knew that as, unlike in high school where he'd sat on the sidelines, his life was now in the public eye. At least to those who were active on social media, watched television, and read self-help books. Which would be one hundred per cent of those attending tonight – the active on social media part, at least; he wasn't sure how many read self-help books.

Dan tapped his foot on the floor of the car as his driver drove into the high school entrance. His mind always did this, go at full speed, round and round, whenever he had a big event coming up, or an important appearance or, as it so happened, a school reunion. He had learned over the years to trust himself and be confident in who he was, but sometimes that ugly self-doubt and imposter syndrome would creep in and try to sabotage his usually calm and charming demeanour. Especially when hit with a thousand memories on seeing the old school building where so much of who he was had been moulded and shaped. The lunchtimes spent sitting on the concrete steps eating cheese sandwiches, which sometimes got flipped up in the air and onto the ground by a passing bully, taught him resilience. The sport classes when he'd get puffed out after fifteen minutes playing basketball, taught him that sport wasn't his thing. The walk home with Katy and Kane, deciding whose house they would hang out at or where they would go skateboarding, until Kane found other friends and Katy started skateboarding with girls instead of the awkward chubby boy she'd known since they were babies, had taught him it was best to rely on himself.

But most of his learning had come *after* high school, when he got into university in Melbourne to study psychology, then did a master's degree, then a few short courses to add depth and specialty to his expertise and offer more to his clients. This had taught him that persistence, determination, hard work, *and* self-belief paid off. And it was with that awareness that he stepped confidently out of the car, ready to brave the faces of the past. He didn't expect the first face he'd see to be none other than Katy herself. He didn't believe in fate, but if it did exist, it sure as hell slapped him in the face at that moment. Okay, so he did want to reconnect with her, but more for curiosity and closure than anything else. He was ready for the next phase of his life and, as he taught his clients, closure and cutting cords from past attachments was crucial to moving forward and having success in future relationships.

Seeing her eyes though...

He gulped. That simple subtle beauty still graced her face, but with a maturity she had grown into perfectly. She didn't have a man on her arm, but that of Jenna Simons, all smiling and colourful.

For a moment he froze, taking her in, then cleared his throat and walked over to the pair, not able to withhold the big grin on his face, as one began forming on hers.

'I didn't think I'd see you here tonight!' Katy remarked, leaning towards him and giving him a quick hug. The welcoming touch was over before it began. He would have liked it to have lasted a moment longer, not being able to process the brief physical contact quickly enough and wondering if it had really happened.

'I didn't think *I'd* see me here tonight,' he replied. 'But as fate has it, other circumstances led to me being back in town, so here I am.' He held his palms out to the side.

Katy smiled but tilted her head. 'I thought you didn't believe in fate.'

Wow. She remembered the deep and meaningful (or D&M as they'd called it back in the day) they'd had on the beach late one New Year's Eve. A group of teens had watched the New Year's Eve fireworks together and they'd hung about longer than anyone else, laying on the sand and discussing the workings of the universe.

'I don't? I mean, I don't. Just a figure of speech.' He gave a nod and turned his focus to Jenna. 'Hi, Jenna, you look lovely.' He gave her a brief hug too.

'Thanks! I thought I was too frilly but Katy said I looked fine. Congrats on all your success,' Jenna said. 'I follow you on Instagram.'

'Oh, thanks, I would follow you back, but I have someone who does all my social media for me so I keep it purely professional.' He had strategic 'follows' recommended by his social media manager, and was advised not to have any personal connections on his public profiles, given his position as a popular celebrity dating coach. The amount of spam they had to block from people wanting a chance to date *him* was bizarre and ridiculous. He often thought, *If only they'd seen me eating lunch on those concrete school steps.* He hadn't wanted to be a celebrity, he'd only wanted to help people become more confident in themselves when dating, like he had wanted *and* achieved for himself. He hadn't known his accessible, practical tips and videos would go viral. It had started out as a bit of fun, making videos where he'd date himself to show examples: switching the camera between *real him* and *fake him* (sometimes dressed up as a *her*), and modelling conversation dos and don'ts. People thought it was hilarious, and then helpful, as he threw all the facades and unrealistic expectations out the window, advising people to get straight to the nitty-gritty and be authentic, while enhancing one's natural charm, as he called it.

'Dating Dan?' a gruff voice said from behind, and he turned to see a guy who looked vaguely familiar apart from the balding head that he hadn't had at school. The guy slapped him on the back. 'Love your work, man. Good stuff. Ladies.' He gave a nod to Katy and Jenna then walked up the same concrete steps where he'd slapped Dan's sandwich out of his hands over twenty years ago.

'Still an idiot,' Jenna whispered. 'Anyway, I think you're going to be popular tonight,' she said, as the three of them walked towards the entrance.

Dan took a deep breath. Maybe he shouldn't have come. He didn't want it to look like he was here for the accolades – *boring boy becomes badass celebrity*. Yes, he'd turned his life around and achieved his dreams, well, most of them, but he was sure many others here tonight had done the same. Singer Drew Williams was another success story from Tarrin's Bay High, but he hadn't been in the same year. And success wasn't defined by one's celebrity status, but their own individual goals and values.

Surprisingly, once they entered and received their name tags, apart from many eyeing him up or their mouths opening wide in surprise, and some coming over to meet his newfound self, Katy received the most attention. She had fulfilled her dream of becoming a nurse and many of the night's attendees were patients or had children who were patients.

'She's the only one my kid will let give her a needle,' said a woman he didn't remember. 'Works magic, she does. See you next week, Katy.' The woman wandered off and hugged someone else just as enthusiastically, as though they too were the best needle-injector in the world.

'I'm so glad you're doing what you set out to do,' Dan said, filled with genuine pride. She had always been good at fixing up his grazed knees from falling off skateboards and bruised elbows from tripping on bulging tree roots. If it wasn't for her, he probably wouldn't have found out he'd fractured his foot once, after trying to be all macho and saying, 'Ah, it's nothing – just a bruise.'

'Thanks, Dan. I love my job.' She smiled and her lips shone with a faint hint of pink.

'Kane not coming?'

Her eyes creased at the edges as she said, 'Nah, he couldn't make it.'

Dan wondered if Kane really couldn't, or just *didn't* want to make it. He had always rebelled from the usual traditions and expectations in the past. Maybe he hadn't changed much in twenty years. Dan had been in touch with Katy briefly when his parents had passed on the sad news that her parents had died in an awful accident. He had felt bad he hadn't been able to attend the funeral due to being on a two-week certification course in Florida. It was such a long time ago now, he didn't know whether to bring it up or ask how she was doing in that regard. But tonight was about fun and nostalgia, enjoying the memories of youth and how everyone had 'grown up'.

As they helped themselves to drinks from a passing waiter carrying a silver tray, a tall, fit looking woman approached with a wide smile on her face. It took a few seconds for Dan to remember her: Stephanie, a sporty girl he'd struck up an unlikely friendship with after the Awkward Incident with Katy – unlikely because he wasn't into sport and it was all she ever did or talked about, but she was great at making people feel comfortable and important no matter what.

'Dan!' She flung her long arms around him.

'Great to see you, still doing netball?'

She flicked her hand. 'Not anymore, I'm now into canoeing, among other things. In my spare time, that is, when I'm not teaching PE at a girls' school in Sydney.'

'Awesome, well done.'

She grinned. 'And,' she twisted her body side to side as though shy, 'I have you to thank for my recent...' she leaned forward and curved a hand around the side of her mouth as though about to tell a secret, '...dating success.'

'Oh, great to hear! You've found a good match?' He always enjoyed hearing success stories.

She flicked her hand again. 'Oh no, not yet, but your advice helped me get rid of the ones who don't deserve my time.' She chuckled.

He raised his eyebrows and nodded. 'That's good then. Don't settle.'

'I won't, believe me.' She held out her hand for a... fist bump? He tapped it with his, and she turned to Katy and Jenna.

'Hey, ladies. Looking great. Love those frills, Jenna.' She ruffled the sleeves on her arms, and Jenna looked both surprised and flattered. 'See you on the dance floor later!' She sashayed off, raising a glass and singing along to the retro music the DJ was playing.

Maybe it had been a good idea to attend after all. Dan's shoulders relaxed and his overactive mind settled as he enjoyed mingling with old friends, acquaintances, and not-friends, most of them partnered but not all.

'Dan, do you have any advice for, you know, couples who are already together but need to...' A woman who had appeared out of nowhere leaned closer to him as women often did when talking about things of a personal nature. '...reignite the spark?' The woman glanced back at a man standing and chatting to one of the waiters, and he recognised him from his school days, so she must be his partner or wife he'd brought along. 'Sorry, I shouldn't have bombarded you!' She tipped her head back and laughed. 'I'm Leanne. Just thought I'd catch you while Brett's in deep conversation with the waiter about football or some other nonsense.'

Dan smiled. 'No problem. It's not really my specialty at the moment, but I may be delving into this topic down the track. Stay tuned online.' He offered a courteous smile, but avoided elaborating. He was often cornered at events by people asking advice and it was hard for him to enjoy a night off without having to think and respond.

Katy seemed to notice the slight intrusion and grabbed his arm. 'Oh, remember this song? We have to dance, c'mon.'

He welcomed the interruption and followed her and Jenna to the dance floor, a couple of other old friends and their partners joining them. He didn't think the particular song held significance to them, but he was glad Katy had sensed his need to have a break from being Dating Dan. Now, on account of his dancing, he was probably Daggy Dan, but he didn't care.

'People are always asking me for medical advice!' Katy said over the music. 'Like, can I just have the night off, please?'

'Well, I do have this sore arm I've been meaning to get checked out,' he joked, 'maybe you can take a look?' He made a show of rubbing it and wincing.

She gave him a light whack on his supposedly sore arm and they laughed, revving up their dancing as a more upbeat song came on. As Dan danced, sang, laughed, and reminisced, he noticed the DJ glancing repeatedly at their group, but more so at Jenna, whose frills were frilling and flying and flapping everywhere as she let loose like it was her first night out in years. Which maybe it was. He discreetly nudged her and cocked his head to the DJ stand. Jenna eyed him curiously but followed his gaze, still dancing energetically. She glanced back at Dan and raised her eyebrows as though to say 'he's hot', and he gestured forward as though to say 'go tell him that!' Her dancing became stiffer as she subtly shook her head in defiance. It was a bit hard to give dating advice in a noisy auditorium, so he had to resort to high school antics of nudging, winking, and gesturing. When the song ended and the MC asked everyone to look up at the screen for a photo slideshow, he spoke into Jenna's ear. 'The DJ was totally checking you out.'

'Really, you think?' She fanned her face, from the flattery or heat from dancing he wasn't sure.

He gave an assured nod. 'I see he's got business cards on display, why not go over and take one, ask what the going rate is for an hour or two of DJing.'

'I couldn't!'

'Yes, you could!' Katy added her encouragement. 'I'm not the only one who needs to move on,' she said, and Dan wondered what had happened to her marriage. 'Go on!'

Jenna smiled nervously, picked up her drink, and walked in as non-awkward a way as possible over to the music table. She picked up a card and inspected it, nodding as the DJ spoke to her. She swayed side to side a little, the music still having residual effects, or perhaps it was her way of showing interest. The DJ smiled and gave her a wave as she walked back to them, grinning from ear to ear.

'I told him I had a friend who's looking for entertainment, which wasn't a lie, Greta is planning a big sweet sixteenth for her daughter's birthday – that's Lexi's best friend. Lexi's my daughter,' she said to Dan. 'And he asked if *I* was looking for any entertainment too, and I said I'm not sure but that I like being entertained, and he said that's good to hear, and I smiled, and he said well please get in touch if you'd like any entertainment, and I said I'll keep that in mind, and then I walked back over to you guys.' Jenna took a big breath, then a swig of her bubbly. 'Woo! I don't normally drink much, I'm not used to feeling this uninhibited.'

Dan and Katy exchanged amused glances, then Jenna pointed to the screen. 'That's us!' There was a photo of the three of them, plus Kane, hanging around a tree, Kane about to climb it and Katy holding out her hands as if to say 'no it's too dangerous!' Dan and Jenna didn't appear fussed and were too focused on the packet of chips they were sharing. He remembered this was taken only a couple of months before everything changed. Amazing how a photo could capture a moment in time, and how hindsight could give everything a new perspective.

'The good old days,' Katy said, and it seemed she was speaking only to him.

'They sure were,' he said, exchanging a knowing smile with his oldest friend.

She nudged him. 'Hey, I'm proud of all you've achieved. Where's that little kid I used to play in the mud with?'

He gestured to his suit. 'I confess I've not played in mud for quite a number of years.' He had learned that, along with sport, getting his hands dirty was also not his thing. But Katy was up for anything, at least she had been, and she'd surely seen many messy things in her career as a nurse.

'I might need to start looking up your dating tips,' she said, and his heart beat a little faster at her words.

'Oh?'

'In a few months, it'll be one year since my divorce.'

'I'm sorry to hear that. Are you okay?'

She nodded. 'Yep, all good. We're actually still good friends, we just stopped being good partners. Grew apart, I guess. And wanted different things. At least it was all fairly straightforward and civil, unlike other divorces I've heard about.'

'That's a positive, then. My advice for now would be not to rush anything. Get used to you as an individual again, then decide what you want from there.'

'Thanks, that's kind of what I've been trying to do. Though last weekend it all went out the window, hence why I think I might need your dating tips.'

Dan could hardly believe what he was hearing. After all these years, she wanted *his* advice? He had been the awkward teenager with minimal social skills who'd tried to kiss his best friend while waiting for a bus back from the shopping centre. He had thought she wanted it too, but had been clearly, and painfully, mistaken. Their lips had lightly brushed together and then their heads had bumped, but more from her sudden shock when he leaned close too quickly, and it had become an embarrassing attempt at a first kiss. She was silent the whole bus trip home. He had said sorry about seventeen times, and though she still acknowledged him each day at school, they never spoke of the incident and lost their usual ease with each other. Soon it became too uneasy to continue their friendship the way it had always been. He had regretted that moment for years, but he also praised it. For it was that moment that inspired him to change for the better... to believe in himself and learn how to understand people and communicate. Fear of another embarrassment had fuelled him towards the life he now lived.

Two decades later, he had enjoyed many dates, many kisses, and a few relationships, but nothing serious. He was a master at dating, but was he a failure at relationships? The dating had to lead somewhere eventually, and he'd been so focused on getting that part right to help other single people that as the years went by it was becoming clearer he didn't want to keep dating for the rest of his life. Teach it, yes, but it was time for something more for himself. Life was too short. He hoped that by the end of his time in Australia, he could somehow find the closure he needed from his past so he could return to the States and implement a new Dating Plan. It was hard when so many people knew his profession, but he hoped to find someone he truly connected with who liked him for who he really was, not who he was in his career. Someone he could build a life with. Not Katy, obviously, because she'd never had any interest in him.

But someone *like* Katy.

CHAPTER FIVE

Katy rubbed her eyes as she walked down the stairs, a yawn stretching sore cheek muscles from all the smiling, laughing, and singing at last night's reunion. She still had a song stuck in her head and she hummed it as she headed towards the enticing aromas in the kitchen.

'Morning, sleepyhead,' Kane said chirpily as he flipped the eggs and bacon. 'Sunday breakfast special, courtesy of Kane's Kitchen.' He flashed her a grin. 'Remember how Dad used to do his Sunday Breakfast Special?'

She nodded and smiled, then cast him a curious glance. 'Why the good mood?' For a moment she worried that he had taken something last night when she'd been out, or taken something less problematic as a substitute, owing to the energy and appetite he so clearly had.

'Aren't I allowed to be in a good mood?'

'Of course,' she said. 'It's... it's so good to see.' She peered into the fry pan. He slid the spatula under the food to lift it and placed it on the plates.

'I just feel a bit, I dunno, like I'm a burden. And I wanted to show my appreciation.' He took their plates to the dining table where he had even put a vase of fresh flowers from the garden. Katy shook her head in awe. She couldn't remember the last time he had cooked for her, or made much of an effort with anything. He was a fish and chips, takeaway food, and Macca's kind of guy. He returned to the kitchen and poured two glasses of juice. The toast popped up from the toaster and Kane flinched slightly.

Still hypervigilant, she noted.

He buttered the toast with a little too much enthusiasm and one of the pieces broke in half. 'Let's eat!'

She grabbed her multivitamin tablets and fish oil capsules and followed him into the dining area, adjacent to the living room and overlooking the ocean. Light streamed in, making the white table shine like glossy satin.

Kane drank half his juice in one hit, then tucked into the steaming food. 'So good, if I do say so myself.'

Katy sliced a triangle from the corner of her toast and popped it in her mouth, followed by a sliver of egg and bacon. With a nod, she agreed. 'Nice work, chef.'

He smiled and pointed with his fork out the window. 'Good swell today, should I go out? I haven't surfed for so long, though, and I'd have to hire a wetsuit and board as I didn't think to pack mine in my hurry to see you last weekend.'

'If you're up for it, though the weather's still a bit cool. And maybe you should do some practise first, build up some strength again.'

Kane always liked to leap into everything or give up on everything, there was no in between. She wanted to make sure he'd be safe in the water having lost a lot of his physical strength and fitness through the drug use.

'Since when did cool weather stop a surfer from riding the waves?'

'Since never, I'm guessing.'

'It's like fishing, it doesn't matter if it's hot or cold, it only matters if the conditions are right and the tide is on the move.'

'Well I'm looking forward to a lazy Sunday in my pyjamas,' Katy declared.

'I crashed out halfway through my binge marathon last night and slept for what felt like forever,' Kane said. 'That doesn't happen often.'

'That'll put anyone in a good mood,' she said. 'The windy weather during the night didn't wake you?'

He shook his head. 'Compared to living in Sydney, it's all peace and quiet here.' He swallowed a mouthful of food. 'Oh, how was the reunion? Did anyone ask about me?' He covered his eyes as though worried.

'Actually, Dan asked about you.'

Kane's eyes bulged. 'Dan Dexter? What was he doing there?'

'Same as everyone else. Although I don't think he came all this way just for a school reunion, he said there were other reasons. Maybe just wanted to spend time with family.'

Kane nodded. 'If you see him again, tell him I said hi. I don't think I'm up to being sociable with anyone at this stage.'

'Will do.'

Katy's phone chimed and she withdrew it from the pocket of her pyjama pants.

> Hey there, how's things? I'm going for a walk/jog around the harbour today, care to join me?

Katy's eyes widened. She hadn't expected to hear from Jon again. She'd texted an apology the day after their date and Kane's arrival, and he'd said it was no problem, that he understood family came first. She had sent a smile emoji and left it at that. She had thought about starting afresh with a new date, but then the reunion had been on and she'd been hesitant to due to her previous plan of waiting a year. But now Jon was asking her. She thought she'd scared him off.

She stopped eating for a moment and nibbled on her lower lip, her finger hovering over the screen.

'Not a work emergency, I hope?'

She shook her head. 'Not on a weekend, thankfully. The doctors take turns being on call for out-of-hours treatment.'

Kane looked relieved.

She typed her reply:

> Hi, thanks for getting in touch. Sounds lovely, but I'll take a rain check. Late night last night and a big week ahead, so a relaxing Sunday it is for me today.

She'd first typed 'lazy Sunday' then changed it. She didn't know why she felt the need to make him think she was as fit and energetic as him, but was conscious of her word choice.

> No worries, enjoy! Maybe next weekend.

She smiled and was about to reply with 'sure', when something twinged inside. Uncertainty. She thought about what Dan had said: *Don't rush anything... get used to you again...*

As much as she liked Jon and really enjoyed their brief but passionate interlude, she now didn't feel ready. With Kane needing support, and her original plan being to wait, maybe it was best to take things easy for a little while longer.

> Actually, I'm so sorry but I think I might take a
> break from dating for a few months. My brother
> will be staying with me for a while, and I'm
> trying to wait until a year after my divorce so I
> can pack up some baggage and move forward
> fully without messing anyone around. Sorry. I
> think you're awesome and I loved our date.
> Hope to see you again down the track, but if
> not, I understand.

She bit her lip as she hit send.

'That seemed like a long text,' Kane remarked. 'Oh, is it that Jon guy? You should invite him over for dinner, I can apologise and cook us all a good meal. Or I can go out for a while and leave you two alone, whatever you prefer.' He shrugged.

'Nah, thanks though. I'm actually going to take a break from dating.'

'Didn't you only just start?'

'Yep, and now I'm taking a break.'

Creases of concern marred Kane's face. 'Not because of me, I hope? Please don't let me get in the way of your life, Katy.' He lowered his head and ran a hand through his hair.

She reached out and placed her hand on his forearm. 'Not at all. I think I was rushing into things, and I'm glad you came. I'll just wait a bit longer before moving on in the dating department.'

She glanced at her phone but there was no reply. She hated letting people down, but one thing she'd learned through her break-up was that it was important to do what was right for yourself first and foremost. Feelings changed, life circumstances changed, sometimes suddenly and without warning. There was no shame in changing your plans, or your mind.

A thumbs-up emoji appeared as a reply. Katy knew that when one replied with emojis only it signalled the end of a text conversation. Part of her hoped she'd made the right choice. Jon was an absolute catch, and she could have gone for a walk/jog with him and enjoyed herself, but then the next bit of uncertainty would ensue: who would call first? Would they go on another date? What would happen next? She didn't think she was truly ready for all that stuff yet.

Surprisingly, when she was about to take the breakfast plates to the sink, her phone chimed with another message.

> I understand. I'm disappointed we won't get to continue where we left off, but I appreciate your honesty, thanks for letting me know.

Katy exhaled deeply. She replied with a *thank you*. So that was that. First dating hurdle dealt with, now back to lazy Sunday.

Kane brought the glasses to the dishwasher, and after loading them in he scratched his head, looking a little preoccupied.

'You okay?'

'Me? Yeah, course.'

She held his gaze. She could see beneath the exterior of his eyes. Twins could often tell what the other was feeling, or when they weren't being completely open about something.

And like she knew there was something more, he knew that she knew. He sighed and leaned on the kitchen island bench. 'Sis, I've made a big mistake.'

Katy's insides curled up into a twisted knot. *Oh no, what did he mean?*

'The money. My inheritance. It's all gone.'

She opened her mouth but no words came out.

'I've wasted it. Oh, man, how could I have been so stupid!' His voice became loud on the last two words and he began pacing the kitchen.

'Oh, Kane.' Katy leaned on the bench and sighed too. 'You

didn't put most of it into that investment fund like we talked about?'

He paused and eyed her only briefly before diverting his gaze. 'I put *some* in, but as soon as the minimum duration was up, I withdrew it again.' He shook his head. 'I just kept living off it. Food, rent, entertainment, and... well, *you know*. And before I knew it there wasn't much left. In a brief moment of sanity, I did put a small amount in a term deposit, but the term's not up yet so I can't access it. And the rest... I dunno, it'll probably last me a week, two at the most. And to think I almost blew it on a fix.'

Katy's heart became heavy. She should have encouraged him to put a deposit on a property like she had, but she knew he wouldn't have the commitment to manage it, even with a property management team. He'd have to be responsible for any maintenance, keep financial records, and he wasn't up to all that, so she'd suggested a managed fund.

'And Centrelink?'

'It's not enough. Rent is too high in my place, not to mention food. I'll have to go back and pack up my things. Without you, I'd be...' He stopped pacing and leaned on the bench again.

Homeless.

'When does your term deposit end?'

'About eight months to go. I could find a new share house with cheaper rent, use most of that as bond, but as for now?' He tapped his foot rapidly on the floor.

'You can stay here,' she said. She knew it wasn't a long-term solution. They loved each other fiercely but would also drive each other mad eventually. And she couldn't be like a parent to him for the rest of his life. 'Eight months, I can help you get back on your feet by then. But you need to keep up your rehab appointments, look after your health, and make a solid financial plan. *And* find a job you can keep.'

He'd only had sporadic jobs, either quitting due to boredom or getting fired for being late or stoned.

She pulled some paper and pens from the sideboard in the hall and sat at the dining table with him, drawing a line down the middle and writing *Expenses* on one side and *Cost* on the other.

'What, now?' he asked.

'Let's start with some basics and go from there, huh? Before another busy week at work.'

He went to the kitchen and flicked on the kettle. 'Coffee?'

'Yes please,' she replied. So much for lazy Sunday.

CHAPTER SIX

A light wind flapped around Dan's face as he stepped out
of his luxury cabin at the Trees of Life Resort in the
Tarrin's Bay hills. Each cabin was named after a tree; his was
the Flame Tree, and on the inside of the front door was a framed
photo with information about it and its history. It was a nice
touch to embrace the theme of the resort.

Sunlight cast speckled patches of light on the pathway
leading to the main building, and his inner child resisted the
urge to hopscotch along them, for now. Maybe he would
unleash his inner child another time. And he might need to
warm up first. And make sure no one was watching, like the
gardener who gave him a wave as he walked past. Reconnecting
with Katy the night before had triggered an avalanche of
nostalgia and memories, and he forgot he was an almost forty-
year-old man. Life sure did seem to be moving faster than it
used to. But for some, including his cousin, Harry, who he'd be
seeing today, it was moving even faster.

He reached the L-shaped accommodation building and
stepped underneath the decorative arch that connected the
rooms with the other parts of the resort, including the reception

office, restaurant, function room, and day spa. From this vantage point, he had a view of the swimming pool and playground below, and the car park in the distance. He strolled along the walkway and went down the steps at the edge of the resort, spotting his parents waiting at the bottom with huge grins on their faces. He'd only arrived in town a few days ago and they had picked him up from the airport, but still they were thrilled to see him again, after so many years living interstate then overseas.

He turned his regular walk into a fancy walk as he descended the remaining steps, and his mum Ellen laughed her high-pitched cackle, while his other mum Sandy smiled and shook her head at his silliness. He held out his arms and they had a group hug, their warmth a comforting presence.

'Your chariot awaits,' said Ellen, ushering him to their Toyota RAV4 Hybrid, expertly parked between two other cars.

'Yet again,' Sandy said. 'Maybe you should become an Uber driver too, Ell, in your spare time.'

'Ha, what spare time?' Ellen replied.

His biological mother ran a local driving school and was always booked out, and in the evenings she did various classes or created artworks on the dining table at home while Sandy read eBooks on her Kindle, and on weekends they did morning yoga and often hiked or swam. He was glad his mothers were keeping fit as they entered what Sandy called their 'silver years' – '*Not quite golden yet, Danny,*' she'd say. Sandy commuted to the city four days a week to her architect firm, which she was in the process of preparing to hand over and sell to one of her associates in the next couple of years so she could retire at sixty-five. As for Ellen, he didn't know if she wanted to retire, keeping busy was her favourite hobby. He had probably inherited that from her. Not that he couldn't *not* be busy, but his mind was always active at least, planning or pondering life and his next step.

'I could have given you your first Uber job last night,' Dan said, explaining how he'd attended the school reunion while they'd been out of town for a birthday party.

'Happy to give you a discount.' She winked as she opened the passenger door for him. 'Was Katy there?'

'Yep,' he said. 'Was nice to see her again.'

'I bet. She's done well for herself and she's such a great nurse. I'm like a proud auntie.' Ellen smiled. Dan and Katy's parents had been neighbours who became friends after both needing fertility assistance to start a family. Katy's mum and Ellen had been pregnant at the same time, and had helped each other out in the baby and toddler days – Katy's mum needing more help on account of having had twins.

Once the car began moving, the air somehow felt still, as though pausing to prepare for where they were headed. Dan swallowed a lump in his throat. 'How is... I mean, is it... really bad?'

'Harry's doing better now he's back home. Likes to be in his own space. But yeah, it's...' Ellen cleared her throat and her grip tightened on the steering wheel.

'Not looking good,' Sandy concluded. 'But he's a strong one, so who knows, he might surprise us all.'

'Did they give a, um, timeframe?' Dan didn't know how to say *how long does my thirty-three-year-old cousin have left to live?*

'Could be a month, three at most, the oncologist thinks,' Sandy said in a sombre tone.

The following silence was like a vice, squeezing his whole body.

'I'm glad I'm here,' he said. 'I just wish there was something I could do.'

'We all do,' Ellen said, manoeuvring the car onto the highway as they headed to Welston, where Harry lived with his parents close to the hospital, having moved there shortly after his lymphoma diagnosis.

'Seeing you will do him good,' Sandy suggested. 'Someone closer to his age to chat to about... man stuff, I guess.'

Dan didn't know what *man stuff* his cousin would be keen to talk about when his life hung in the balance. Harry probably didn't have any need or want for dating advice in his condition, but he *was* a trained psychologist and perhaps he could provide some emotional support as a relative and a professional.

Ellen turned up the radio, which he knew was her way of saying let's not get bogged down in all the negativity.

Soon, they were doing car-karaoke to old songs, or *car-a-oke* as Dan called it, and Dan's conflicting eagerness and apprehension to see his cousin dissolved as he let himself be in the moment with the two women who, along with a sperm donor they had met through Katy's parents and made a discreet arrangement with, had given him life. He wished he could somehow give life back to Harry, but that would take a miracle, and he didn't know if he believed in those.

***

'Dan, so good to see you,' Robbie, Ellen's brother, said as he welcomed them into their home, giving him a brief hug.

'You too, Uncle Robbie, it's been a long time.'

He nodded and they entered the small living room where his wife, Eliza, stood with difficulty from the couch, rubbing her hips. He embraced his auntie and she wiped the corners of her eyes.

'Harry awake?' Dan asked softly.

Robbie nodded. 'This way.'

'You go first,' Ellen said, 'better if we don't all bombard him. We saw him in hospital only recently too.'

Dan nodded and followed Robbie to Harry's room, where various sounds were coming from the television or computer. The first thing he noticed was a gaming controller in Harry's spindly hands and a small smile lifted the corners of his mouth. He was reminded of gaming with him when they were younger, though the technology back then was more Super Nintendo than PlayStation.

The next thing he noticed was how Harry seemed to be half the size he was when he'd last seen him. Although he'd been in contact via phone, text, and video during his treatment, there was nothing quite like seeing the reality of his situation in person. His arms were bony and slender, his skin had a grey tinge, there was only a shadow of stubbly hair across his scalp, and his face was sunken.

'Just one sec,' Harry said, pressing the buttons urgently on the controller. 'Yes!' he exclaimed, then released his grip. 'Sorry, bro, had to get the bad guy.' He smiled, and for a moment Dan wondered, *What if the doctors had it wrong, what if he wasn't going to die anytime soon? Was there still a chance?*

Dan approached the side of the bed and held out a hand, Harry tapped it twice then clasped it, doing their old handshake. 'Ha, you still remember it.'

'I think it's ingrained into my subconscious.'

'What are we playing?' Dan asked, sitting on the side of the bed.

'We?'

'Yeah, don't you have an extra controller?'

Harry glanced to the side of the PlayStation. 'Sure do, though it doesn't get used much. Dad tried to play with me a few times but spectacularly failed.' He chuckled.

'I heard that!' Robbie called out, his footsteps then retreating down the hallway.

Dan got up and grabbed the controller, resuming his position on the side of the bed.

Harry set everything up and soon they were fighting the bad guys with much enthusiasm, and Harry said it helped him imagine that his immune system was fighting the cancer. 'Beats the meditations they want me to do,' he said. 'I'd much rather go out fighting than surrendering.'

Dan's heart pinched. 'Whatever makes you happy, that's what's important. Oh no!' He got hit by one of the bad guys. 'I'm out of practice. Or too old.' He laughed.

'Never too old,' Harry replied, and Dan realised Harry would never get to be his age. He probably wouldn't see his thirty-fourth birthday next year. Dan was damn lucky. But life was so unfair sometimes.

After a few games, Robbie came in with some medications for Harry and a cheese sandwich. Harry swallowed the tablets with an upward shake of his head and took a few bites of the sandwich, but chewing and swallowing seemed a lot of effort for him and he placed the rest of the sandwich down on the plate. 'Maybe later,' he said.

'Nothing like a plain cheese sandwich,' Dan said, and his stomach grumbled a little.

'Feel free to have the rest,' Harry said. 'I don't have much appetite these days.'

'No, I'll leave it here. Maybe you can have a tiny bit every now and again.'

Dan wondered how much of terminal illness was terminal because of the illness or because of malnutrition and weight loss.

'I'll try.' He shrugged, then yawned.

'So,' Dan said, 'any of your friends dropped by?'

'A couple. They feel a bit awkward around me and don't stay long, though. They don't really know what to say. Neither do I, to be honest.'

His eyes went distant and his breath seemed to slow, like breathing was also an effort.

'If there's anything you want to talk about, I'm here. And if you don't, I'm also here.'

'Thanks,' Harry whispered, casting a brief glance his way. 'Just send me funny texts sometimes, like memes and stuff. Distraction helps.'

'Consider it done.' Dan gave a nod.

'How's work?' Harry asked. 'You going on that new show?'

Dan nodded. He had accepted an offer to be a coach and co-host on *Love, Unfiltered*, a television show that exposed singles and couples to the reality of dating and relationships in the modern world, encouraging truthful communication, authenticity, and vulnerability in order to find the right mate. 'Starts next month. So, some time off for me now, and plenty of time to game with you whenever you want.'

'Cool.' Harry's eyes brightened a little.

'Want to play again?' Dan asked.

'Nah.' Harry pushed the controller to the side. 'Too tired. But thanks.' He wriggled slightly back on the pillow and pulled the blanket higher up as a shiver ran through his body.

'Need a heat pack or anything?'

He shook his head and yawned again. 'Damn meds make me drowsy, along with the damn cancer.'

His fun mood from before seemed like a distant memory. Dan scratched his head and stood. 'How about I let you rest for a while. I can come back tomorrow. And anytime you need company or help, let me know.'

Harry nodded weakly and gave a limp thumbs up.

He was about to exit the room when Harry said, 'Dan?'

He turned to face him.

'You found anyone special yet?'

Dan scratched his head again, which was by no means itchy and he didn't have lice or anything, but seemed to help him think about how to respond to certain questions. 'I've had no shortage of dates, a few decent relationships, but nothing lasting yet and nothing that was really...'

'Love?' Harry suggested.

Dan nodded. 'It's hard sometimes, being seen as an expert but not having found your own perfect match.'

'Each in their own time,' Harry said. 'Though I think my time's run out in that department. I mean, who wants to date a dying man?' He raised his arms briefly and they flopped to his side.

'Hey.' Dan sat back on the side of the bed, his heart plummeting. 'I can't imagine how hard it is, how hard *all* of this is for you. But I do know that each of us are living on borrowed time. Some people know when they're going to go, and others don't and could be gone sooner than expected. I could die tomorrow. All we can do is milk each day for all it's worth, huh?'

Harry nodded and sighed.

'Easier said than done, though, I know.' Dan stood and held out his hand and Harry managed a weaker version of their handshake. 'You're doing great, man. And I love the idea of fighting those bad guys through your gaming.'

The rims of Harry's eyes reddened and he rubbed the back of his neck. 'I'll be okay. I mean, seriously, I get food brought to me in bed, gaming whenever I want, binge watching the best shows. It's like I'm living the dream here!'

'That's the spirit.' Dan smiled. He guessed Harry's mood probably shifted countless times a day.

'And I'll be watching you on that show.' Harry grinned, then his smile flattened out. 'At least, I hope to. If I'm still here.'

'Hey, it's only a few weeks away, of course you will.' Dan *really* hoped he would be. Not to watch his show, that didn't matter, just for him to still be... around. As long as he wasn't in too much pain.

Dan went to the door again.

'Promise me one thing?' Harry said, and Dan raised his eyebrows. 'When you feel it with someone, that... *love*, don't waste the opportunity. Tell them. Have the love that I won't ever get to have.' His voice cracked on the last few words and Dan had to bite his lip to hold back a tremble.

'I promise,' Dan said. Taking a risk with someone when they might not feel the same way was daunting, and the aftermath of rejection even worse, but Harry was right. Life was too short not to take risks and he still had life and risks to take.

CHAPTER SEVEN

'Lexi?' Katy asked through the car window, noticing the short awkward-looking teenager with dyed purple curls hanging around outside the clinic when she was about to drive out of the parking lot. 'Your mum left two hours ago; did you need a lift home?'

She shook her head.

'Does your mum know where you are?'

'Told her I was hanging with friends, but they've gone now.'

Curiosity and concern prickled Katy's skin. Jenna's daughter liked her independence, but she wasn't the type to get into trouble or cause havoc. The girl fiddled with her hair. 'Do you want to talk or anything? I'm not in any rush.' Though she was keen to get home and see if Kane had had any luck applying for casual work.

'Umm, maybe. Yeah, guess so. Just need to ask you something.'

'Sure.' She turned off the engine and got out of the car, then placed a gentle hand on the small of Lexi's back. 'Wanna come inside? There's no one else in the clinic.'

Lexi nodded.

They went around the back and once inside, Katy made Lexi a hot chocolate with one of the powder sachets in the staff kitchen.

'Thanks, just realised I haven't eaten since lunch.'

'Oh.' Katy found a muesli bar from the stash in one of the drawers. 'Here.'

The girl munched away and Katy waited for her to finish before asking how she could help.

'Don't say anything to Mum, please.'

'Okay. But I'm sure if there's something you wanted to talk to her about, she'd be willing to listen.'

'I don't want to worry her, she has enough on her plate.'

She did? Katy knew that Jenna sometimes struggled with self-esteem and juggling life as single parent, especially after her difficult past, but her life also seemed quite in order with work and home life with her daughter, who she was close with.

'I didn't want to go to the chemist either, but do you have… can I get…' Lexi's cheeks were pink and Katy knew.

'A pregnancy test?' she asked softly.

Lexi nodded. 'Don't tell her, she'll say I'm too young. And I am young, but it just happened. Noah and I are kind of dating and, I dunno, is it too young to fall in love? I think that's what I feel. I mean, he's said it to me but I haven't said it back.'

Katy smiled. The confusion, exhilaration, and uncertainty of being a teenager was ever present in her memory, especially as she dealt with many in her teen health workshops.

'Love is something that just happens too. It might be, it might not be, only you can figure that out. But don't say something just because he's said it unless you feel it. And don't do anything that doesn't feel right. Did it feel right?'

'Yes, I think so. I mean, at first it was a bit awkward, the next couple of times it was better, didn't hurt. But now...' She bit her lip.

'You're late?'

She nodded.

'Any stress at school?'

'Just the usual stress of being forced to sit in classrooms studying things I probably won't need to know in my lifetime when I could be doing something else.'

Katy smiled again. 'Did you, um–'

'Oh yes,' Lexi said quickly, as though she didn't want to hear Katy say the proper words, clearly embarrassed as it was. 'But nothing's a hundred per cent, is it?'

'Sadly, no. Close, but there's always a risk.' She ushered her down the hall. 'C'mon, let's get you a test and go from there.'

Lexi exhaled a shaky breath.

'It's okay,' Katy reassured. 'Whatever happens, we'll work it out. Okay?'

'Okay.'

She took one of the tests from storage and gave Lexi a cup. When she returned, she dipped the test strip in then left it on the bench, waiting the full three minutes without looking, just to be sure, while they chatted about random things.

The timer went off and Katy glanced at the test. She picked it up and showed Lexi.

'There's a line, does that mean...'

'No, there's only one line. For a positive there needs to be two. It's negative.'

'Oh, thank God.' Lexi buried her face in her hands.

'If there's still no sign of your period in the next few days, you let me know, okay? Here, I'll give you my personal number.' She typed it into Lexi's phone. 'Cycles at your age can be irregular, your brain is getting used to figuring everything out.

But it's a good idea to keep track so you know if things seem too out of balance. Any issues with acne, excess hair, sugar cravings?'

Lexi shrugged. 'I love sugar, but like, I don't *need* it. And yeah, I get pimples but not as bad as some of my friends.'

'There's also the pill, but that would be something to discuss with your mum and one of the doctors. Starting it too young can sometimes disrupt the hormonal regulation later on as your brain is still getting things established, which can take a few years. But the pros and cons are worth considering, or you can continue with what you're currently using.'

'I don't want to take any pills,' she said.

'Okay. But if you do want to discuss it at any time, let me know, and we can work out how to bring it up with your mum.'

Lexi covered her face with her hands. 'I can't think of anything worse.'

Katy placed her hand on Lexi's forearm. 'Your mum and I, we were teenage friends once, like you and your friends. Times have changed, but some things haven't. Please know that she'll understand if you want to talk. We've all been there.'

'Eww, I know. Thanks.'

'Anyway, good news, eh? Don't forget, let me know if you have any problems.'

'Thanks, Katy, so glad my mum's best friend is a nurse.'

'So glad my best friend has such an awesome daughter.' She curved an arm around her and walked her out of the clinic. 'How about I drop you home anyway, tell your mum you bumped into me after your friends went home. It's getting dark.'

'Okay. Thanks.'

Katy drove her to the back of town where she and Jenna lived in an area with cheaper rent, based on the fact it was alongside the railway. She waited till Lexi got through the front door, offered a wave, then left. Thank goodness the test was negative. A teen pregnancy was not an easy thing to navigate. She'd seen a few come through the clinic and it was always hard on everyone involved. But the ones she'd seen through the whole experience now brought their babies to the clinic, and somehow, they just managed. She couldn't have imagined being a mum at that age, couldn't even have imagined it in her twenties. Now, at thirty-eight, she knew time was getting on a bit, which was why she'd frozen her eggs at age thirty when she still wasn't ready for a family, but knew all too well the difficulties faced by older mothers. Her own mum had tried for years to conceive naturally, then through IVF. It took eight cycles to get a positive, and along she came into the world with her twin brother. Her mother had been told she was too old and her eggs were bad quality and it most likely wouldn't happen, and that they should probably give up, but she said 'one more go', and miraculously, it worked. Two embryos out of three made it to day five, implanted, and became her and Kane. That wasn't the case for everyone, many didn't get that lucky. Katy knew her life was a miracle, even more so now her beloved mum and dad were gone.

She squeezed back the tears that began to spill, thinking of them again. And then more came when she thought of how her marriage had broken up, and along with it, the chance for a family. Maybe it was easier not having had children yet, it would have been hard sharing custody. But now what? Was she going to meet someone new and start trying for a baby right away, or use her frozen eggs if they had no luck? It's not the sort of thing that usually gets talked about on a first date, and she hadn't brought up anything of the sort while getting to know Jon. Katy had been thinking lately, if she did not enter a new relationship by age forty, or forty-two at the most, she'd consider going it alone with a sperm donor so she could experience motherhood. It wasn't the ideal situation, but Dan had been born that way, though he had two parents raise him. She didn't want to wait around forever.

Anyway, it wasn't worth thinking about right now, she wasn't in that much of a rush and was looking forward to making the most of single life.

As soon as she got through the door at home, Kane greeted her with a smile. 'Got an interview,' he said.

'Oh? That's great! What's the job?'

'Sorting stock and carrying heavy loads to people's cars at the farming store further south.' He made a fist and flexed his biceps. 'Need to build up my muscles, though. Or maybe that'll happen on the job. I hope they don't take one look at my puny build and say, "Sorry, mate, you're not cut out for the job".'

'I'm sure they won't. They'll have trolleys, and they probably have occupational health and safety regulations to avoid lifting over a certain weight.'

'What do I wear to the interview? It's not like I'd be needing a suit.'

'Smart casual, I reckon. If they hire you, they might give you a uniform or tell you what to wear.' Katy ruffled his hair. 'Better give this a wash. And when is it, do you need a lift? I'll be at work but I can see if I can sort something out.'

'It's okay, the shop is only a fifteen-minute train ride from here and an easy walk from the station, so I'll check the timetable and make sure I get there on time. Tomorrow, 10am.'

'Good luck, though I'm sure you'll do fine. You've got past experience at that warehouse, remember?'

'Yeah, the only employer not to fire me. Maybe it was good that I left when I did, even if I did give a fake excuse.'

'As long as you did your job decently, that's all they'll want to know.'

'What if they ask why I haven't got any other references?'

'Just tell them the truth; you've had some health issues and that took up a lot of your time. You're okay now and looking for a fresh start.'

His shoulders softened and he sighed. 'Thanks, that makes me feel a bit better.' He went upstairs. 'Does it matter if my hair smells of your fruity shampoo?' he called out.

Katy laughed. 'They might not even notice it being around all the animal feed and farm smells!'

'True!'

She chuckled and went to the kitchen to heat up some leftovers, and while waiting for the microwave to beep, a message chimed on her phone.

> Hey there, hope you've had a nice day. Wondering if I can ask for some advice? Happy to chat on phone or meet up and shout you a coffee. Dan.

Advice? She wondered what he could need advice about. Health? Fun things to do in Tarrin's Bay?

Typing dots appeared on the screen and she waited.

> It would be good to catch up some more too, was so much fun at the reunion!

She smiled and typed a reply:

> It sure was! Sounds good. Lunch break tomorrow, should be around 12.30 or so. Meet me outside Tarrin's Bay Medical Clinic and we can walk and talk?

Perfect. I have all the time in the world at the moment.

Lucky guy. See you then.

And all of a sudden, she was reminded of meeting up after school and buying bubble gum at the shops, seeing who could blow the biggest bubbles, and ending up with sticky pink faces. A smile tickled her lips. She had an idea.

CHAPTER EIGHT

When she'd finished with a patient's iron infusion at work the next day, Katy took a moment to check her phone.

> Interview went well, they're going to let me know today or tomorrow!

Relief flooded her body. This was exactly what Kane needed, a simple job with no pressure, to rebuild his bank balance *and* his confidence. Something that would keep him busy, use up his nervous energy and not put him in any risky situations.

> Ooh! Let me know as soon as you hear xo

She checked the time then put her phone away. Half an hour till lunch. A buzzer went off and she checked a patient's arm for any reaction to their vaccination, then sent them home. Next up was a wound dressing, and before she knew it, she was freed up enough to take her lunch break five minutes early.

'See you after!' She gave Jenna, who'd be taking a break after hers, a quick peck on the cheek.

'Say hi to Dan for me,' Jenna said, and Katy nodded.

When she went outside, she stopped on the sidewalk and looked both ways. She checked her phone again, and when she looked up he was rounding the corner from the main street. She smiled and waved, as did he, and when he got closer he did a funny little skip thing that made her giggle. He used to do that sometimes as a kid.

'Still got that boundless energy from twenty years ago, I see.'

He shrugged. 'Sometimes I think I do, then overdo things and realise the next day that I don't!'

'Ha, I can relate. I do Pilates occasionally and lots of walking, but when I don't, my body feels like it's getting older and achier day by day.'

'Use it or lose it, so they say, or so my mums say.'

'True. How are they? I see them around sometimes and at the clinic occasionally, but not as often as you'd think in a small town.'

'They're great. Sandy's busy as always in the city but planning her retirement, and if Ellen retired, she'd probably fill up her spare time with another job or hobby.'

'It's great they're doing well. Say hi to them. Oh, and Jenna says hi too.'

Dan nodded and cast a small wave back at the clinic as they walked in the direction of a small café down the road, around the corner from Home restaurant.

'Coffee?' he asked. 'My shout.'

'Sure, thanks. Caramel latte, please.'

Dan placed their order, him choosing a sweet chilli chicken wrap and Katy a toasted cheese and tomato sandwich.

They wandered over to the harbour and sat at a picnic table, wind whooshing sporadically around their faces like the air was singing a tune. Katy tightened her ponytail and sipped her coffee.

'How's it feel to be back?' she asked Dan, noticing the fine creases around his eyes. He had a hint of fine greys among the brown of his hairline, but they were only noticeable if you really looked.

'Surreal. Both familiar and different at the same time. It's been a long time between visits. I heard you'd moved to Welston a while back?'

'Yeah, with Erik. My ex-husband. Only been back in the bay a short time, couldn't pass up this dream job. Best hours ever for a nurse, and I love making a difference in the local community.'

'It's important to put the lifestyle you want first. I'm realising that more and more now, redefining what I want and not always chasing the next big thing. I'm being drawn to more simplicity and slowness, though it's challenging when you have a lot of commitments and your brain likes to be stimulated all the time.'

'Oh yes.'

They ate in silence for a few moments and Katy remembered he wanted some advice. 'Was there something you wanted to ask about?'

He gave a nod. 'My cousin, Harry. Terminal cancer. I mean, I know how to talk to people, give emotional support, that sort of thing, but when it comes to someone you know, well, it's... different. Difficult. Any tips for dealing with cancer patients? What not to say, that sort of thing? Did I already say "that sort of thing"?' He placed his hand on his forehead.

'You did, but that sort of thing's perfectly okay with me.' She smiled. 'I'm sorry about Harry, I've seen him in the clinic a few times, but then not for a while. I assumed he was getting care in Welston's oncology department.'

'Yep. He's reached the end of the road, they say.'

Katy's heart ached. She'd nursed many cancer patients over the years, not that she'd worked in oncology, but they'd often presented to the emergency department, where she'd worked for a few years, with various urgent complications that needed tending to. She exhaled deeply. 'It's tough. There's not really any *right* thing to say, just be there, I guess. Be present. Listen. Do things they need done, but don't... how can I say it? Don't... hover. Like, making them feel like you're waiting for something to happen or for them to die. Patients sometimes told me that although they liked having family and friends around, they felt uncomfortable if they hung about awkwardly, or got too much in their personal space. Cancer patients, or any patients with ongoing issues for that matter, don't get a lot of personal space. People are always in their face, prodding and poking, checking vital functions, asking questions. That in itself can get exhausting. Being in hospital can be exhausting, they often don't get much rest even though they're in bed all day. So be there, but also give them space.'

Dan nodded slowly, as though taking it all in.

'I don't know if that's helpful, or really answering your question. But I think listening is more important than talking. Let them feel safe to say anything that's on their mind. They might be worried about being a burden or their family feeling grief, they might be scared of dying, so let them know they can share anything they wish.'

'That is very helpful, thank you. I hadn't thought of it that way. I mean, as a psychologist we were taught about active listening and the appropriate responses to validate what they're feeling and saying, and encouraging them to delve deeper. But I hope I can do that without him feeling like he's in a psych session.'

'I'm sure he's grateful to have you here, and for your expertise.'

Dan sipped the last of his coffee then stood and tossed it in the nearby bin. He gazed out at the ocean, then at Katy. 'I'm glad to be in Tarrin's Bay, and glad to have bumped into you again.'

She smiled. 'Me too. Fancy you seeing me at a school reunion, what are the chances?' She raised her hands in the air and chuckled.

He chuckled too and sat back down. 'Well, I *was* hoping to see you there, and I did have a feeling you might be.'

Katy marvelled at how much time had passed and shook her head. 'Life's short, huh?'

'Indeed.'

'Oh,' she reached into her pocket, 'almost forgot!' She handed him a packet of bubble gum, similar to the ones they often had when they were young. She'd had the idea yesterday to buy some for him. 'I think the graphic design on the packaging is a bit more advanced than in our day.'

Dan's eyes widened and his mouth opened. 'Are you sharing this with me or is it all mine?' He winked.

'Happy for you to enjoy it all yourself.' She grinned. 'I remember how much you loved your bubble gum.'

'I remember when you gave me your last piece after the shops had closed and you took some out from your stash so we could both have one but there was only one left.'

'I felt bad and didn't want to be greedy!'

'And then I felt greedy having it all to myself.'

'I know, you offered to break it in half, remember? But I said it would reduce the bubble size and that at least one of us should enjoy it in its entirety!' Katy laughed.

He laughed too. 'And I honestly think that was the biggest

bubble I ever blew, because I had all this pressure on me to make the most of the cherished last piece.'

They stood and threw their lunch wrappers in the recycling bin. It didn't feel like a work day anymore and Katy had a funny feeling they should get to school before the bell rang.

As they walked closer to the harbour's edge, Katy checked her watch to make sure she still had enough time, and Dan stretched his arms up and gazed out at the horizon.

'What do you love most about your job, apart from the hours and making a difference?' Dan asked. 'Like, what are the daily things you do and love?'

It wasn't often Katy got asked about the details of her work. As a nurse, people usually assumed what her basic tasks were but didn't always realise how varied the role was. 'I like meeting the patients and caring for regulars, seeing their journey progress, sometimes getting better, sometimes the opposite. But it's all an honour, being part of their lives.'

Dan nodded and waited for her to continue.

'I love working with teenagers the most, actually. Because that's where you can really make a difference. They're young and easily influenced, so I think it's good to have a professional and caring voice in their ear, helping them make good choices and letting them know I'm here if they need to talk. Mental health and safety, not just physical, is such an important thing to be on top of these days.'

'Absolutely. I've seen in many of my clients how their mental health affects their social life too. In my work, sometimes it's about dating advice and sometimes it's about supporting mental health, so they have the self-esteem, confidence and desire to make authentic connections with other people. And knowing that they don't have to be perfect.'

'You would have made a good nurse too,' Katy said.

'And you would have made a good psychologist,' Dan replied.

'Maybe we should career swap for a year!' She laughed.

'Oh no, I may be able to talk to people but I have no idea how to give an injection or administer medication. I'd probably kill someone!'

'Okay, let's stay as we are. But I reckon I could learn a thing or two from you. Actually, my patients could too...' She eyed him curiously, an idea simmering within.

A seagull landed nearby as though to eavesdrop, then got bored and flew away. 'I run workshops on different topics for patients and have a regular teen group. Sometimes I have guests come and share their expertise. Nothing fancy, just a general chat for a half hour or so.'

Dan's eyes widened. 'Would you like me to visit?'

'It just occurred to me, but you don't have to.' She flicked her hand. 'I mean, we can't afford to pay anyone, the clinic only pays my wage.'

'I don't expect payment,' he said. 'I'd love to come and have a chat with them. Do you mean on mental health, or on dating and relationships?'

'Dating, for sure. Like maybe, things I wish I'd known about dating as a teenager or something,' she suggested with a shrug.

'Ha! I could write a whole book on that. Actually, I kinda did. Not with that particular topic or title, but you know.'

'I know.' She smiled. 'A celebrity dating coach, I think they'd think that was pretty cool. Or awesome. Or whatever teens say these days, I can't keep up.'

'Didn't we say "rad" or "sick" or "mad"?'

'Probably, I think rad was before my time but there were definitely a lot of things that were "mad" back in the day.'

'Before your time? You and Kane were born only a month before me, remember?'

'I know, you were practically our triplet.' She winked and he gave a brief smile but glanced away. A twinge of regret twisted inside, as she didn't want him to think he was only like a brother to her. That was what he'd thought after she rejected his kiss at the bus stop all those years ago. But it wasn't that. They were friends, best friends, and the kiss was unexpected and weird and something she totally wasn't prepared for. And it all happened too quickly, and then she couldn't think straight about it because of the awkwardness and didn't really know what she thought or felt. So she kept ignoring it and hoped the memory would go away. But of course, those sorts of memories never did. She still felt bad about it, but hoped he had gotten over it by now. Of course he had, what was she thinking? He was a grown man. As if something like that would weigh on his mind for twenty years.

Her phone chiming gave welcome relief to the awkward moment.

'Sorry, you probably have to get back,' he said.

'No, I still have a bit of time left. It's Kane.' She read his text message.

> Got the job! I start next week. Mon-Fri 9am-4pm, and every second Saturday morning.

'Yes!' Katy exclaimed.

'Good news, I take it?'

'Kane got a local job. So it looks like he'll be staying with me a while until he gets back on his feet.'

'I meant to ask how he was doing.'

'Up and down. We have a lot of years to catch up on!'

'We do. Fancy another coffee catch-up sometime?'

Katy tilted her head slightly. 'Is that one of your sneaky dating tricks? A casual "fancy another"...'

'Sure is. But it's also just a natural way to ensure we continue such a *rad* conversation another time.' He winked.

Her cheeks warmed. 'Sounds good. And I'll be in touch soon about the teen workshop. How much notice do you need?'

'I could do it now, no problem.'

'Right this minute?'

'Yup.'

'Okay, maybe I'm the one that needs the notice. I'll draw up a plan and get approval, set a date, then let all the kids know. We might be a full house for this one.'

'Ready when you are.' He gestured in the direction they'd come. 'Shall I walk you back to work?'

'Sure.'

And they wandered back, Dan handing her a bubble gum along the way, both of them blowing the biggest bubbles they could muster.

CHAPTER NINE

D an read through the approved workshop proposal Katy had sent him two days later, and chuckled. She was a very good organiser, as well as nurse, by the looks of it.

```
Teen workshop topic: Things I Wish I'd
Known About Dating As A Teenager
   Presenter: Celebrity dating coach and
psychologist, Dan Dexter
   Agenda: Introduction to Dan, Dan's
talk, Q&A, info about the clinic's teen
services, refreshments and mingling,
info on next workshop. Clean up.
```

It was to be next Tuesday at 4pm. There were some legalities and an online form to sign, and soon he was all booked in for probably the smallest, but hopefully most helpful, presentation he'd done in years. Although his stomach fluttered slightly at the thought of Katy seeing him in action. She'd probably seen him online doing his thing at some point, or maybe she hadn't, but doing his job with her present in the room, at her workplace, was somehow more nerve-wracking than talking to a room of one-thousand people. He sent her a quick reply too, saying he'd filled everything out and would prepare some notes for the talk, even though he knew he could wing it. He wondered what sorts of questions the teens would ask. He would have to ponder that and be prepared with some answers, as he usually dealt with adults.

He stepped out onto the verandah of his cabin at the resort and breathed in the lush cedar-scented air. The gardener was planting some seeds alongside the pathway and he waved. The guy had a tanned and slightly weathered face with a wide, relaxed smile.

'Nice day, eh?' the gardener said.

'Beautiful. Nothing beats being back in Australia.'

'You from here?'

'Grew up here, moved interstate then to America for work.'

'Nice. My partner worked in America too,' he said. 'Make-up artist in Hollywood and beauty therapist.'

'Wow. And she moved back here?'

'Yep. True love and all.' He held a hand to his chest and laughed. 'I'm Nathan.' He took off his glove and held out his hand and Dan leaned over the railing and shook it.

'That's awesome. I'm Dan.'

'What kind of work do you do over there?'

'Psychologist by trade, but I actually specialise as a dating coach. Helping people connect and communicate with others, find confidence on the dating scene, and increase their chances of fulfilling relationships.'

Nathan's eyes opened wide. 'Wow, I meet a lot of different guests here but I've never met a dating coach. I could have used your advice when I was trying to navigate long-distance romance!'

'Sounds like you didn't need it though, everything worked out in the end, huh?'

'Thankfully. It took a while, but we got there. And I actually had some good advice from an elderly widower in the community when I did her garden makeover. She gave me some words of wisdom that helped me take a leap of faith.'

Dan gave a slow nod. 'We should always listen to those older than us, not much can replace a long life of experiences.'

'Too true, mate.' Nathan eyed the garden bed. 'Better get back to it. You off to lunch?'

'Yep. Only had a coffee in my cabin for breakfast, late start to the day for me. I'm starving.'

'Enjoy, the food here is amazing, though they don't usually let me in the restaurant to eat amongst the guests with all my garden mess, but I do get some samples and packed meals when I don't bring my own. Perks of the job.' He smiled.

'It must be a great place to work. I'm usually in front of a screen or a group of people. Nothing beats nature.'

'Ain't that the truth.' Nathan offered a wave as Dan descended the steps and walked to the main restaurant, a huge expanse of a room with floor-to-ceiling windows and an outdoor seating area with a firepit and fairy lights. The tall trees surrounded the building as though they were the walls, and he could tell how it got its name as the Trees of Life Resort.

'Welcome, Mr Dexter,' said the restaurant manager, who had introduced himself on his first day at the resort as Gabriel.

'Thank you, Gabriel, and please call me Dan.'

He gave a precise nod and led him to a table. 'Here is today's specials menu along with our regular fare. Please call me over when you're ready to order.' He gave another nod and glided away as though he was an elegant ice skater.

Dan's mouth salivated as he perused the menu. He decided on the mushroom arancini with truffle mayonnaise, and the potato and leek soup with home-made crusty sourdough and garlic butter. After getting Gabriel's attention and placing his order, he took a sip of water and gazed outside, each tree reached to the sky and his eyes followed as natural filtered light filled the restaurant with a calming glow. He thought of Harry and his inability to eat a simple cheese sandwich and guilt panged inside. Even if he were to bring a gourmet meal such as what was served here, Harry probably wouldn't feel like eating it. He made a note in his phone, along with Katy's tips, to ask Harry if there was anything he felt like eating – anything at all – and he would endeavour to find it and bring it to him, even if he had to get a custom chef order. Since there was probably not much that diet could do at this stage to change his prognosis, he might as well eat whatever he wanted. But loss of appetite was never a good sign, especially when he remembered Harry loving his food when he was younger.

Despite feeling indulgent when his food was placed (also elegantly) in front of him, his voracious appetite took over and he decided it was better to make the most of the gift of being able to eat, let alone a meal as delicious as this. The arancini was perfectly crispy on the outside and melt in the mouth on the inside, and in moments it was gone. The soup was warm and comforting on what was a cool but pleasant day, and with the warmth of spring soon to appear, he knew that soups would disappear from the menus in all the cafés and restaurants in town. It'd be freezing by the time he returned to the States in December. At least, that's when he planned to return – he hadn't confirmed a return ticket yet – to allow time for his work here to be completed, and see how Harry went. Though he didn't want it to happen and he hated to think about it, in a bittersweet way he hoped he would still be here for Harry's funeral. But at the same time, he hoped his cousin would outlive his prognosis and prove them wrong, even if it meant he had to say goodbye and leave the country due to his upcoming speaking tour in January.

He allowed his thoughts to roam as he ate, something he advised clients to do when eating alone, to avoid distracting yourself through social media scrolling, and simply be present with yourself as you ate, acknowledging any emotions or thoughts that arose. *Become comfortable with being on your own*, was one of his tips, surprisingly, as he knew that when that was possible, dating and relationships became a bonus rather than a requirement for oneself to feel good. And he had eaten many meals on his own both in his apartment, and at hotel restaurants or via room service when he travelled for events. He always tried to avoid looking at his phone until he was finished. *Minimise phone use,* was also one of his tips, for when spending time with others. *Show them that they are more important than the latest viral video.*

Interestingly, it was when he dabbed the napkin to his mouth and placed it back on the table having finished his meal, that his phone beeped, as though someone knew his boundaries and had been waiting for him to finish.

> Thanks for filling in the form! And for doing
> this. Looking forward to it!

Katy was probably on her lunch break now. He sent a *no worries* and a thumbs up.

> Hey, how long do you think you'll be in town? It
> probably depends on Harry, yeah?

Also interesting that she was texting about something he had moments ago been thinking about.

> Aiming till December, but yes, it somewhat depends on Harry. I have commitments back overseas in January. I'm also in town for something else: a new reality dating show. Don't cringe – it's not a cheap, shallow, 'everyone is botoxed' kind of show. It's real, unfiltered, diverse singles and couples taking on dating challenges and sharing their experiences and feelings – live! There'll be pre-recorded edited content too of course, but interspersed with a live chat format with an audience.

He hit send.

> Oh wow! I don't watch much TV but let me know when it's on and I'll check it out. So you'll be travelling to Sydney for the live shows each week?

> Yep. Every Tuesday night. Starts in September.

> What's it called?

> Love, Unfiltered.

> Nice. Sounds interesting! All the best with it. You've really done well. Proud of you!

> Likewise.

He smiled and what he felt inside was as comforting as the soup he'd eaten. It was nice that two decades had mostly dissolved any awkwardness between them and they could just be mature adults. He'd made many new friends over the years, but he hadn't realised until now how much he'd missed his *best* friend.

CHAPTER TEN

Katy finished the rest of her tuna salad quickly and rinsed out the container in the staff kitchen sink. It was a quick lunch today as they were extra busy and had fallen behind when a patient had fallen following a drop in blood pressure and hit their head on one of the chairs. Katy's skills in emergency nursing had come in handy, and an ambulance had taken the patient to hospital. Sometimes she missed her old job: the excitement, the diversity, the rewards when patients recovered and were sent home. But she didn't miss the shift work and long hours with barely a moment to eat or go to the bathroom. She was glad to be in a less demanding environment, and getting to know the patients and see their progress was a new kind of rewarding.

Jenna came into the kitchen while one of the part-time nurses was treating patients. 'Think I've got time for a quick bite to eat.' She rummaged in her large bag and pulled out a container of soup. 'Thank God for processed food.'

'At least it's soup, can't be too bad.'

'Chicken and vegetable. I won't look at the other ingredients with various numbers I don't recognise. Mark was telling me I need to have food with less additives and make batches of meals at home to bring in, but it's so time consuming, and I'm so tired when I'm at home I just want to binge watch the latest shows on Netflix.' She popped the plastic bowl in the microwave. 'He also said I should minimise microwave use and plastics. Oops.'

Mark was the clinic naturopath, and often gave them tips here and there when they crossed paths. He sometimes did nutrition talks for groups of patients too, and had done one on healthy eating for teenagers, which didn't get a big turnout at the start, but once some of the teens found out he had brought tasty food samples, they'd texted friends to come along and the crowd had grown. Katy had enjoyed his simple meal and snack ideas and had even adopted some of them for herself, like the savoury muffins that were easy to make, freeze and bring to work for a quick and balanced lunch.

The microwave dinged and Jenna withdrew the soup and sat at the table, just as Katy poured herself a cup of herbal tea then sat to join her. Steam rose upwards and Jenna blew across the surface before sliding her spoon in and having a tentative sip. 'Yum,' she said. 'Those numbers sure taste good.'

Katy laughed. 'Oh hey, so Dan is all booked in to do a talk for the teenagers. Tuesday. Can't wait to hear what he has to say.'

Jenna's eyebrows rose and she took another sip from the spoon. 'I don't know whether to suggest that Lexi go along or if I'm inviting trouble. My little girl is growing up.'

'You're worried about encouraging her with dating and boyfriends, I assume?'

She gave a nod. 'I mean, she has a boyfriend, at least *I think* he's still around; she's been quiet the last couple of days. Maybe the talk could help... make sure she learns some communication skills and how to navigate the intense emotions of adolescence.'

Jenna shrugged. 'We had no such help back in the day, I think we just made things up as we went along.'

'I'm sure Dan would have their best interests at heart, and I don't think it would encourage anything more than what they're already getting up to. It might actually help them be more informed, aware, confident, and safe.'

'True.' Jenna put her spoon down. 'She did speak to me last night after her quiet spell. Asked if I had ever taken the pill. Wasn't something I was expecting to come out of her mouth as she tends to shy away from uncomfortable discussions.'

'Oh?' Katy didn't want to break patient confidentiality. Lexi was sixteen which meant she could see a doctor or nurse on her own, unless the practitioner deemed it necessary to contact their parents for their health or safety.

'Yeah, she said she was getting some annoying pimples and had heard it could help, but wasn't sure whether it was worth taking.'

Oh. So she hadn't mentioned the *other* reason for asking about the pill.

'Personally, I don't know what she's worried about, I mean her skin isn't that bad, nothing out of the ordinary for her age.'

'Teenagers do feel more self-conscious than us.'

'True. Anyway, I told her I had only taken it for a few months but it made me feel sick, so I stopped. That was years ago, though, and I guess the pills are a bit different now.'

'There are some different options depending on the purpose of taking it... acne, hormone imbalance, or contraception, for example.'

'I did mention that if she were to take it, the other benefit would be birth control if necessary, but she soon changed the topic of conversation.'

'It's understandable. Can be awkward to talk about those things.' Katy sipped her tea then added, 'Well, I'm always here if she wants to talk about anything, or she could discuss it with Sylvia.'

'Yeah, I'll mention it. But I don't want her to take medication just to make her skin look better, she's still so young.'

'The important thing is to let her know you're comfortable answering any questions she may have. The fact she brought it up with you is a good sign, even if only briefly.'

Jenna nodded. 'Thanks, guess I'm doing something right.'

'Hun, you're doing a lot right.' Katy reached her hand across the table and placed it on Jenna's forearm. Jenna clasped her hand on top. 'Get her to come along on Tuesday. I know it's when you've finished work and she probably won't want her mum hanging around listening to everyone chat about dating, but I'll be there.'

'So glad you're working here now,' Jenna said with a smile, her eyes with slightly red rims.

'You okay?'

Jenna swiped the corners of her eyes. 'Yeah, yeah, probably just hormonal myself.' She chuckled. 'I don't know, sometimes I just feel... a bit down, you know? Like... flat. Even though people say I'm bubbly and even funny sometimes, inside I feel a bit worn out, I guess. A bit aimless.'

Katy nodded slowly. 'That's okay. Are you taking much time for your own self-care? Not just binge watching, but doing other things you enjoy?'

Jenna's lips twisted to one side. 'Hmm, not really, though I keep rearranging our house and redecorating. Cleaning, tidying.'

'You were always good with decorating and design. What about doing something artistic? Taking a class?'

'Maybe. I like buying cute décor for the house at Kmart but then I spend too much and have to cut back, but maybe I should do something more creative. Lexi sometimes draws pictures and she enjoys art at school.'

'You could even do something together. Creative time *and* mother–daughter bonding.'

'Could be an idea. If she wants to.'

'If not, do something for yourself anyway.'

'Thanks, Nurse Katy.'

Katy smiled and stood, sipped the remainder of her tea, then washed the mug and exhaled. 'Back to the madhouse I go.'

'Have fun, see you back in there soon. For now, I'm going to enjoy the rest of my number soup and maybe look up some art classes or something.' She gave an affirmative nod.

'Sounds like a plan.' She gave a little wave, even though she'd see her again in fifteen minutes. It was like when they were at school, they'd hug each other whenever they'd see each other, between classes, on lunch breaks. Female friendships were so important at that age and, although many disappeared over the years, maybe even more important now. Something niggled as she recalled Jenna's red-rimmed eyes. She'd seen that in Kane sometimes, and although his situation was different, it made her wonder if Jenna was suffering from mild depression. All she could do was offer support like she had just now and see how things went, but if the niggling feeling returned, she would bring it up with her and maybe suggest she have a chat with one of the doctors, or even book in with a counsellor or psychologist.

Jenna had been through trauma, Katy knew that, and had come out the other side strong and independent. But she was sure some of that trauma remained and affected her sometimes. Just as her own trauma did. Often when life was a bit monotonous and routine, when things felt safe and even a bit boring, that's when trauma would often spring up out of nowhere again. It was the brain's way of processing it at a time when it felt safe, when there was no other current threat going on. Losing her parents suddenly in a car accident had been too much to process when it happened and she had been in shock for so long. Counselling eventually helped her unpack most of it later on, but sometimes, when she least expected it, like when she was washing dishes, having a shower, arranging flowers in a vase, or watching the ocean waves, horrendous visions of their mangled car and broken bodies would pop in her mind. She'd have to physically shake her head to try and dislodge the images, and then turn her focus to something else. She had done EMDR therapy too, to reduce the impact of the memories. It helped, but they never fully went away. She wondered if it was like that for Jenna now that her life was safe without her abusive ex-partner in it.

As she walked down the hallway to the nurses' station, she heard a few sniffles from the kitchen and paused, ready to go back in but a patient walked past and said, 'Good timing! I'm here for the shot in my butt!'

Katy made a note to check in with Jenna later as she prepared the medication for the next patient and was soon swept up in the busyness of her work. Jenna had returned to her desk with a smile on her face and a joyful voice as she spoke on the clinic phone. The patients needed them and, as usual, their own concerns would have to wait until their own time.

CHAPTER ELEVEN

Katy allowed Kane to play his choice of music in the car instead of her usual audiobooks on their drive to southwest Sydney. The windows down a little, fresh air streamed in and ruffled her hair as she thought about everything while Kane drummed his fingers on the door in time with the music. Most of the traffic was headed in the opposite direction, people travelling south for a weekend on the coast. But today, there'd be no beach walks, lazy café lunches, or browsing local shops, only packing up Kane's belongings and selling or giving away anything else so that he could be out of the share house before his rent ran out. His roommate Cal had taken photos of his bed frame and a few other items on his behalf, and Kane had managed to arrange a couple of Marketplace buyers to arrive today. Hopefully they would pay in cash. It wouldn't be much, but something. Anything left he'd have to leave out the front for free. No point hanging on to old things, and Kane didn't own or need much. He'd have everything he could want or need at Katy's for the time being, and then he would have to start again once he'd saved enough money from his new job and the withdrawal of his term deposit when the time came.

'Oohh, ahh, oh-oh-oh,' Kane sang along to some song she didn't know, and she smiled. At least he was happy at the moment. Maybe he was distracting himself from the job ahead of them. If Katy had to pack up her things at short notice, she would need several days, a week at best, not just one day. She'd done her best to simplify her belongings, but still they accumulated. Sometimes, in strange moments, she wondered how Kane would manage if she passed away and he had to sort through everything. Like they'd done with their parents' lifetime of belongings. It had been so hard, they'd had so much stuff, and obviously had not expected to die before their time. Who did? Some of their things Katy had kept, but much of it they had to sell or donate. At least they'd had up-to-date wills, which had been the only silver lining in the chaotic, shocking, and devastating time of their deaths.

'Hey, I should take you to this café I like, they do the best coffee.' Kane took a break from his car-a-oke.

'Okay, but we won't have much time so how about we go there first and get takeaways?'

'Sure.'

Katy was desperate for some time out after a busy work week, but this was important and had to be done. Kane needed a hand, and she had one to give.

She followed his directions to a street of shops, found a parking spot in a side street, and walked to the café filled mostly with twenty-somethings adorned with tattoos and body jewellery. They ordered and waited, Kane chatting to one of the baristas like they knew each other, which they probably did. They took their coffees and wrapped sandwiches and as they left, Kane called out to the barista, 'Take care, mate, might not be back for a while.' He waved and the barista did too, with a curious look on his face.

'He looked like he wanted an explanation for why you wouldn't be back. You didn't tell him you were leaving the area?'

'Nah, I don't want anyone to ask questions. Better to avoid the details.'

'Fair enough.'

They drove into his street, thankfully finding a spare parking spot not too far away so they could bring things easily to the car. When they got inside, Cal was chucking some things in the bin, and then grabbed his keys. 'Gotta go out, I'll leave you guys to it. Hi, Katy.' He held out his hand. 'Sorry, didn't have time to clean up.' He gestured to the lounge where cushions were strewn about as though someone had been having a pillow fight. The curtains were only partly open and the room was dark, dusty, and had a faint smell of cigarette smoke.

'Hi, Cal, been a long time.' She'd only met him a few times, and each had been brief. She knew he was probably also involved with drugs, but he was also functional in society and had a job in construction. Their other roommate, Ben, was hardly ever around, and if he was, he kept to himself in his room. Cal said on his way out that Ben would be back sometime later.

'Place to ourselves,' Kane said. 'We can sing as loud as we want.'

'Well, you can. I might put my earphones in.' She winked. 'Okay, down that coffee, bro, and let's get to work.' She put the sandwiches in the fridge to have later and went to Kane's room.

The first thing she did was get him to strip the bed and put the sheets and blankets in garbage bags, not to throw out but to wash and use at her house in the spare room. 'Now the bed is ready to be sold. Let's hope the buyer turns up, you never know with these online sales.'

They removed everything from the desk and bookcase so they too would be ready for pick up. Kane didn't own many books but there were graphic novels and various novelty books like *Guinness Book of World Records* from five years ago and some pub trivia quiz books. 'Want to keep these?' she asked.

'I think all those world records have probably been broken by now.' He laughed and Katy smiled. It was good to see his sense of humour emerge from the darkness sometimes. 'Chuck everything out except...' he flipped through the graphic novels, '...these ones.' He put them in a box marked *keep*.

He also chucked out some random items littering the room, checking a few pens to see if they worked, keeping the ones that did. 'So much crap,' he said. 'How do things accumulate in life?'

'We keep more things than we throw away,' Katy replied. 'I still have some decluttering to do, but I've made good progress, and boy, it makes such a difference to how I feel.'

'At least I only have a room full of stuff. Oh, apart from...' He dashed out to the lounge and unplugged the old Xbox. 'Sorry, Cal,' he said even though Cal wasn't there. 'You'll have to get your own.' Kane grinned. He put the Xbox in the *keep* box and said, 'And sorry, Katy, for the noise that's about to overtake your TV.'

She shrugged. 'Maybe I'll just join in.' She nudged his arm and continued sorting.

'Oh.' Kane dashed back out again and returned with a mug that said *I'm the better-looking twin*. 'Can't leave this now, can I?'

Katy laughed and shook her head. 'I guess I can make room for one more mug.'

An hour later the bed, desk, and bookcase had been sold, and the bedside table was being left for Cal, so Kane put it in his room.

Kane had taken all his clothing and footwear out of the wardrobe and after allocating some for donation, packed the rest in a large clothing bag Katy had brought along. There were some old shoeboxes and plastic containers in the wardrobe, and Kane chucked some out without even looking. 'Don't need all that stuff.'

Katy didn't ask any questions.

Kane took the lid off one of the containers and sat on the floor, his shoulders sinking. He pulled out some old photo frames with pictures of their parents, them as a family, plus Katy and Kane as babies.

Katy sat next to him. 'Oh,' she sighed.

Kane swiped some dust off them and looked at the photo of their parents; their mum with her dark curls and wide smile, and eyes that were weary but content. Their dad had started balding at that time and his coarse sandy hair held hints of grey.

'I think that was taken when we were little kids,' Katy said. 'Maybe by one of Dan's mums.'

'Speaking of Dan.' Kane held up a photo of the three of them as four- or five-year-olds.

Katy laughed. 'Oh God, how time flies.' She could hardly believe that the suave, successful man she had reconnected with was once this chubby, silly, fun, and cute child making faces at the camera along with her and Kane. 'I don't think I have a copy of this one.' She took out her phone and snapped a photo. 'Dan will get a laugh out of it.'

'You catching up with him again?'

'Yeah, he's giving a talk at the clinic next week.'

'Nice.' Kane tapped the photo against his chin. 'Might be good to see him again. I kind of went AWOL as a teenager and we lost touch but, man, we had some fun as kids, didn't we?'

'The best childhood ever,' Katy said.

'Invite him over if you want,' Kane said. 'Dinner or something?'

'You sure?'

He shrugged. 'Dunno, but maybe it'll be good for me.'

'I think it would be and he won't judge, don't worry, he's qualified in psychology and understands all the different issues people have.'

Kane nodded, then looked again at their parents' photo. His chin trembled. 'I feel like a failure,' he said, lowering his head.

'Hey, don't say that.' Katy rubbed his arm.

He looked at her again. 'I want to do them proud, Katy.' His eyes welled with tears and he grasped her forearm. 'Please. Help me do them proud.'

Her eyes stung and she blinked. 'You always do your best to pick yourself back up again, that's what matters,' she said. 'Take one step at a time, starting with your new job on Monday.'

'Yep. 'Bout time I tried something new.'

'And hey, maybe you can help me sort through the rest of my stuff that's packed away in the wardrobe at home.' She winked.

'Hmm, not sure, I'm going to be a busy working man now, might not have the time.' He straightened his posture and raised his chin.

'Oh, haha. That makes us both busy working people.'

'But yeah, one step at a time. I'll show them. I'll show them I can turn my life around.'

Katy sure hoped his will was as strong as his resolve. She stood and held out a hand for him to grasp. 'C'mon, better-looking twin, let's eat before we do any more. I'm starving.'

Kane smiled and took her hand. It had not been the first time she'd helped him get back on his feet, literally and metaphorically, but she hoped that someway, somehow, it might be the last.

CHAPTER TWELVE

Dan looked again at the photo Katy had sent him of the three miracle babies who became best friends. He chuckled at his chubby cheeks, enhanced by hooking two fingers on either side of his mouth to make a funny face. Kane had done the opposite, pushing his cheeks together so his face was squished, and Katy simply had her tongue out and her eyes bulging wide. Life was simpler at that age. He taught his clients to let their inner child loose and have more fun, not get so caught up in the seriousness of adult life. It was hard sometimes, especially when the reality hit you hard on the face like with Harry's situation, but then again, maybe that was even more reason to live in the moment and create more enjoyment.

Although he was here for work and for family, he decided, after seeing the photo, that he would also make time for some old-fashioned fun. And maybe encourage Katy and Kane to do the same. Unless they already were. He hadn't seen them in so long, for all he knew Katy could be the Queen of Fun and might be able to teach him a thing or two. But so far, having spoken and caught up a little bit, it seemed like she was a hard worker and a caring sister, and they were her priorities. She seemed more serious than he remembered, but growing up tended to do that anyway. And there had been her marriage breakdown, which must've taken its toll too.

As for Kane, he wasn't sure why he was living with his sister when he'd been so keen to get away and live his life on his own terms. Maybe he was just in transition, needing some family support in between jobs and rent leases. He was looking forward to catching up with both of them tonight after the workshop. When Katy had invited him to dinner he'd been delighted. He was unsure how Kane would warm to him considering how long it'd been and the fact that they'd grown apart and gone their separate ways, but obviously she wouldn't have asked him if Kane didn't want to be part of it. Dan's mind often ran through various possibilities when it came to understanding people, he always aimed to understand first and not judge, and his ingrained training made him curious about people and their backgrounds, motivations, and what caused them to be who they were.

He put his phone away and started the engine of the rental car he'd hired to save having to order taxis or Ubers and his parents from having to pick him up whenever he wanted to go somewhere. It was strange having the steering wheel on the right side and driving on the left side of the road again. He'd grown accustomed to life in the USA.

He drove towards town, past Honeydew House, which he knew was owned by singer Drew Williams and his wife who ran yoga and music retreats there. He'd never been much into yoga though he had tried it, and he was a fan of meditation, but for exercise he preferred HIIT – high intensity interval training – which had been what he'd got into during his university days. It had helped him transform his body from wobbly and weak to sculpted and strong. Not so much that he was like a body builder, but enough to improve his health and fitness and feel confident in himself. It was something he could do easily wherever he happened to be: at his apartment, in a gym, or in a hotel.

He passed Tarrin's Bay Caravan Park, reminding him of times they'd spent as kids at the small beach in front of the cabins, collecting shells and getting tangled in seaweed. He eyed various new houses and units, shops as well, that he hadn't seen before and marvelled at how development was always happening, things were always changing.

He'd been back in the country to see his parents but Katy hadn't been in town at those times. He was glad they'd finally reconnected now she'd moved back, but it was also bittersweet, knowing that not only would he have to say goodbye to Harry, but to Katy as well, at least in terms of giving closure to the past and moving on back in America.

Soon he arrived at the medical clinic and drove to the rear of the building where Katy had said she'd put a reserved sign on a parking spot just for him. He saw it and smiled; a piece of cardboard stuck to the fence on the side that said: 'Reserved for VIP'.

He saw a back door but decided to walk around to the front entrance. A lady with the name tag Joyce greeted him with a friendly smile.

'Nice to meet you, Dan,' she said, gesturing in the direction of where to go.

He walked down the hallway and sprayed his hands with the sanitiser positioned at the entrance to the nurses' clinic. Jenna came out from behind the desk, handbag draped over her shoulder. Katy appeared from around the corner with a smile.

'Welcome and goodbye!' Jenna laughed. 'Gotta go do grocery shopping, ah such joy. Will use up my whole weekly wage.'

She smiled and as she walked past him, he whispered, 'Any luck with that DJ?'

Her cheeks brightened and she whispered back, 'I've been trying to pluck up the courage to get in contact. I did give his details to my daughter's friend's mum, but that's it so far. Any tips on how to initiate something?'

'Keep it casual. Say you enjoyed the music and you're keen to see a local band or performer, and does he want to meet up with you there for a drink?' Dan suggested. 'Or something similar if clubs aren't your thing. A coffee in the park? Nothing ventured nothing gained.'

'Eek, I'll see what I can do. Thanks.' She tapped him on the arm and walked past, her curls bouncing along with her.

'I took the last parking spot, hope the VIP doesn't mind,' he said to Katy with a wink.

'I'm sure they won't, just this once.' She held her arm out to the side to show him the clinic. 'Here is where I fulfill my life's purpose.'

'Which is?'

She looked at him with a creased forehead like he'd asked a silly question.

'Nursing, I know,' he said. 'But how would you put it into words that are more specific and exciting?'

'Nursing people and helping them?' she suggested feebly.

'How about...' Dan tapped his chin. 'Tending to the individual health care needs of patients to help them achieve greater well-being, comfort, and confidence?'

She clamped her lips together and nodded slowly. 'Not a bad way of putting it.'

'I teach my clients to be more specific about what they're looking for in a date or a partner and what their purpose with dating actually is, so that they're highly focused on achieving their desired outcome and more likely to do so.' He shrugged. 'Thought it might also be relevant for career-based purposes.'

'Clever. And what's your career purpose?'

'Educating and empowering people to be their best self and communicate authentically to bring meaningful new social connections and relationships.' He gave an assured nod.

'You prepared that earlier, didn't you?' She crossed her arms.

'It's printed out and framed in my home office.' He grinned.

'So, what would be an example of a dating purpose?'

'Hmm, depends on what the individual is looking for, but off the top of my head... seeking out enjoyable casual dates with those who share my interests or... using online dating to meet with only those I feel truly connected to on the phone first, and continuing until I find a meaningful long-term relationship.'

She uncrossed her arms. 'Ah yeah, cool. So, it helps them get clear on what they actually want so they don't waste time or settle for second best.'

'Yes. Without a clear purpose for their dating life people can get caught up in lust and intense emotions, which is fine if that's what they're after, but not if they want something to become deeper. In which case they need to be aware of that and also communicate what they're looking for to the other person so there's no miscommunication or false expectations.'

'So definitely no mind games or putting on an act.'

'Not if you want something real and healthy.'

Katy nodded. 'Sounds like you're somebody a lot of people need.'

He chuckled. 'I wouldn't say I'm an essential for a single person's life, but I can be... helpful.'

'Modest, I see. Well, I'm proud of you for going after your dreams. And speaking of dreams...' She moved to the side table that had an array of refreshments. 'These cookies are an absolute dream. Here, try one.' She held up the small marshmallow-topped cookie with flakes of coconut and chocolate.

He stepped forward and allowed her to pop it in his mouth in one go, his lips brushing against the tip of her finger.

'Wow,' he said in between chewing. 'This is delicious. Hold me back or I might eat all of them.' He held out his hands and made grabbing gestures. Her laughter lightened the air in the room.

'At least leave some for the teenagers. They'll start trickling in soon. Jenna's daughter is coming by the way.'

'Oh good. Well, let me get organised. I take it this is my spot?' He gestured to the stool beside a small table displaying his business cards, some fact sheets, and one of his books that he'd dropped off at reception yesterday.

'Sure is. Hope it's suitable? I can give you one of the regular chairs if you prefer, but I find it good to have the presenter a bit higher up than everyone else. And it beats standing!'

'It's fine. Thanks. He tested it out and stood again. 'As long as I don't fall off the back and make a fool of myself.'

'I always worry about that when I'm sitting on a bar stool!' She smiled.

'We never got to that stage, did we, hanging out at bars? I mean, I did eventually, but not in Tarrin's Bay with you.' He wondered if he should have said that but the words were already out of his mouth. He needed to stop talking about the past if he were to have closure and move on from his old life, and her.

'No, we didn't. Too young. But I did too, later on. Especially after uni lectures.'

'Same.'

The sound of footsteps came down the hallway and a girl with purple curls entered the room.

'Oh, am I the first one here?'

Katy and Dan nodded.

'Dan,' Katy said, 'this is Lexi, Jenna's daughter.'

'Hi, Lexi.' He held out his hand and she grasped it tentatively. 'Thanks for coming.'

She smiled feebly. 'Did you really go to school with my mum and Katy?'

'Indeed.'

Her smile widened. 'You're, like, famous and stuff. I looked you up on Insta.'

'I guess you know all my secrets now.' He chuckled.

'You've got, like, over a million followers, dude, that's insane.'

He chuckled again. He was reminded of how he was at that age. Back then there were no followers, just real-life friends. If anyone was following you it was considered stalking.

Lexi took a seat at the back and checked her phone. Three other teens came in, chattering away, then a girl on her own, a group of girls, and two guys. As he expected, the audience was predominantly female. Many of the male clients he'd met had been reluctant at first to admit they needed help in the dating department, but when he began running groups for men, more became interested and supportive of his teachings.

Katy stood in front of the group. 'Hi, guys, thanks for coming. If you could all pop your phones on silent during the talk that'd be great.' She waited while they did so, then said, 'For those who are new, I'm Katy, one of the nurses, and I'm excited to introduce you to Dan Dexter, a trained psychologist, author, and an expert dating coach. He loves educating and empowering people to... be their best self and... communicate authentically... to bring meaningful new social connections and relationships!'

Katy smiled and Dan couldn't believe she'd remembered his

career purpose word for word. She was one smart cookie, just as she'd been in school, with an eye for detail and a knack for remembering things. Which also made his presence in town a bit awkward, knowing she probably remembered that moment in high school every time she saw him. But that didn't matter now, the teenage years were experiential, formative, and filled with a smorgasbord of possible choices, directions, and outcomes. Like a choose your own adventure novel. It was a crucial time that could be a stepping stone to a rewarding life or a troubled one. If he could play a small role in helping teenagers navigate their emotional connections, it would be rewarding in itself.

'Thanks for the warm welcome, Katy, and thanks to you all for coming.' He took a moment to smile and connect with the gazes in the small crowd. 'This is a fairly casual talk and there'll be time for questions too. I've planned it around the topic of things I wish I'd known about dating as a teenager, because...' he put on a sarcastic voice, 'I know I look ancient, but I was once just like you, growing up in Tarrin's Bay.'

There were a few giggles. Dan ran a hand over his dark brown hair that was still thick and full, unlike one of his best friends in the States whose head was becoming balder year by year. 'All genetic,' his friend often said, 'thanks to my dad.' Dan only had one faded photo of his biological father, who also had dark brown hair. And he could see he had a similar nose with a slight upward tilt. When Dan was young, he was curious about his origins and his mothers said they could help him get in touch with the donor when he was eighteen if he wanted to, despite the agreement that he would simply be providing half the genetics and not be part of his life. But when he reached that age, for some reason, his desire to know had lessened. He had realised he was only ever meant to have his two parents and although without the donor he wouldn't exist, without Ellen and Sandy he wouldn't either. So he'd decided against finding out more about his history, and set out to discover himself instead, to work on his future. Maybe at eighteen, especially after his let-down with Katy, he didn't want to be disappointed in some way, or *be* a disappointment in some way. But for whatever reason, moving forward had felt better than delving into the past.

'And somehow, over twenty years later after moving away, here I am, back in the bay.'

'I can't wait to move out of this little ol' town,' one of the guys said.

Dan smiled. 'Now, I know that these years of your life are confusing at times, fun at times, and hard at times. And that's normal. Friendships, dating, and relationships often take centre stage as hormones surge and we strive for freedom as we come to know ourselves and the types of people we want to hang out with. It can feel like both the best and the worst years of your life.'

'I agree!' one of the girls called out. 'I cannot *wait* until I'm eighteen, life will be *so* much easier when I'm *finally* treated like an adult.'

'It'll be here before you know it.' He knew that on turning eighteen a whole host of other things in life changed, and along came more responsibilities and expectations, but she would realise that soon enough and he wasn't here to preach to them.

'Back in school, I wasn't one of those guys who was good at everything and I wasn't sporty in any way. I thought I was probably a bit boring, to be honest, but I had a few good friends and we had an absolute ball growing up.' He stole a brief glance at Katy who was listening intently. 'But in the teenage years, things change, friendships change, and *we* change. Don't let those changes throw you off course or get you down. Know that they're a normal part of young life and keep moving forward on your own path.' He adjusted his position on the stool and leaned slightly forward to engage more with them. 'So back then, I wish I'd known that it was okay to be me. I didn't have to be good at everything, I didn't have to love sport or anything else that wasn't my thing. I had my own skills, like reading books superfast, and somehow knowing what to say or do when people were upset. But apart from that, I didn't think I was very interesting. Now I know those skills were to help me in my future career.'

'Cool,' someone said.

'Nice to know young people still say cool,' he said with a smile. 'So I want you to know that you don't have to try to be someone you're not, in order to fit in or get someone to like you. Because that stuff can't be maintained and your true self will eventually show itself, so it's better just to be authentic from the get-go. Yes, it might mean you *won't* fit in with some people, but you know what? High school is such a fleeting experience and you'll spend a much longer part of your life immersed in other things and spending time with other people you'll meet along the way.'

The lone girl wriggled slightly and raised her hand. 'But how do you get through each day knowing that nobody gets you, that everyone thinks you're weird or boring?'

Dan's heart ached with the memory of what that felt like, except he'd had Katy and Kane, at least for a while. 'That's tough, for sure.' He nodded. 'But as hard as it is, try not to be too concerned with what others think about you. Most of the time, they're so preoccupied with worrying about themselves and what others think of *them*. And... everyone is weird in their own way. I'm kinda weird, and I've grown to actually like my own quirks.'

'Yes,' Katy piped up. 'I've known Dan for a long time, and he does this weird thing sometimes where he does a little jig, or some kind of daggy dance move, whenever he's walking down stairs, or walking towards anyone who's watching.'

Dan lowered his head, his cheeks warming. 'I do, I do.'

'Show us!' a couple of the girls called out.

'No, it's okay, I'm sure you get the drift.'

'Show us! Show us! Show us!' everyone chorused.

Dan turned his head towards Katy and held up his hands in defeat. 'If I must.' He stood, and although there were no stairs to give the full effect, he walked to the reception desk, turned and faced them all, then started walking back, but did a little hop, skip and jump, followed by a few sharp movements à la *Karate Kid* style.

They all laughed.

'See? Weird. I can't help myself,' he confessed.

The lone girl managed an amused smile. Lexi turned to her and said, 'I don't think you're weird or boring.'

The girl's eyes widened. 'Thanks. But no one ever talks to me or sits with me for lunch.'

'I will,' Lexi replied. 'Bella, isn't it?'

She nodded. 'I was named after you know who from *Twilight*. So embarrassing.'

Lexi chuckled. 'That's kinda nice. I think my mum chose my name just because, no reason. It's not even short for Alexa or Alexia, or anything. Just Lexi.'

'I like it,' Bella said. 'Sounds sassy.'

Dan's heart warmed. Although he liked to follow a general structure for his talks, he knew with teenagers it was better to allow them time to process information and have some fun with it, otherwise their attention spans waned. This was good. Yes, he was talking mostly about dating, but friendships were the cornerstone of a teenager's social life, and if this talk helped one lonely girl find a new friend and give her confidence, he was glad to be part of that.

'Great,' Dan said. 'Thanks, Lexi. Sometimes reaching out or taking the initiative with other people can help not only you, but them. The more kindness we show others, the more we'll receive. No one needs to feel alone. There is always someone out there needing connection just as much as you. It's up to us to take steps to interact with new people, and if you see someone sitting on their own at lunch, why not ask them if they want company?'

The group nodded and the trio of girls glanced at Bella. 'You can join us for lunch too,' one of them said.

Bella's eyes became slightly red and glossy behind her glasses and she rubbed at the corner of one.

Dan continued sharing the things he wished he'd known back then, including how to communicate better, how to actually ask someone out on a date and choosing the right words to use, how to make connections with like-minded people who shared your interests and values, and how to be kinder to yourself and not see anything as a failure.

'Last of all, I wish I'd known to just be open and honest. To say something if I feel something for someone, instead of letting it build up to the point where you can't think about anything else, and then it blurts out of you one day and the other person has no idea and is a bit overwhelmed and then...' He glanced discreetly sideways at Katy. 'Well, the chance is gone.'

She clamped her lips together and her cheeks looked slightly rosy.

'So, if you like someone, just come right out and tell them?' a girl from the trio asked. 'I mean, it's so embarrassing and risky, and what if they don't like you back, or they laugh at you, or tell the whole school?'

'Firstly, yes, you can tell them straight up, but it doesn't have to be verbally. You could say it indirectly, like in an old-fashioned letter, or a Facebook message, or even a small casual gift to show that you know them and like them. Like, share a packet of chips with them after school, or bubble gum, or whatever.' He looked at the group, catching the gaze of a few. 'Do you guys still chew bubble gum, or is that just from the olden days?'

A few chuckles sounded. 'Yeah, but it's kinda lame to go around blowing bubbles,' a girl said. 'Chewing gum is better, or M&Ms, or just Tic Tacs.'

Dan smiled. 'Noted. Personally, I've always loved the orange Tic Tacs.'

'You gotta try the berry ones, man.' A boy with tangled wavy hair said, digging something out of his pocket, handing a few to Dan, then catching eyes with the girl who had spoken and giving her some too.

'Sorry to ask,' another boy spoke, scratching his chin, 'but are you single?' He quickly held out his hand, palm facing Dan. 'Sorry, I don't mean... Oh, man.' He lowered his head and covered his face as a few people giggled. 'That sounded inappropriate!' He raised his gaze again. 'I mean, did all this stuff you teach help you find the one?'

Dan was used to answering this question and, as had happened a few times, being ridiculed by journalists saying he mustn't be a good dating coach if he was still single. 'As with many things in life, there are no guarantees. I can't guarantee that by following my dating principles every person will find the one they want to be with, but I can guarantee that no matter what happens, they will help you find yourself, and *keep* yourself.' He gave a nod. 'So many people lose themselves in relationships and wonder how they got to where they are. By starting at the beginning, we can prevent that. A good relationship with another person starts with a good relationship with yourself.' He cleared his throat. 'And to answer your question, yes, I am currently single.'

A few woo-woos and whistles sounded and the teenager turned bright pink.

'As I teach my clients, unless something feels completely *right*, or it doesn't feel equally two-way, I don't continue.' Dan briefly caught the gaze of Katy who glanced away.

'So you have standards and just kinda stick to them no matter what?' Bella asked.

'Yes. But you guys, you're still young and figuring out what you do and don't want. All I can advise is to notice when things don't feel right, and speak up or move on.'

Lexi raised a feeble hand and leaned forward. 'Umm, what should you do if someone wants you to do something, or to be a certain way, and you're not sure you want that too?'

'Tell them it doesn't feel right. If they understand and accept that, great. If not, time to cut ties. It's not worth being with someone who doesn't honour your perspective or feelings.'

'Thanks,' she said softly, settling back into her chair.

'When you treat yourself with respect, you'll find other people do too. Or the ones that matter at least.'

After a few more questions and bouts of laughter from the group, Katy concluded the session and handed out flyers for the clinic's free services for adolescents to support physical and mental health, and the teenagers eagerly accepted the snacks and drinks as they chatted and showed each other things on their phones.

After they had all left, Dan helped Katy with the clean-up despite her insistence that he didn't need to. As they put the chairs back in 'waiting room' arrangement, Dan said, 'Sorry if anything I mentioned brought back memories. I was just using a bit of our past as fodder for my talk. Real-life experience, you know? So hopefully they can see that I was just an uncertain kid like them once.'

'Sure, I know,' she replied. 'And it was actually interesting to hear your perspective.' Katy gave a half smile and stopped what she was doing. 'I'm sorry about what happened, back then. It was no reflection on you at all, it was just as you said; I was overwhelmed and confused with the sudden, unexpected nature of it.'

'Hey, no need to explain. Of course. I get it.'

'And I guess after that, things just got...'

'Weird.'

'Yes.' Katy lowered her head, then raised it a moment later and looked Dan right in the eyes. She came closer, her arms reaching out slowly, and before he realised what was happening, she had embraced him. He softened and did the same.

'I'm glad we grew up together,' she said. 'They were some of the best years of my life.'

'Mine too.' Dan held her a moment longer then pulled back a little. The feeling of her body touching his and her eyes seeing him truthfully after all these years sparked a small flame within. It burned gently and lingered, even after she returned to cleaning up. He thought he'd extinguished that flame years ago, but there it was again: reignited, warming his soul, tiny embers flickering throughout his body.

CHAPTER THIRTEEN

Katy started the engine and a strange but comforting energy buzzed between her and Dan as they sat in her car. They'd decided to travel together so they could pick up a few items from the supermarket for tonight's dinner. She'd drive him back to the clinic's car park later so he could drive his rental car back to the resort.

They wandered the aisles for ingredients, and she was reminded of when they used to wander the general store for all the best snacks and treats. But tonight they'd have to eat more than salty chips, chewy snakes, and Maltesers.

'Chicken schnitzel okay with you?' she asked, her stomach grumbling and wanting something quick and easy to cook up.

'Anything, I'm easy. But I plan on helping you cook, just so you know.'

Normally she'd tell a guest that no, she would provide the hospitality but her familiarity with Dan, despite the years of absence, made her self-imposed expectations to be the perfect host dissolve.

'That'd be fun,' she said. 'Thanks.'

'You know what'd be nice? Fry them, then top with tomato and cheese, then grill for a bit.'

'Ooh, like a cheesy melt, but on chicken instead of bread.'

'Sound good?'

'Let's grab some tomatoes.' She turned and headed to the fresh produce section with an eager smile.

Dan chuckled. 'Hungry?'

'Just a bit.' She chose a bundle of tomatoes. 'Next, cheese. Mozzarella?' She grabbed that too. 'I already have some salad at home we can use. Any other ideas, Dan the Dating *and* Cooking Guru?'

His grin brightened under the overhead fluorescent lights, and she remembered that same smile, though softened by youth and chubby cheeks, when he'd mastered a few basic skateboarding skills under her tuition. It was the smile of satisfaction, of achievement, and of being accepted.

'Hmm, I think my guru status ends at grilled tomato and cheese.'

'Salad it is then,' Katy said. 'Although...' She wandered to the frozen section and Dan followed. 'French fries?'

'*Oui.*'

She grabbed them from the freezer and placed them in the basket Dan was carrying. 'Easier than making from scratch.'

'My tastebuds can hardly wait. Let's go!'

They rushed through the checkout as though they were kids about to get caught skipping school (which they'd never actually done, though Kane often had).

Soon they arrived on the driveway in front of her house, and she suddenly realised Kane might be feeling a bit nervous, though he'd seemed eager to see Dan again regardless. 'Oh and by the way, a bit of a heads-up...' She turned off the engine. 'As you know, Kane got in with the wrong crowd in high school.

But, without giving away his privacy as I haven't asked his permission to tell you, he got into *more* trouble after school. He's not quite stable yet. Getting there. But for now, he's with me until he gets things back on track.'

'Understood,' Dan simply said. 'I don't need details unless he wishes to share them with me. And if there's any way I can help, I'd be happy to.'

Katy nodded, happy to leave it at that. They carried the shopping bags and she unlocked the door. Welcomed by an enticing smell of garlic and herbs, she called out, 'Hello, anybody home?' knowing full well Kane was doing something in the kitchen when she'd told him not to worry.

'Welcome to Kane's Kitchen, table for two?' He smiled as she fully opened the door.

'Make that three,' Dan said. 'Long time no see, man. How're you doing?' He walked over and they gave each other a quick hug and pat on the back.

'Looking good, man, Hollywood agrees with you,' Kane said.

'Not quite Hollywood but close enough.' Dan smiled. 'We brought ingredients, but it looks like you've beaten us to the kitchen.'

'I know you told me not to do anything, Katy, but I only made garlic bread, nothing fancy. It's just about ready!'

Phew. Katy was pleased Kane was getting excited about daily life and also helping out at home, but she was *really* looking forward to the grilled cheesy chicken schnitzel.

'Smells delicious,' she said as he opened the oven and, with oven mitts, withdrew the tray with crispy browned bread sticks with a deep slice longways down the middle. 'The way Dad used to make it?'

'Yeah. Butter soaking into the centre, fresh garlic, herbs, mmm.'

'I was hungry before, but now, even more.' Dan leaned closer to smell the garlic bread.

'Give it a minute to cool then you can try some.' Kane placed the tray on a trivet. 'What else are we having?'

'Chicken schnitzel with grilled tomato and cheese. Oh, and fries. So leave the oven on.'

'We should have guests more often,' Kane said, smiling at Dan.

'Happy to visit any time I'm wanted,' Dan replied.

It almost felt like the old days when it was just the three of them, except they didn't have to prepare meals back then with the luxury of having two sets of parents doting on them. Now, only one set remained. Life was moving fast and always had unexpected twists and turns. She was so glad Dan still had his parents and his aunt and uncle, despite Harry not having much time left. Whether she would still have a chance to have a family of her own yet she wasn't sure. She thought the time would come fairly soon but now with her marriage breakdown, that chance was gone.

They each shared the cooking of dinner while chomping on pieces of garlic bread, and soon their tastebuds were fully satisfied by gooey cheesy goodness.

'Yum, sooo good.' Dan wiped his mouth with a napkin. 'Thank you.'

'Thank *you*,' Katy said and glanced out the window, the blinds not yet closed for the night. 'Such a nice evening, spring is on its way.'

'I can feel it in the air,' Dan said.

'Might finally head out for that surfing session, or at least get some refresher training. I'm a bit out of practice,' Kane confessed.

'You'd still be better at it than me,' Dan said.

'You never were one for sports, were you?'

He shook his head. 'PE was my worst nightmare. But after school I got into interval training, which suited me better than having to navigate waves and sand.'

'Sounds fancy,' Kane replied, taking a sip of his lemonade. Katy hadn't bought any wine for the dinner, knowing that any addictive substance, whether alcohol or otherwise, could potentially trigger desire again within him, even though he'd never been that keen on wine anyway. But when one fix was missing, there was always a substitute to half fill that void.

Maybe Dan had noticed. 'I haven't had lemonade for years,' he said. 'So refreshing.'

'You prefer a cold one, I guess?'

'Beer? Nah, wine mostly, occasionally. Everything in moderation.'

Kane eyed Katy. 'Doesn't work for everyone,' he said.

'I'm sorry?' Dan raised his eyebrows.

'Moderation. I tried that and could only be all or nothing.'

'Oh, I see.' A slight hint of realisation showed in Dan's compassionate eyes. 'Well, lemonade is just as good a choice as anything.'

'Guess Katy told you about my drug problem.'

Dan almost spat out his lemonade. 'Um, no, she didn't actually.' He exchanged glances with her.

'Really?' Kane said with disbelief. 'It's okay, you don't have to pretend. It's not exactly a huge secret. Everyone knows I'm a bit of a dropkick.'

'Kane,' Katy said, reaching her hand out across the table and touching his arm. He flinched and pulled it away. 'I didn't tell him.'

'Yeah, she didn't, mate. She said you'd had some ups and downs and were staying with her to sort a few things out, that's all.'

Kane eyed them both as though trying to ascertain if either were lying.

'I'm your sister, I wouldn't share your personal details without your knowledge.'

'Jenna knows.'

'Jenna's always known, she saw you years ago when you were high and knows how hard it was for you. She doesn't judge. She just wants you to be okay.'

Kane shrugged.

'What matters is you're taking steps to move forward. That's what counts,' Dan said.

'Oh, what would you know?' Kane stood and the chair skidded against the polished floorboards.

'Kane,' Katy repeated, this time with a stern tone. She stood too.

'It's okay.' Dan placed a hand on her arm. 'It's okay.'

'No, it's not. Kane, you need to show some respect, Dan's our guest.'

'He's not our guest, we were childhood pals, practically siblings, playing in the dirt together, and now we're supposed to be all grown up and perfect, well, except for me, and–'

'Kane!' Katy stepped out from behind the table and followed Kane over to the window where he gazed at the ocean and ran a hand over his head. 'What's got into you?'

'Nothing!'

'It's obviously something. Did anything happen with your new job? I thought your first couple of days had gone well?'

'I can go,' Dan said, 'if you need some space.'

'No,' Katy said, turning back to him. Kane was not going to interrupt another nice evening at her house, even if Dan was simply an old friend.

Kane turned to look at Dan, his face reddening. 'You've gone and made a life for yourself. An amazing, successful life.

And my sister helps people and makes a difference. And me? What do I do? Nothing, that's what. There *is* no moving forward, *mate*. I may be off the drugs for now but nothing's ever changed for me and nothing *will*. It's hopeless, and no psych guru can tell me otherwise.' He turned back to look out the window.

Katy eyed Dan and mouthed, 'I'm sorry.'

He waved his hand as if it was no problem. Clearly, he wasn't perturbed by people losing it in front of him, he'd probably seen a lot. Dan picked up the plates from the table and took them to the kitchen.

'Kane, what's going on?' Katy stood beside him and gently placed her hand on his back. This time he didn't flinch.

'I don't know, maybe seeing him again triggered my low self-esteem. It's the reason I didn't go with you to the reunion. I didn't want to feel like I was being compared. Like a failure.'

'You are *not* a failure. You get knocked down but you keep getting back up. I'm proud of you.'

He gave a single disbelieving snort. 'I don't deserve your pride.'

Katy sighed. They'd gone through this so many times before. She always tried to support him and give him reassurance and praise, but did it really help? She walked away into the kitchen to give him some space.

'I'm sorry, Dan. He's clearly not doing as well as I thought,' she whispered.

'Really, it's okay. We had a nice dinner. I've had a nice day. We can call it a night.' He offered a small smile.

Katy's chin wobbled and her eyes stung. It *had* been a nice day, but a long one, and she wished she could just enjoy a simple nice evening with a guest without any drama.

Dan noticed. 'Hey, don't worry.' He placed his palm on her cheek. 'You're doing the best you can, and so is he.'

Kane cleared his throat at the entrance to the kitchen. They turned to face him. Katy wiped away a tear that had only just fallen. Kane lowered his head and shook it. 'Oh, man.' He sighed.

There was a moment of silence, then he tentatively approached his sister. 'Sorry, I didn't mean to upset you.'

She turned her face away a moment, then back again, no words forming.

'And I'm sorry, bro.' He looked at Dan.

'It's okay.'

'No, it was rude. I don't know what happened, sometimes my thoughts take over and I can't control the things that come out of my mouth.'

'I understand. Thanks for apologising.'

Kane leaned against the kitchen bench, exhaling. 'A guy at work was talking about how he's just gotten married, and another one has almost finished saving for an adventure holiday, and I guess comparison got the better of me and I felt bad about myself again.'

Compassion softened Katy's heart. 'Ah, yes, it's hard when you get talking to people,' she said. 'Once you settle in more to the job, I'm sure those feelings will calm down too.'

'She's right. Give it time,' Dan added.

Kane shrugged. 'Guess so. And then seeing you again.' He looked at Dan. 'It kind of added to it. Sorry you took the brunt of my low self-worth.'

Dan held out his hand and Kane shook it. 'We're friends, even though we lost touch for many years, we'll always be friends. I'm here if you need anything.'

'Oh, man. Why do I deserve such compassion? Thanks.'

'Getting an addiction doesn't make you a bad person.'

'The things I've done to maintain my addiction do, though.

But yeah, I got caught up in the wrong way of life and once you're in it, it's hard to get out.'

Dan nodded his understanding.

'You're right, what you said. I guess it does matter that I'm here and taking steps forward.'

'Absolutely.' Dan plucked his phone from his pocket. 'What's your number?'

Kane gave it and Dan texted him. 'Let me know if you need some company or help with anything while I'm in town. A surfing buddy even, though I'll probably watch from the sidelines.' He laughed.

'Okay. Will do.'

Katy leaned over and draped an arm around her brother. Crisis averted. He hugged her back.

'I promise, I'll get it together and leave you in peace as soon as I can,' Kane said.

Katy shook her head. 'Hey, whatever it takes. Go at your own pace. I'll never leave you on your own, okay? We're in this together.'

'Okay. But I'm still planning on leaving you in peace once my term deposit is up.'

'Okay.'

'Okay.'

'Right, how about some dessert?' Dan rubbed his hands together. 'What do we have?' He opened the freezer like he was, in fact, part of the household and not a guest, which each of them used to do at each other's houses anyway. 'Mmm, mind if I have some?' He held up a tub of Neapolitan ice cream.

'As long as I can have most of the strawberry,' Kane said, rushing to look in the tub.

Dan held it back. 'Really? Damn!'

'C'mon, you guys, you can have equal amounts of the

strawberry flavour.' She took the tub from Dan. 'I'll scoop it all into bowls so it's equal, okay?'

She placed three bowls on the bench and placed one scoop of vanilla and chocolate in each, followed by two scoops of strawberry in each, and then, before putting the lid on the tub, quickly scooped an extra strawberry and plonked it in her bowl and rushed off to the couch in the lounge room. 'Haha,' she said in a cheeky voice, feeling like a child again.

CHAPTER FOURTEEN

'Thanks for your help trying to defuse the situation before,' Katy said as Dan got into her car. Kane had said he was off for a shower and bed so he could get up on time for work.

Dan fastened his seat belt with a click. 'I don't know if I was much help, but I'm glad he was able to regulate himself and own up to his actions. That takes real guts and maturity.'

'Thanks for saying. He gets so down about himself, it's hard to help build him up again and again.'

Dan noticed the weariness in her voice. 'It must be draining for you.'

Katy nodded, starting the engine. 'How nice is the moon over the ocean.'

He glanced across the street and took it in. 'Stunning. Do you think a photo on my phone would do it justice? I could send it to Harry.'

'Not from here. We could stop by Lookout Point if you want?'

'Sounds good.'

The small fire within Dan continued to burn. It looked like their night wasn't over yet. He wasn't a tiny bit tired.

They parked and walked up to the lookout, and Katy rested her petite hands on the railing that had supported many hands over the decades as the breeze danced with her wispy hair.

'I remember not being tall enough to reach this very railing as a kid,' Dan said.

'Ha, yes. How time flies.'

'I'm surprised no one else is out here,' he added.

'Just wait for the October school holidays,' Katy said with a hint of annoyance. 'No parking, tourists galore flocking to all the town's landmarks.'

'Ah yes. Well, I'll have to revisit all the best the town has to offer before then... be a bit of a tourist myself. I don't think I fully appreciated the beauty of where we lived when I was younger.'

'Me neither. You just grow up alongside it and think the whole world is like this, until you venture away.'

'True. Oh, almost forgot.' Dan took his phone from his pocket and angled it upwards, centring the glowing moon. He took a few shots, and although they didn't replicate the real-life version, it was enough. He sent it quickly to his social media manager for them to do an Instagram story with, something about stopping to appreciate the moment and to see the light in others. Then he sent it to Harry with the caption: *It's not a funny meme, but the moon looks awesome tonight. Funny memes to follow as soon as I find some...* He would have a browse online later.

'Let's do a selfie,' Katy said, grabbing his phone, which made him chuckle. 'Can you imagine if we had selfies back then? We had to wait for our parents or someone else to take photos of us and then wait for them to be printed and hope they looked good.'

'Yeah, and we could never capture the best moments when

we were having adventures by ourselves because no one was there with a camera!'

'Yes. Sad in a way, but also good. We have to rely on our memory.'

'Personally, I'm kinda glad not many photos were taken back then, no doubt someone would find them and put them online and ruin my distinguished reputation!'

'Well, let's ruin that reputation now with a replica of that old photo, minus Kane though. I recall you had your fingers underneath your cheeks and I poked my tongue out.'

'Lucky you're holding the phone.' Dan hooked his fingers inside his mouth and pulled the funniest face he could muster.

A laugh exploded from Katy's mouth as she tried to poke her tongue out with as much effort as her childhood self. She snapped a few pictures and then took a 'normal' one of them laughing. 'Oh, that's a nice one,' she said. 'Send them to me. But no posting them online!'

'Wouldn't dream of it, don't you worry.' He took his phone back and sent her the images. 'Hey, we should do another replica with the three of us too, sometime. If Kane is up for it.'

'Good idea. It'd be nice for him to be reminded of his youth before he took a different path.'

Dan nodded. When he'd worked with clients who were depressed or suffering low self-esteem in the past, he'd encourage them to remember what they enjoyed about childhood and to bring some of that back into their adult lives. Some would discover long lost talents, and others would simply find more joy in the moment by pursuing an enjoyable hobby. He remembered one such client who, at the age of forty-three, got back into her teenage love of dancing and ended up opening her own dance studio. Life could always turn itself around if we just let it.

'What's this?' Katy asked, looking at the photos on her phone. 'I think you sent me an extra one by mistake.'

Dan's chest tightened, hoping he hadn't accidentally sent one of the selfies he'd taken in his room at the cabin in order to find a suitable snapshot for social media. But he relaxed on seeing it was of the stepping stones at the resort leading to a pond in the garden. 'Oh, oops. But a nice picture to accidentally send.'

'It's beautiful. I'd love to go visit the resort sometime and check it out, I've heard it's so nice and the landscaping is unique.'

'They might not let you in unless you happen to be invited by a guest.' He winked, though he wasn't sure if she saw it.

'Oh. Of course. Hmm...' She tapped her chin.

'How about on Saturday?'

Her brows rose. 'Saturday? Um, sure.'

'We can have lunch at the resort's restaurant too. It's like fine dining in the middle of a forest.'

'Wow. Count me in.'

'Invite Kane if he wants to come.' He didn't want her to think he was trying for a long-awaited second chance, which he wasn't, he just wanted to enjoy some reconnection and be able to leave town this time with a happy heart. And he wanted to help Kane feel included and supported.

'I'll ask. Wandering around gardens isn't really his thing though. He might get the urge to climb a tree and throw berries and twigs at passers-by like he used to!'

'Oh, I forgot about that. He got all of us into trouble a few times, didn't he?'

Katy nodded, then held up the moon photo. 'Amazing really, how this little device can capture a moment in time, as though it's paused forever.'

'It is. Technology, huh? So confusing but so amazing and useful.'

A memory swirled and Dan tried to grasp it. It popped up to the surface just as he was about to forget. 'Oh my God. Do you remember, back when we were, what, ten or eleven? That thing, we buried it.' He held out his hands as though holding the object.

Katy's eyes bulged. 'The time capsule! Oh, wow, I had literally forgotten. How could I forget?' She held a hand to her forehead.

'Life gets busy and filled with other things.' He shrugged. 'But yes, the time capsule!' He grasped her arms eagerly. 'Do you think it's still there? Probably been dug up by now or shrubs planted there or something.'

Katy held up her hands. 'Who knows? Only one way to find out.' She started walking down. 'Oh, but wait! Didn't we agree to open it in fifty years' time?'

'That was when we were ten and fifty years is when we'll be sixty. Who knows where we'll be then?' He thought of Harry. 'No, let's do it now. There's no time like the present. Sometimes, it's all we have.'

'You're so right. Let's go!'

They giggled and ran down to the base of the lookout, got in the car, and drove to the other lookout by the beachside cabins where the grand Tarrin rock formation stood. They parked in one of the parking bays, and he eyed the scattered lights shining in the row of cabins long the beach... such a beautiful sight. People enjoying holiday time, family time, couple time, and making the most of this beautiful location. He could have rented one of them but they'd all been booked out, so he'd opted for the new resort.

A couple were walking hand in hand down the pathway

from the lookout, chattering cutely to each other. They turned quiet on passing Katy and Dan then resumed once out of earshot.

'Wait, don't we need a digging implement?' Dan said.

'We didn't bury it that deep, we could probably just use sticks.' She laughed.

'Got a crowbar? Or whatever they're called here.'

She shook her head. 'They always have those in cars in horror movies.' She shivered. 'Oh! But I do have a picnic basket.'

'A picnic basket?' Dan eyed her curiously.

'It has knives and forks and plates and stuff. Hardly use it. I should, really, but that's for another day. Anyway, yes, knives and forks!'

'Knives and forks it is!' Dan laughed and shook his head. 'Are we really doing this? What if we get in trouble?'

Katy looked him in the eye. 'I've heard that many times from you and have I ever got you in trouble? Kane maybe, but me?' She put on an innocent expression with pouted lips and wide eyes.

Dan's smile grew and his nerves tingled with anticipation. They got the picnic basket from the car and walked on the other side of the pathway's incline where there was a grassy area obscured from the nearby houses by trees and shrubs. A small park bench sat in front of one of the trees, and he was sure many first kisses had happened here. Thankfully, no one was around. At least if anyone approached, it would look like they'd simply enjoyed a late-night picnic, and were not two suspicious people digging something up.

'Was it somewhere here?' Katy gestured to a small tree next to a larger tree.

'No, it was this one, over here, remember?' Dan pointed to the bare patch of earth where the pathway above curved around a little... it was an awkward small space that he was sure town planners or maintenance gardeners would've filled in with shrubbery, but it looked like they'd kept all the natural trees and plants from years ago.

'It's been twenty-eight years, it might be too lodged in with overgrowth and a more developed root system, or it might've disintegrated.'

'Hope not.' Katy knelt on the ground and looked up at Dan. 'Ready to get your hands dirty?'

'I've heard that many times from you in the past too! "Let's make mud pies, let's set up the farm animal figures in the dirt, let's set up a desert hospital in a war zone with the army figurines..."' He laughed and knelt down too, rolling up his sleeves.

'I'm not afraid of dirt or blood, you know that,' Katy said.

'I never would have done half the things I did if it wasn't for your encouragement, or should I say forcefulness?'

She whacked him lightly on the arm. 'Encouragement always.' She smiled. 'And aren't you glad I did? Gave you lots of fun times to remember.'

'Sure did. Okay, let's see. May I make the first dig?'

'Go ahead.'

'Knife and fork, please.' He held out his palm like he was a surgeon awaiting a scalpel. She placed them gently onto his hand. 'Good thing they're proper metal ones and not dodgy plastic ones.'

'No need to skimp when it comes to picnics. Although, the plates are plastic, sorry. We can use them to scrape away the dirt once we get in there.' She got a couple at the ready. He noticed the rock they'd put there to mark the spot had disappeared. As expected, not everything would be where it was.

'Hope your dishwasher has a heavy-duty cycle for these once we're done.' He smiled, then stabbed the fork into the dirt. It was hard and crumbly, but as he got further in it became softer and denser. He used the knife to scrape away dirt and the fork to dig deeper each time. Katy got in on the action and they giggled and dug, reminding each other to shush occasionally so as to not attract any attention should someone be walking nearby.

'I hope we've got the right spot or we might have to dig a much wider hole.'

'I'm sure it was just... about... here.' He grunted as he dug deeper and the fork hit against something. 'Ooh!' They kept digging and using the plates to scrape dirt away, eventually revealing a large rectangle gourmet biscuit tin.

'Woohoo!' Katy exclaimed. 'Could you imagine us as sixty-year-olds doing this? With arthritic knees and aching backs.'

'Yeah, we probably would have needed to bring those low camp chairs to make it easier.' He laughed. He brushed away dirt from the surface of the tin, which he recalled being given to Katy's family by his family one Christmas, hence why they decided to use it as a combined time capsule for the both of them. Kane hadn't wanted to take part and had gone on some bike racing thing the day they buried it. Katy's mother had been storing wool in it but said they could have it once she heard about their plans.

They dug their hands either side of the tin and loosened it from the soil, lifting it out. Dan gripped one side and tried to prise the lid open. Katy tried but it only budged slightly. Dan brushed off some more dirt and banged on the lid a few times, and then was able to get it open with a pop. His heart beat fast with excitement.

With eyes wide they peered into the tin, the moonlight providing enough light to see the polyester scarf wrapped around two glass jars. 'Mum's old scarf!' Katy said. 'I forgot.' She held it to her nose and breathed in, her eyes closing a moment. 'When I told her what we were doing she helped me decide what to use and said to wrap it in her scarf as it wouldn't break down as easily as other fabrics.'

Dan noticed her eyes shining in the moonlight and had the urge to reach out his dirt laden hand and touch her cheek, but he held back. Katy gave the scarf a shake and wrapped it around her neck, then picked up one of the jars that had her name written inside on faded paper. Dan picked up his jar.

'Ready? I hope we can open these now!'

They pulled the metal clasps down and the air released with a pop from under the lids. Twenty-eight years of preserved memories unleashed.

'Again, lucky we don't have arthritic fingers yet,' Katy said.

'Yet? Speak for yourself.'

'Most people over sixty have some degree of it, can't always escape the ravages of ageing.'

'I'll try not to think about it.' He delved his fingers into the jar, lifting out a piece of paper with the date from twenty-eight years ago written on it, and his childlike handwriting:

DAN'S TIME CAPSULE! IF YOU FIND THIS, PUT IT BACK! WE WILL OPEN THIS IN FIFTY YEARS.

He folded it back up. He took out a Matchbox car. 'My Ferrari Testarossa! I should have kept the box, maybe it'd be worth something today.' He pulled out a coin. 'Same with this, the Sir Henry Parkes one dollar coin. Wonder if it's worth anything? I'm going to do some research later!'

'I should have put something valuable in mine too, I only have my favourite hair scrunchie, my Strawberry Shortcake figurine,' she held it to her nose and breathed in, 'which, oh my God, still smells nice! And the first-place ribbon from winning the eight hundred metre final in the athletics carnival when I was nine.'

'I remember that day. You were way ahead right up till the end.'

'Only because my best competitor got a bindii from the grass track stuck in her foot halfway through, and another one fell over and twisted her ankle.'

'Still. It's an achievement.'

'I think that's why I put it in here and didn't keep it. I felt bad for them!'

Dan smiled. 'Do you have the list we wrote? Let's read our answers together.' He took out a piece of typewriter paper he'd taken from Sandy's home office, which had been rolled into a scroll.

'Got mine too.' Katy cleared her throat. 'Okay. On this day, my favourite book was: *The Famous Five* by Enid Blyton.'

'Mine was any of the *Goosebumps* books!'

'I liked those too! And *The Babysitters Club*. Okay, next question. My favourite place to go: the beach or the rainforest.'

'Mine was,' he cleared his throat, 'the library.'

'Next: What I think life will be like in fifty years' time – ooh, we still have to wait for that one – I said there'd be no more wars. Hmm, not looking good. Also, we'll have a female prime minister. Been there, done that. And school will only be four days a week instead of five. Ha!'

Dan chuckled. 'Oh God, this is mine: In fifty years, I'll be married to a wonderful wife and we'll live in a top-floor apartment with shiny things everywhere.'

Katy laughed. 'Is your apartment in the US shiny?'

'Yes, but I don't have a wonderful shiny wife.'

'There's still time!'

'And...' he continued, 'we'll be able to travel to different countries in only a few hours via special cars that fly and follow a holographic road system to keep everyone in the right spot. People will travel to the moon to celebrate birthdays and special occasions at the Moon Hotel. Me and Katy and Kane will have a party at the Moon Hotel each year to celebrate our birthdays all at the same time.'

'Oh wow, I want to jump ahead to the future now!'

'But wait, that's not all… old people will no longer have grey hair, thanks to scientists curing the cause of grey hair.' He burst out laughing at his silliness.

'Dan, oh my God! I had no idea you wrote all that, were you actually being serious?!'

'Um, yes I think I was!'

'Well, lo and behold, forget about diseases, let's prioritise a cure for grey hair!' She cracked up with laughter and slapped her thigh.

'Well, I thought that would be nice for many people.' He shrugged. 'But yes, a bit naïve of me.' He thought how much he wished there was a cure for Harry's cancer.

Inside the jar he also found an old rock with some flickers of quartz crystal throughout. 'Cool. I mean rad. I remember collecting a few interesting rocks when you force– *encouraged* me to go on all those long explorational walks.'

She peered closer and shone her phone light onto it. 'Nice. Did your parents write a note too?' she asked, holding a folded piece of paper carefully in her hands. 'I don't know if I can read this.'

His breath halted. A note from her mum and dad who were no longer here.

'I'll look at mine first.' He pulled it out. It was rolled up like a scroll and tied with red ribbon. He unrolled it and luckily the ink was still readable and not smudged.

Dear Daniel,

We are writing this together, Sandy and I. Well, I am writing and she is adding words as I go. A time capsule, eh?

What a cool idea! I do hope you can find it again in fifty years, and I do hope we will still be alive when you do. Please show it to us if we are! We want you to know how very wanted you were. It wasn't easy for us back then, women like us weren't as accepted as I hope they are in your future. And having a baby was usually not an option or not an easy one. We found a way to bring you into the world – Thanks to Katy and Kane's parents who got chatting to a donor in the waiting room at the IVF clinic. They were able to put him in contact with us, and he was happy to help, and we are forever grateful. We hope we have been good parents to you, and that we were enough. We hope you are as proud of us as we are of you. You are the best part of our lives and we love you to the moon and back.

If there's something you want to do in life, go for it. We support you. And you can achieve anything you set your mind to. Oops, by the time you read this you'll be sixty, so we hope you have already followed your dreams and achieved what you want! We will make sure to tell you this anyway, in person. We hope you can look back on your life and say 'I did it. I did what was right for me and didn't let anyone tell me what I can and can't do. I've built a great life for myself and I am surrounded by love and friendship. Life is good!'

Always look after your health, listen to your intuition, and we know you'll have a great future.

Love always,

Mum and Mum xo

Dan's heart fluttered and his eyes warmed with tears. He slotted the letter in his shirt pocket. He would bring the jar back, of course, but wanted the words close to his heart. 'I'm so glad we opened this now and not another two decades or so later.'

Katy lightly touched his arm, then slowly opened her letter. She held it between them so they could both read it. Her chest rose high and a shaky breath emerged as her chest fell.

Dear Katy,

Our miracle daughter. We were so lucky to have you and your brother after years of infertility. I had reached the point where I thought it might not happen, and I knew that we only had one more chance, because our money and energy had been exhausted. IVF was still in the early stages back then. But our final cycle yielded two good quality embryos and it worked! The doctor advised that we try one embryo at a time and freeze the other one, but freezing was still experimental back then, and I was insistent that we wanted one last try with both of them together. I never would have thought that both would work, let alone one, but you two were obviously meant to be in the world.

We know that by the time you read this, you'll have hopefully lived a long, healthy life and still have many years ahead of you. We certainly hope we'll still be around then too, but we'll be getting on a bit! Whatever the future holds, don't worry, don't stress, just enjoy each moment. Stay connected to the world, reach out if you need help, and hold your friends dear.

You have always been curious, resourceful, helpful, caring, patient, and practical. You give anything a try and have immense courage. Don't lose that. Even if things don't go to plan in life, trust that you can always turn your life around at any time. You can always start again. Your life is yours to live and enjoy, so do what makes you happy, and

*don't lose touch with that child inside who loved to play
and explore all day.*

*As we get older, we've realised that youth really is
fleeting. Make the most of it, well we hope you have by the
time you read this! If at this point in time there are still
things you want to do, do them! Don't hold back, don't think
you can't, and don't wait. Life is now. Enjoy, love, and
laugh.*

Love,

Mum and Dad.

Dan held a hand to Katy's back as her upper body shook a little and tears fell down her face. Despite the dirt on his hands, he wiped the side of her cheek before tears fell on the letter. She looked across at him, her face soft, her eyes glossy under the moonlight. 'I wish I could thank them,' she said. 'I wish I could rush over to them and hold up the letter and say "I finally got it!"'

Dan's heart ached for her. He would be able to do that, but she couldn't. He hoped opening the time capsule early had been the right thing to do and would not trigger her grief. He would make sure to check in on her over the coming days to make sure.

Katy sniffed and wiped the corner of her eyes with the back of her wrist. She went to fold the letter but paused. She lifted the page and saw that another one was behind it.

'There's more?' Dan asked.

'It's for Kane,' she said with a smile. 'Even though he didn't take part, they still left a note for him too.' She looked Dan in the eyes. 'Do you think it will help him to read this now or make things harder for him?'

Dan twisted his lips. 'Depends what it says, I guess.'

Katy read it and Dan looked away to give her privacy.

'It's similar to mine but it also touches on his spontaneous and energetic nature, his curiosity also, and his trusting of other people. They say to be careful of letting life sweep him away and to find his roots, his base, his foundation and build from that. Interesting though, that this is life advice intended for a sixty-year-old who's already been through the ups and downs of life. It's almost like they knew they would be leaving this world early and that we'd be opening it sooner than expected.'

'Perhaps it'll help him. Even if it rattles him a little at first, I do believe it will be a positive thing overall.'

Katy nodded. 'I'll show him tomorrow after work. And I'll ask him if he wants to visit the resort on Saturday as well.'

'Sounds good.'

Katy leaned over and put her arms around him. 'Thanks, Dan. This has been... emotional, but fun. I feel like a kid again!'

They put the things back in the jars and filled the hole in the ground with dirt.

'They did say to not lose touch with your inner child, so maybe there are more things you can do to embrace that. It's something I teach actually, as it helps people remember who they are at their core and what brings them joy.'

'Apart from digging in the dirt, which we've done tonight, I loved riding my skateboard.' She laughed. 'Can you imagine me, thirty-eight, flying down the road on a skateboard?!'

Dan patted the top of the mound of dirt and shrugged. 'Why not? Age shouldn't stop you.'

'But I'll probably fall off and hurt myself.' She drew a heart shape on the dirt mound.

'Wear knee pads and elbow pads and a helmet.'

'We never did that when we were young.'

'We're not young anymore, and you do need to be careful of those arthritic joints.' He winked.

'Okay.' She stood. 'I promise I'll give it a go. *If* you do too.' She pointed at him.

He gulped. He'd never been that good at skateboarding as a kid and he doubted anything had changed in two decades. 'As long as it's somewhere private.'

'So I take it you don't want to go to the skate park that's filled with kids doing fancy moves?'

'Hell, no.' He shook his head. 'We can figure something out at the weekend. Let's get going so you can get some sleep, it's a school night, remember!'

'Haha, yes. I have patients to see from 9am. Need to be refreshed.'

Dan picked up the biscuit tin along with his jar, and Katy carried the picnic basket with the now-dirty cutlery along with her jar to the car.

They drove in relative silence to the clinic car park where Dan's rental car sat in isolation.

'Thanks for a great night,' Dan said as she put the handbrake on.

'It was eventful, that's for sure. And great, once Kane's disruption was sorted out.'

'I'd already forgotten about it.' He smiled. 'And the time capsule, it's given me an idea for Harry.'

'Oh, good. When do you see him next?'

'I'll visit tomorrow.'

She nodded, then yawned. 'Well, safe driving back to the resort.'

'Of course. You too, back home.'

For some reason he didn't want to get out of the car. He held her gaze and he saw something different, in her eyes. Something softer, but also more alive. What was it? It was as though there was something lingering, a floating string in the air between them that he couldn't quite grasp. Unspoken words perhaps, or a maybe just the exhumed grief. He realised she was probably waiting for him to say goodbye and get out of the car, but when he did, and waved at her through the window, the look in her eyes remained. It was like they were trying to pull him to her, like their hug from before had not ended. He was tempted to tap on the window to ask if she was okay, but stepped away, waving again. It was enough for one night. He would see how she was tomorrow. In fact, he had an idea for her too, and he smiled as he got into the car and mentally planned his day and the surprise that would await Katy at the end of her work day.

CHAPTER FIFTEEN

'Thanks, Sylvia,' Katy said as Dr Greene finished up with one of Katy's patients in the clinic.

'All good to go now, Mrs Berton.' Katy helped the elderly lady up from the bed. 'Do you need assistance getting out to your taxi?'

'Oh, no, thanks, dear. I'll be right as rain. This infusion will have me at my best in no time.'

'Well, take your time and let us know if you experience any dizziness or excessive fatigue.'

She nodded. 'Cheerio. And you have yourself a lovely evening, Ms McKenzie.'

'You too.' Katy smiled. She especially loved her elderly patients. They were always so polite and friendly; had been through a lot and didn't complain about trivial things the way some younger people did. Well, most of them. She did have a few older patients who were grumpy and grizzly, but often it was simply from being in chronic pain or being tired, and she did her best to have patience with them. She also knew that a patient's mood could be an indicator of other health issues such as diabetes or blood sugar fluctuations, vitamin deficiencies, memory issues, or neurological issues, and always noted down their demeanour on their file, if it was anything out of the ordinary, for their doctor to review at the next appointment.

Katy glanced at the clock above reception where Jenna sat yawning. 'Almost home time, hun, just a bit longer,' Katy said.

Jenna smiled, then leaned under the counter and pulled out a packet of Tic Tacs. 'Want one?' She held up the berry flavoured pellets. 'Lexi brought some home yesterday after Dan's talk and I think I've found my new addiction.' She held the packet out and Katy took a few. 'Oh, sorry. I shouldn't joke about addiction.'

Katy waved her hand away as berry flavour burst through her mouth. 'It's okay. No biggie.' She glanced down the hall and saw a familiar face walking towards the nurses' clinic. 'Speaking of Lexi...'

Jenna got up from behind the desk. 'Sweetheart, what are you doing here? Wasn't I going to pick you up from Noah's?'

Katy noticed her forearm. There was a line of blood streaked across it. Instinctively she went to her and grasped it gently.

'What happened?' Jenna approached her daughter and put her hand on her arm.

Lexi sniffed and her eyes and cheeks were a bit pink. 'I just scraped it on a branch. Will I need stitches?'

'Looks superficial,' Katy said. 'But still a decent gash. Let me take you into one of the treatment bays so I can take a better look.'

'Can I do anything?' Jenna asked.

'Want a cup of tea or hot chocolate, Lexi?' Katy asked.

'Um. Okay, hot chocolate.'

'On it,' Jenna said. 'Be back soon.' She went off down the hallway towards the staff kitchen.

Katy wanted a chance to talk to Lexi privately. She took her to the treatment bay and she sat on the side of the bed. Katy turned on the overhead lamp and inspected the gash. 'A branch, eh?'

'Yes. I lost my balance, tripped, and tried to catch my fall.'

Katy nodded. 'No stitches needed. But we'll need to clean it up and close the wound with a dressing.' She gathered the supplies and began cleaning the wound. 'May I ask...' she lowered her voice to a whisper, 'did you end up getting your period?'

Lexi nodded. 'All good.'

Phew. 'And how are things with Noah?'

She bit her lip and blinked her eyes. 'We broke up.'

'Oh, Lex, I'm sorry. Are you okay?'

She nodded.

'Was this because of the advice in Dan's talk?'

'Partly. It helped me know I was doing the right thing. Noah wanted me to take the pill so we wouldn't have another pregnancy scare, but I looked into it and it just didn't feel right to me, so I said no. And he said he didn't want to risk it and that maybe we shouldn't be together. But,' she sniffed again, 'I'm sad. I really liked him.'

'I know. It's so hard, hun. But if he didn't respect your decision about your own body, then maybe...'

'For the best.'

Jenna's footsteps became louder. 'One hot chocolate coming right up!' Jenna popped her head around the curtain.

Lexi's chin trembled.

'Sweetheart, are you okay? Does it hurt?'

Lexi shook her head. Katy kept quiet, giving Lexi time to speak if she wanted to tell her mother. She disinfected the wound and closed it up with a waterproof padded dressing. 'Keep this on and dry for a few days. You can shower with it on. I'm just going to go check your tetanus status on the computer.'

Katy smiled and exited the treatment bay. As she searched her vaccination history, she overheard Lexi sniffling with tears, telling her mother what happened with Noah.

'How did you trip?'

'I lost my balance suddenly. Noah was upset about breaking up, and–'

'He didn't hurt you?' Jenna asked urgently.

'No, not at all. But he got kinda... agitated, and he just said "well I guess this is it then" and grabbed some twigs off the tree and chucked them. It was sudden so it kinda gave me a fright, and I flinched and stumbled backwards, tripping on a tree root. I grabbed a branch and another one scraped my arm. I feel so silly.'

'Don't feel silly, it's a normal reaction. As long as you're sure he didn't hurt you in any way?'

Lexi was quiet and Katy assumed she was nodding.

'Okay then. Drink up, take a few minutes, and then we'll head home. I'll just close down some things on the computer system, okay?'

'Okay.'

'You don't need another tetanus shot, your last one is still valid,' Katy called out.

'Okay,' Lexi called back.

'You okay?' Katy whispered to Jenna, who looked more upset by the wound and break-up than Lexi did.

'Just got worried for a minute that he'd hurt her.'

'Understandable.'

With Jenna's history of being in an abusive relationship with Lexi's father, it was bound to cause post-traumatic stress for both of them. And it explained Lexi's automatic reaction to Noah's behaviour.

Jenna finished up her work quickly and grabbed her handbag, giving Katy a peck on the cheek before escorting her daughter out of the clinic. Lexi mouthed, 'Thank you' when she glanced back and Katy offered a reassuring smile.

After returning a phone call to a patient, Katy closed up and drove home. On the way, she found herself thinking about Dan and all that had happened the night before. But most of all, she found herself remembering a strange sensation she'd felt on dropping him off at his car in the car park. She'd been ready to call it a night and go home, but at the same time she'd wanted, needed, something else. She wasn't quite sure if it was just the need for comfort in her grief, but there'd been a warmth in the air between her and Dan. He was so familiar to her, but after such a long absence he also felt so new to her, like finding an old family heirloom that had gone missing. She wanted to keep feeling that warmth, keep it close and wrap it around her like a warm, cosy blanket.

When she entered her house and kicked off her shoes, she did a double take at a brightly coloured item near the inside of the front door. *What the...*

'Ah, you're back. Dan left that on the doorstep, it was waiting there when I got home.' Kane eyed her with curiosity.

Katy chuckled at the multi-coloured graffitied skateboard with a huge red bow wrapped around it. She bent down and picked it up. 'And I thought he would try to forget about it.'

'Forget what?'

'Ah, just that he said I should try skateboarding again to get in touch with my inner child. I said I'd do it if he did.'

'Does that mean you have to buy him one too?'

She shrugged. 'Guess I can't forget about it now either! Wonder if I can still ride these things.' She turned the board around to examine all its parts and curves.

'I'll give it a go, gimme.' Kane went to grab it.

'Not so fast.' She pulled it away. 'I do remember you broke yours once.'

'Yeah, along with my wrist. I gave it up after that.'

'My point exactly.' She grinned. 'I actually can't wait to try it out! But not here, somewhere suitable and after I've warmed up properly so I don't hurt myself. It has been a while.'

'That's so cool. How come you took so long coming back last night?'

'I thought you'd gone to bed early.'

'Yeah, but I was still awake and hadn't heard you come home.'

'Sorry, I should have texted. Dan and I stopped by the lookout to take a photo of the moon, and,' she plucked the letter from her handbag, 'we dug up our time capsule two decades earlier than planned.'

Kane's eyes widened. 'Really? It was still there, all intact?'

She nodded. 'It was so much fun. I wish you'd taken part too, but guess what?' She handed him the letter. 'Only open this when you're ready. It's, a, um, letter from Mum and Dad.'

His eyes bulged.

'Written when we were ten on the assumption we wouldn't be reading it until we were sixty. Let's just say I'm glad we opened it earlier. But it did make me emotional, so you have been warned.' She went into the kitchen and poured a glass of water. 'Here for you if you want to talk about it later.'

Kane shifted from one foot to the other, gripping the letter as though it might fly away. 'Okay, I might look at it later. After dinner. I'll see how I feel.'

Katy nodded. Kane went upstairs and she popped a frozen pizza in the oven. She didn't feel like cooking tonight, and Kane (apart from his foray into garlic bread) was not that great in the kitchen. She really should teach him a few more skills while he was here. But not tonight.

She sank into the couch and put her feet up on a cushion, opened her text messages, and sent one to Dan.

> What a surprise! I love it. Thank you. But you need one too, don't forget.

He responded with a photo of another skateboard with love hearts and smiley faces all over it.

> I figured this one was most suitable for a dating coach, even if I'm going to look ridiculous on it. Besides, I'm going to donate it to a needy family at the end of the year before I go back home.

> That's a good idea. So, shall I bring it on Saturday?

> Yes. But no need to drive here, I'm going to pick you up this time. That way I can have more control where we go for our skateboarding, LOL. About 10.30am?

> Sounds good. Do I need protective gear?

> I've got it covered. Is Kane coming?

> No, he said he'd give it a miss, and is actually meeting up to go fishing with a couple of the guys from work, so that's good.

> Great. Okay, see you on Saturday!

She sent two extremely happy smiley face emojis. She had been going to ask how his visit with Harry went, but it didn't feel appropriate now. It also didn't feel appropriate to feel that warmth again but there it was.

CHAPTER SIXTEEN

Dan faced the phone camera towards his face and pulled a worried expression. He sent it to Katy with the text:

> This is how scared I am about today's skateboarding.

After a few minutes, she replied:

> This is how much I'm looking forward to watching you be scared.

Then she sent a photo of herself laughing.

> Meanie.

He sent a wink emoji.

He put his phone in the pocket of his cargo pants, grabbed a bottle of water and his keys, and a duffle bag of protective gear which he'd hired. His skateboard was already in the car as he'd left it in the boot, covered by a windscreen sun shield for security. He paced around a few times, thinking he'd forgotten something, but realised it was just his confidence. He paused at the door and took a breath. If he was to encourage people to make changes in their life or utilise strategies, he had to be willing to do the same. A good psychologist practises what they preach. Even if that meant going skateboarding.

He stepped outside and looked up. Blue skies and only sparse clouds. *Damn.* He was partly hoping it would rain and he could get out of embracing his inner child for the day. But another deep breath and he was on his way.

When he'd had dinner with his parents the night before, they'd applauded his plans to take Katy skateboarding. 'That woman needs to let loose, she works so hard,' Ellen had said. 'She was always such an active and joyful child.' He'd shown them the letter they'd written for his time capsule and they'd all shared a few tears. He'd told them how grateful he was to have them, especially knowing Katy no longer had hers, and they vowed to catch up with her more often and make sure she was okay after he went back to the States.

Dan played loud nineties music on the drive over, singing along and hoping it would get him into the zone and boost his confidence, but it only reminded him how bad a singer he was. He laughed at himself as he arrived at Katy's.

She was already opening the front door when he was about to get out of the car, clearly keen to get going and reignite her skateboarding skills. He gulped when he saw her, dressed in black exercise tights that moulded to her slim yet curved thighs and hips; a slinky but slightly loose-fitting purple T-shirt, and her hair in a low ponytail with wisps whooshing around her heart-shaped face in the light breeze dancing across from the ocean.

'Hi!' She waved, then flung a canvas knapsack over her shoulder. She started walking towards the car then did something that he usually did – a little jig.

He laughed. 'Are you embracing your inner child or mine?'

'Both!'

She got into the car and when the engine came to life, loud music blared. He pushed the volume button repeatedly. 'Sorry! Was getting into my teen spirit.'

'Cool. Turn it back up.'

They sang along as he drove to where he was hoping would be private, no witnesses in sight.

'High school oval car park?'

He smiled and nodded as he pulled into the deserted area. 'Will we get in trouble for trespassing?'

'Don't think so, it's kind of public. There's no sport on till September though.'

'How do you know; do you take part or coach?'

'No, I see the injuries that come into the clinic each spring.'

'Ah, of course. Well, hopefully no injuries today!'

'If there is, don't worry, you've got a trained nurse at your disposal.' She got out of the car and pushed the door closed with her hip. The movement made his stomach flutter.

'Be prepared to try something new,' he said, though he thought he was thinking it, not speaking out loud.

'New? This is old hat to me.'

'Sorry, I was just recalling one of my dating principles. I encourage people to try something new, whether it be for a date itself, instead of the usual dinner, coffee, or drinks, or on their own to discover a new experience to enrich their lives and have something else interesting to talk about with a date.'

Katy placed her hands on her hips, surveying the scene and no doubt scouting out the best places to skate. 'That's really good advice. For anyone, I think, dating or not.'

'Exactly.' He grabbed the duffle bag and skateboard from the boot.

'Here, let me put your water and keys into my knapsack.' She grabbed his loose items and secured them in her bag.

She walked and he followed. 'I'll have to read one of your books, Dan. I would have earlier to show my support, but being married, I didn't think I had the need.'

'And now?'

'It's still early days after my divorce. But it's been so long since I've dated, they probably do things differently now! I did have one date recently, but it was also the night Kane arrived on my doorstep, so it fizzled out pretty quickly.'

'I see. Well, happy to give you tips any time.' Something awkward and uncomfortable twisted inside his belly. 'Not that I think you'd need them much.'

'But I like what you told the teenagers, that unless something really feels right, you don't continue.'

'Yep. Too many people get into relationships because they're lonely and the thought of being alone again is worse than being in an unfulfilling relationship, so they stay. But I promised myself I'd never do that,' he explained.

'I like your integrity.' She glanced back and smiled. 'Now, I'm thinking that slope over behind the stands on the oval would be good for some rad moves.'

Dan scrunched his face. 'Umm, how about we start on flat ground to get used to the board first?'

'Oh yes, good idea, sorry. Getting ahead of myself. This is going to be so much fun!'

He tried his best to flash an excited, though nervous, smile.

They dropped their bags near some parking bays on the side of the oval. There was also a curved driveway that went around the back, and it sloped downwards behind the school grounds. At the very least, he could sit on the board and roll down the hill. Less chance of an injury or making a fool of himself.

'Okey dokey. Let's warm up, shall we?'

'Definitely. I can do some of the warm ups from my HIIT classes, or do you have any better ideas?'

'Some stretches would be good, but let's do your warm up first to get the blood circulating.'

'Okay.' He swung his arms back and forth and she copied. Then he walked on the spot a few steps, then walked a few steps to the right, then back again, then on the spot, and then he increased his speed and raised his knees high with each step before slowing down again, and repeating. After several minutes, his muscles became warm and energised.

Katy stood on one foot and balanced for a while, before swapping to the other leg. 'This will activate your core balance and your hip tendons, to make sure you can be ready for sudden impact and for all the squatting and bending on the skateboard.'

'I don't know how much squatting I'll be doing unless it's to sit down and take a break, but I'll do what the expert says.' He smiled and copied her movements. They stretched all the major muscle groups and soon were feeling as ready as they could ever be.

'You should come to Pilates class with me sometime, you'd probably like it,' she said.

'Hmm, maybe. It could be good for me to try something new, as I recommend.'

'Exactly. Now, let's get on these boards!'

They put on their padding and he watched her first, as she used her foot to push against the ground and gain momentum, riding the skateboard along the level path. He got on his and did the same. Nothing hard about this, but he didn't know if he would do anything much beyond this and sitting on it.

She approached a parking bay block and tilted the skateboard up onto it to a stop.

He tried to do the same, although when he stopped it wobbled and he lost his footing. 'Oops. Think I'll practise that a few more times.'

She gave him a thumbs up and left him in peace to practise while she rode back and forth, raising one end of the board and flipping it to the side to turn around. 'Yeah, baby. I've still got it.' She laughed. 'This is fun.'

He smiled widely at her happiness in the moment. It was nice to see. Dan tried to turn the board around. It was a bit awkward at first and not as smooth as her performance, but he managed the basics. Soon he was riding back and forth, smiling and laughing, losing his footing a few times, but it didn't bother him and so far, no injuries.

'Ready for the slope?'

'I'm game if you are.' Of course she would be.

Katy walked to the top of the slope then rode down, doing a slight jump and grabbing hold of the board with her hands before landing easily, and bringing herself to a stop further down the path.

He shook his head. Where had the time gone? It was like they'd teleported back to their teenage years and he was watching her skills as he normally did, admiring her athleticism and joy.

Dan walked to the top of the slope, sat on the board, and let himself roll down the hill. 'Woohoo!' he called out, and raised his arms up into the air. He allowed his speed to slow and stopped the board. 'That was awesome,' he said. 'Don't think I'll try your little lift thingy just yet, but I really want to do that again!'

'Go for it!' she replied. 'In fact, I'll join you. Race?'

She eyed him with cheeky determination and they ran up the slope together, boards in hand. Huffing and laughing, they sat on their boards and gave themselves a push off down the slope, going at about the same pace, until Katy started using her hands to push herself along and she took the lead.

'I think the Olympics are waiting for you,' he said with a chuckle on stopping the board.

'Ha, well you never know. I don't think they have a roll down the hill race though.'

'Well, they should.' He stood and glanced at the slope. 'Again?'

She nodded, and they spent the next hour and a half trying out different moves and different locations, and they each took photos and videos of each other.

'Thanks,' Katy said when he'd finished filming her doing an ollie. 'Something to show my grandkids one day!' She laughed and rode off again, and Dan's smile softened, his mood dropping a little.

He had been honest throughout his dating life that he'd decided not to have kids. Some women had left the date then and there, others were totally fine about it. He'd thought when he was younger that he'd wanted them, could picture himself reading to his future children one day, but as he grew older things changed, and now, nearing forty, he didn't know if he wanted to upend his lifestyle to start a family.

He breathed in deeply and exhaled quickly through pouted lips making a bubbly sound. It was a technique to reset the nervous system when feeling stressed or uncomfortable. He didn't know why he was feeling uncomfortable, but the thought of Katy becoming a mother and being with someone else had always been an uncomfortable feeling to him. But it was just his old memories resurfacing and being triggered again, that was all. And a reminder that they were never meant to be more than friends. She would make a great parent, and he genuinely hoped she got to have that chance one day.

They finished up and got back to the car, puffing and sweaty. 'That was so good. Thanks, Dan, for encouraging me.'

'Thanks for *force*-encouraging me.' He winked. He saw that look in her eye again, the one from the other night, only without the grief this time, just pure joy and connection. If there was such a thing as a soul-friend, he was sure she must be his.

CHAPTER SEVENTEEN

'Wow, it *is* like fine dining in a forest.' Katy glanced around in awe at the Trees of Life Resort Restaurant, trees surrounding them from outside the glass.

'I know, right? Where would you like to sit?'

She eyed the tables. 'Over there.' She pointed to a cosy corner near the beginning of the floor-to-ceiling windows.

Gabriel, the manager, who Dan had introduced her to, led them to their table and handed them the menus before bringing a carafe of water. As she perused the choices, she noticed Dan watching her with a smile.

'What is it?' she asked, his curious eyes twinkling.

'Having a great day, that's all. And, I've already memorised the menu.'

She smiled. 'I'll have to make sure I keep up with my skateboarding now. And I should eat out more often too, depending on the funds.'

'Well today is on me. Already asked them to add it to my bill.'

'Oh, thank you. I really appreciate it. So, what would you recommend?' She glanced at the options.

'I recommend whatever you feel drawn to. Everything is good, so you can't go wrong.'

She liked how he always encouraged people to make their own decisions.

'Mushroom arancini first, I think, then the paprika chicken,' she decided.

'The arancini is the best. I'll have that too, and the wagyu steak with braised vegetables.'

They placed their order and sipped their water. Dan cleared his throat. 'So, may I ask, how did Kane react to the letter from the time capsule?'

Katy recalled that night, after eating pizza for dinner on the couch and watching an episode of *Virgin River* on Netflix, Kane had come down to reheat his share of dinner and sat next to her.

'Any good?' he'd asked.

'The show or the pizza?'

'Both.'

'Then, both,' she'd replied with a smile.

He ate his pizza and after a few minutes asked, 'Why are there so many old ladies in this show?'

'Kane!' She'd whacked him on the arm. 'What's wrong with old ladies? I'll be one soon. And anyway, there are also old men on the show.'

He shrugged. 'Just making an observation. I like that one.' He pointed. 'She's kinda hot for an older lady.'

Katy shook her head and laughed. 'They are all interesting characters, older or otherwise.'

'Do you ever wonder what Mum and Dad would have been like, you know, older?'

'Um, I haven't really. When I think of them, I just see them as I last remember them.'

'I think Mum would have kept her long hair,' he said. 'I

remember she used to have it in a long braid down one side, and I used to pull on it.'

Katy smiled. 'I remember that. And I used to do Mum's braid when I got older.'

'I think Dad would have kept going for his early morning walks. Even if he got frail.'

'True. He was never himself if he didn't have his morning walk.'

'I should start doing that,' Kane had said.

'I think that's a great idea. Though you'd have to get up earlier to get the train in time for work.'

'Yes. No more sleep-ins for me. I think I might try morning walks. I want to honour them more. Mum and Dad.'

Katy pressed pause on the TV and turned to face her brother. 'Did you read the letter?'

He nodded, and he clamped his lips tight as his eyes became red.

'Oh.' She shuffled closer to him and put an arm around his shoulder. 'Special, hey.'

He nodded. 'They had high hopes for me, and I feel I let them down.' He covered his face with his hands.

'No, you didn't. And life is still evolving, every day is a new day to start again.'

'I'm trying.'

'And that's the main thing.'

'Was I really that fun to be around, like they said?'

'Absolutely. You were always the life of the party. Never could sit still or not give something a go.'

'Hence the trouble I got into.'

Oops. Maybe she should have worded that differently. 'What matters is what you're doing now. And they also said you were strong and resilient, remember?'

'Yeah.' He ran his hands through his hair. 'Man, it was so

weird seeing Mum's handwriting again. I wish there were more letters to come. I wish they could write some from the other side and send them down.'

'Me too, bro, me too.'

Kane had started sniffling, and soon after, sobbing. Not a loud, messy, ugly cry, but a soft, resigned, tired sob, like it was all he had left in him after grieving for so long. Katy had shed a few tears but once again she had remained the support, the rock, holding them both up.

'So it *was* probably good for him?' Dan asked as their entrees arrived.

'A good cry is always helpful. And he got up the next morning and went for a walk before work.'

'That's a positive sign. Walking is a great antidepressant too, not to mention the health benefits.'

'Maybe it can be his new fix, a substitute in a way, something he can get hooked on in a healthy way.'

'Many survivors of addiction do get into other hobbies in an almost obsessive way, I've found. Especially things that give a quick boost, whether it be exercise or reading a good book. It stimulates their dopamine production, as well as serotonin.'

'I can see how that might happen. Well, it's a good thing then.'

Her mouth watered at the arancini, and she sighed on tasting the melting cheese within. 'Oh my God. I could eat a whole plate of this.'

'Want mine? Happy to give you extra.'

'Oh no, I couldn't. You have it all. I'll save room for the chicken too.'

They smiled and ate, in a much more refined way than they used to when they'd catch the train to Macca's at Welston and eat a burger and fries on their walk to the shopping centre, Dan throwing out his pickles on the side of the road, and Kane slurping loudly on his thickshake.

'Were your mums surprised that you'd opened the time capsule?' Katy asked, wondering what it would have been like had she been able to show her own parents.

'Yes, and Ellen said "Wait, are we in the future and you're now sixty? Because we are all looking pretty damn fine for our age if I do say so myself!"'

Katy laughed. 'She always has a good sense of humour. And I think she – both of them – will definitely be looking pretty damn fine when they're older.'

'I reckon they could do a few tricks on a skateboard, that's for sure.'

'Totally. And,' Katy cleared her throat, hoping it was okay to broach the subject, 'how did your visit with Harry go?'

Dan put down his knife and fork and waited for Gabriel to take their plates away. 'Nice. And difficult. He had some breathing issues while I was there. Got worried for a minute, thought "what if this is it?" you know? But Robbie and Eliza were able to sort it out thankfully.'

'Oh, that's hard. Are they getting help with palliative care?'

'Yeah, a nurse visits regularly.'

Katy admired palliative care nurses so much. She couldn't do it. Helping people feel better, yes, but when there was virtually no hope? She didn't think she had the strength for that.

'He wasn't up for any gaming, but when I told him about our time capsule, he perked up a bit, thought it was so cool.'

Katy warmed. She never thought their trip back in time would be inspiring for more people than just her and Dan and Kane.

'I suggested if he was up for it, that he consider writing letters to his parents, and to anyone he wanted to express anything to, while he still could. I said I'd handwrite them for him if he couldn't, or type them up and he could sign them.'

'What a great idea.'

'At first he was hesitant, but then he agreed it would be good. He even said if we ever did another time capsule, can we put something of his in there and a note with it to remember him by.'

'Oh, do you think we should? Or are we all time-capsuled out?'

'Could be fun. Maybe before I go back overseas? We could bury it in the same spot since that one stood the test of time.'

Katy giggled. 'I feel like I'm a teenager all over again.' She eyed Dan and observed the way he sat confidently with his hands intertwined on the table, unlike the awkward boy she'd grown up with who was always shifting uncomfortably, gazing off into space, or scratching his head or something. She wondered if they'd met now, as adults, would it have been any different? Would she even... date him? He was attractive in a simple, refined way – nice hair, clean-shaven, a kind face, well-dressed (they'd showered and changed after their skateboarding adventure). And he was emotionally intelligent, caring, and calm. Most of all, they had a good connection. Something 'clicked' whenever they were together.

'Let's see how things are after my TV show is finished and work it out from there.' Dan held out his hand.

'Sounds good.' She shook his hand. 'Something to look forward to. Maybe I can get Kane to take part this time.'

It would be exciting, but also bittersweet, knowing that Dan would be honouring Harry through the capsule as well, and that unless he defied the odds, he would most likely be well and truly gone by then.

CHAPTER EIGHTEEN

The first thing Dan did when they left the restaurant with full stomachs, was show Katy the stepping stones near the pond from the photo he'd accidentally sent her.

'Even better in real life,' she said.

Each stone was a different size and shape, and had a different engraving on it: a lotus, a flower, a heart, a swirl, a sun, and a star. It reminded him of a meditation technique he taught where he'd show clients a picture of a symbol, then get them to close their eyes and continue visualising it, choosing a positive emotion or state of being to associate it with. With each breath he'd get them to imagine breathing in that emotion and letting it settle into their mind and body. Whenever they were under stress, or about to react in an unhealthy way to a situation, they were instructed to get into the habit of remembering the symbol and picturing it, breathing in the emotion they wanted to feel, such as calmness, acceptance, understanding, or peace.

Katy stopped in front of the pond, ducks flapping about and enjoying the water and mud around it. She tightened her mother's light scarf around her as a cool breeze greeted them.

He looked up at the light grey clouds, the sky having been clear and blue earlier.

'Looks like rain is on its way,' he said.

Katy looked up and nodded. 'I better get a good look around before that happens then.' She turned and smiled, and then her eyes looked further past him. 'Is that a tree swing? Are we allowed on it?'

'It was one of the first things I did when I got here!'

'Let me at it,' Katy said, breaking into an eager walk.

Dan followed her, and realised how much of his life he'd spent following her around like a shadow, and how she'd never complained, never got sick of him, and always treated him kindly. It was only after the almost-kiss that she started behaving differently around him, but now, it was as though that had never happened.

Katy reached the swing and lifted herself onto it. It was a large thick plank of wood secured with bolts to a heavy-duty rope and looked secure enough for even the heaviest of people to use.

As she swung, she smiled. 'Whee! This is the life.'

Dan took out his phone and filmed her. 'Another one for your grandkids,' he said and she gave him a thumbs up. *Your grandkids. Not the grandkids, and certainly not our grandkids, but yours.*

A little girl came up and waited for the swing. Katy immediately got off and gestured to it. 'You want a turn?'

The girl nodded eagerly and her carer helped her up and pushed her gently to get momentum.

'Might have to come back and visit again so I can have another go.' She chuckled. 'Wow, so many beautiful trees around here, I can see how it got its name.'

'They had to clear a few, obviously, to make room for the building, but I think they've done an amazing job at creating a sustainable oasis for tourists or anyone wanting some time out.'

'Might even book a cabin for myself sometime,' she joked.

Dan held out his hand. 'C'mon, let me show you something else you'll like.'

She took it and it fit as though their hands were puzzle pieces being put in the correct spot. They walked along a curving pathway with various native plants interspersed with sculptures, moving away from the forest area and around the side of the property where there was a large cleared area with a gazebo surrounded by roses, and further along, a paved seating area with a big round firepit in the middle.

'Oh, I've always wanted one of these,' she exclaimed, their hands separating, and Dan only just realising they'd held hands the whole way. 'Don't think it'll fit in my small yard though, or on my balcony.'

'They put it on at night, a few people gather and chat, snuggle on the pod chairs, and even have sing-alongs.'

'You know what? I could retire and move here. Tomorrow.' Katy held out her arms. 'Absolute paradise.'

'Me too. Though something tells me neither of us could give up on our careers at this stage.'

'Yeah, you're right. Besides, it's not perfect here yet, they'd need to add a skateboard ramp to really entice me to move in.' She flashed a grin, and the low afternoon sun behind the darkening clouds and trees gave her skin a warm, pinkish glow. He wanted to capture this moment in a photo too, but it didn't feel appropriate to whip out his phone camera right now. Some moments were best left uncaptured, and just for his memories. This is how he wanted to remember Katy when he left; happy, youthful, and joyful, the changing sky as a backdrop to her smiling face, as though she was part of the landscape herself.

Thunder rumbled through the air and Katy jolted a little.

The clouds were moving more quickly now. 'How much time do you reckon we have?' she asked, glancing up.

A few pinpricks of water tickled Dan's nose. 'Not much! C'mon, let's head over to the cabin before it starts pouring.' He held out her hand again and she took it. This time, she followed him as droplets landed in splotches on the pathway in front and soon, rain pelted full force down on them.

'Quick!' Dan said, as they ran as quickly and carefully as possible, hand in hand, laughing along the way, around the property and along the pathway up to the private cabins. Dan's was one of the cabins furthest away, more private, and his thighs were starting to hurt both from the skateboarding and the dash up the hill.

Katy was giggling and trying to cover her head, Dan was laughing. He didn't really mind getting wet but somehow rain triggered a protective response in people to get somewhere dry.

'Here we are!' he said when they reached Flame Tree cabin. They walked up the steps and stopped, puffing, under the cover of the verandah roof.

'Oh my God, that was exhilarating!' Katy said in between puffs.

'I definitely feel alive!' Dan added, though he also felt tired and sore.

They leaned on the wall and caught their breath, smiling at each other as deafening rain poured down. He unlocked the door and they dashed inside, kicking off their shoes. 'I'll get a towel!' Dan went into the bathroom and returned with a large fluffy white towel. He wrapped it around Katy and dabbed it at her hair, forgetting about himself. When he was sure she was as dry and comfortable as could be, he glanced down at his own dripping clothes. 'Oh, I forgot.' He went and got another towel and returned, ruffling his own hair.

Katy stood still, holding on to the towel at her collar, and looking at him with curious, caring eyes.

Dan paused. 'What is it?'

'Nothing.' She glanced away briefly. 'Just... you've always looked out for me. Cared about me. Thank you.'

Dan's heart warmed. 'It's nothing.' He shrugged. 'It's just what people do, isn't it?'

'Not all people.'

'Well, it just feels natural to me. I want to make sure you, and anyone else I care about, are safe and comfortable and happy.'

'I am. Very much.' Her cheeks were a soft shade of pink, shining with leftover raindrops.

'You've still got some water here.' He reached out and wiped her cheek with the corner of the towel.

'And you've got some... pretty much everywhere!' She took his towel and wrapped it around him with a grin.

Dan's heart raced. All rational thought drained away and he stepped closer. Despite the cool rain, warmth radiated between them and flashes of unexpected desire stoked the fire simmering within his body. Katy's chest rose high and she looked at him the same way as she had in the car that night, only this time he was sure he was looking at her the same way too.

He slowly reached a hand out and touched her cheek again, this time not to wipe away the rain but to feel the softness of her skin, imprint it into his memory, and... whoa... his other hand moved as though of its own accord, reaching around her shoulder, both their towels dropping to the floor but neither stopping them. Katy ran her fingers along his forearm, spreading tingles throughout his arm as he caressed her cheek.

'Katy,' he whispered, unsure what he wanted to say. He leaned closer and their foreheads touched, their arms slowly wrapping around each other. He felt a familiarity in this moment that scared him, but also a new, different sensation, as though things were moving in slow motion.

Her face moved ever so slightly, separating their foreheads but bringing their lips within a breath of each other. As quickly as their lips brushed lightly against each other, an unseen force turned her head to the side. She exhaled slowly. 'I'm sorry.'

Dan's heart continued to beat fast, this time increasing from confusion, and then it slowed on realisation. It was happening all over again. They'd been caught up in the moment but reality was settling in, and she was rejecting him again. She just didn't feel that way about him.

'No, *I'm* sorry,' he said, stepping back. 'I shouldn't have let things get out of hand. I just got... lost in the moment.' He exhaled.

'Me too.' She lowered her head.

'I know you don't feel what I've always felt for you, and that's okay,' Dan said, slipping his hands into his pockets before they decided to act with a mind of their own again. 'Even though we lost touch over the years, you're the best friend I've ever had and I'd never do anything to jeopardise that.'

'I wouldn't want to either. But it's not that I don't feel anything, it's just... the timing, it's not right. I need time on my own to get over my divorce, rediscover myself and what I want, and I don't want to jeopardise that either, or get in the way of your precious limited time here.'

He nodded, though he knew she was also trying not to hurt his feelings again.

'It probably sounds silly, but I made a promise to myself to not get involved or do anything with anyone until after my,' she made quotation marks with curved fingers, '"divorce-a-versary" in November.'

Dan gave a small nod. 'I understand. And that's a good idea. It's not silly.' All rational thought had returned to his brain. He was sure that even after her divorce-a-versary she wouldn't go any further with him. Even if he didn't have to go back overseas, even if he was living back in Tarrin's Bay – friends were all they were clearly ever meant to be. Even though he didn't believe in fate, maybe fate was urging him to at least believe the cold, hard truth.

'I better get going,' she said. She went to turn for the door then turned back. 'Oh, I didn't drive here.'

Dan withdrew his hands from his pockets and grabbed his keys. 'Of course, I'll drive you. The rain's settling to a slow fall now, we can take an umbrella.' He grabbed it from the wall hook near the door.

They walked back at a normal pace this time, no giggles or laughter, no hand-holding, just two friends walking side by side in the rain, until they got to his car, and he drove her in relative silence back to her home.

When he parked alongside her house, she looked across at him, semi-apologetically, and squeezed his hand as it sat on the handbrake. 'I had a wonderful day, Dan.'

He managed a smile, though his heart felt ripped open and laid bare. 'I did too. The best I've had in a long time.'

And he didn't know if there would ever be another one like it.

CHAPTER NINETEEN

K aty closed the door behind her and let out a deep breath. 'Kane, you home?' she called out, to no answer. She dumped her bag on the side table and got out her phone, sending a text to Jenna.

> Hey hun, you free tonight? Want a girl's night?

Within a few minutes she replied.

> Hi! Sorry, I'm actually going on a date tonight, with DJ guy! It was all kinda spontaneous, but I took a risk and he said yes. So we're just having a casual dinner at Café Lagoon, they've got Barry Reynolds playing tonight.

Katy's shoulders sunk at first, but then she straightened up and smiled at Jenna's progress.

> Wow, I'm so excited for you! Please let me know how it goes xx

> I will! I'm free tomorrow, wanna come over for coffee and cake? I was so nervous about the date I baked carrot cake today to keep myself occupied.

Katy smiled, already looking forward to it.

> I'll be there! Will let you know when I'm up (and more importantly, to see if you're home yet from your date!).

> Oh don't worry, I don't plan on going too fast. Lexi's staying with a friend tonight, but still, I'm not ready for any kind of shenanigans.

> Look after yourself and I'll see you then.
> Have fun!

Jenna replied with a kiss emoji and Katy took her shoes off and went into the kitchen to make a cup of tea. She tapped her fingers on the kitchen benchtop while waiting for the kettle to boil. She needed to debrief about what happened with Dan. She had a few other friends, but most were colleagues too and since moving out of her marital home, her other friends hadn't been in touch as often, whereas her friendship with Jenna had been strengthened on moving back to Tarrin's Bay.

She texted Kane.

> How was the fishing? Up to anything else?

He didn't reply.

She took her tea to the balcony, sat on a chair and watched the waves of the ocean as the darkened clouds muted into a soft grey and a haze from the rain filled the sky. It was peaceful, and perfect for pondering.

Had she made a mistake? Should she have kissed him and

allowed whatever felt natural to happen? Or did she do the right thing in stopping it before it started?

Confusion swirled in her mind as she stood and leaned on the railing. It was so much simpler to be friends. But since Dan's return, she'd realised how much she'd missed him, and how much she still got on well with him, and how connected she felt – more connected than ever before.

In high school his attempted kiss had felt wrong. This time it had felt strangely right, but at the wrong time. She sighed. If there was anything between them it would surely make itself known before he was due to leave. Now, there were too many competing priorities going on: time for herself after the divorce, Kane's ongoing rehabilitation, Dan's upcoming TV job, and his limited time with Harry. Anything else would complicate matters and she couldn't risk their renewed friendship at this time.

Her phone chimed with a text.

> On my way back. Feel like helping me cook fish tonight?

Katy smiled. Maybe it was good that Jenna wasn't available tonight.

> Had a good fishing trip I presume?

> Yes. I had some help though and we shared the fish around.

Typing bubbles appeared again then disappeared, then appeared again.

> They went to a pub afterwards, I got as far as the table and almost ordered a beer, but pretended I had a message and needed to get going. I didn't know what to do.

Katy breathed a sigh of relief. Although alcohol wasn't his problem, it could be a gateway and couldn't be risked.

You did good. And if it happens again, don't be afraid to tell them. Sometimes being open and honest is a good thing.

He sent a thumbs up.

See you soon. I'll start preparing a salad to save time.

Her stomach was grumbling, despite her satisfying lunch. And she was now sure she'd made the right decision, stopping today's romantic interlude before it complicated things. It had been an amazing day, but family and her own self-care were top priority and that would surely be Dan's as well.

When Katy stepped into Jenna's house the next day, she held out a small posy of camellias she'd picked from her garden. 'For you. Happy Sunday.' Katy smiled.

Jenna's tired-looking eyes brightened. 'Oh, thank you, they're beautiful.' She took them to the kitchen and put them in a vase as Katy followed her in.

She noticed another bunch of flowers nearby; roses. 'Wait, are they from...'

'DJ Mike.'

'Nice!'

'Two bunches of blooms, aren't I a lucky gal!'

'I take it the date went well?'

'Let's sit on the patio with some cake and coffee and I'll fill you in.' Jenna gave a nod.

'By the way,' Katy said, admiring Jenna's extra shiny, curly, and bouncy hair. 'Hair looks great, did you go to the hairdresser yesterday?'

'I did it myself. No more frizzy, frumpy fossil Jenna! I followed the curly girl method, have you heard of it?'

'With this hair?' Katy held up a wisp of her own hair and it slipped from her grasp. 'No.'

'It's a whole movement. There are very specific rules, Katy, *rules*.' She laughed. 'But it works. I've been looking into it for a while, so I picked up some products and tried it out yesterday morning, luckily it dried in time for my date as I let it air dry.'

'Well, it looks amazing.' Katy reached out a hand and bounced a ringlet under her fingers. 'You're so lucky! I've got boring straight hair. Maybe I could start my own movement: the Straighty Katy Method.'

Laughter burst from Jenna's mouth as she placed two mugs next to the coffee machine. 'Why not? But,' she leaned closer, 'does it have *rules*?'

'I'll be sure to make some strict ones,' Katy replied with a wink.

'Because there are people in the curly Facebook groups who will hunt you down if you don't follow the rules correctly. I got a bit scared when I posted about whether occasional hair straightening damages curls and got some backlash like "why would you do such a thing?" And "this group is only for talking about *curls*".'

'Wow. Anyway, it looks great and you just do what makes you – and your hair – happy.'

After preparing their morning tea, Jenna placed everything on a tray and carried it outside, setting it on the small outdoor table for two.

'Lexi still at her friend's house?' Katy asked.

Jenna nodded. 'She said they're going roller-skating in

Welston. I didn't even know they had a rink. Remember roller-skating? I didn't know anyone still did that.'

Katy laughed. 'Well, not so much roller-skating, but you remember how much I loved skateboarding.'

'Oh yes, you were fab.'

'I did some yesterday, actually. With Dan. But I'll tell you about it later, first I'm *dying* to know all about DJ Mike.'

Jenna's eyed bulged. 'You got on a skateboard again? Oh, you are so brave, how awesome.'

Jenna held up a hand and Katy high-fived it, then lifted the coffee mug from a colourful coaster. 'These are pretty, where did you get them?'

'Lexi made them! She got a coaster making kit with paint pens and glaze. Aren't they great? I told her she could try selling them.'

'Good idea. I'll buy one.'

'Thanks. It'll give her something to focus on after her break-up.'

Katy nodded. 'So,' she circled her hand, 'details, please, on last night.'

'Oh yes.' Jenna cleared her throat. 'Okay, so, it was... interesting! He's lovely. And funny. And talkative, like me. We listened to Barry Reynolds singing a bit and talked in between sets.'

Katy ate a chunk of carrot cake and sighed. 'Delicious.'

'Isn't it? Even if I do say so myself. Anyway, so we basically gave each other our whole life stories. He's been a DJ since forever and does some music production for video games. He's also separated, like me, and has a twelve-year-old son he has shared custody with.'

'Sounds promising, so you're both back in the game?'

'Well, that's the thing. I thought I was, but I just don't think I'm fully ready.'

Katy's mouth fell open. She thought Jenna was ready and raring to go. It'd been three years since she left her partner.

'I waited until the end of the night to be honest about it, as I wanted to see how things unfolded naturally first. But what got me thinking was that he told me about his past and what led him to music and DJing. And it hit a chord with me, pardon the pun. I think I need more time to sort a few things out for myself.'

'Oh?'

Jenna sipped her coffee. 'He said he suffered with depression for a couple of years and it really affected his life. He was single, unemployed, and had to live with a cousin as his family is back in New Zealand. It was after a relationship break-up and a prolonged illness where he just kinda burned out and couldn't get his mood back. He tried medication, therapy, and all those things, but he said the one thing that really helped was music therapy, and making regular time to spend on his passion, DJing. He'd let it go during the illness and he said he just wasn't himself. So after a while he recovered and now he calls himself a go-with-the-flow guy. He's started teaching his son DJing too.'

'That's great. How nice that he was open and honest about himself. Dan said how important that is.'

'Yeah. So I thought I'd be open and honest with him. Told him briefly about my past toxic relationship and how we had to escape one night, and about starting fresh, just me and Lexi. He was really good at listening and showing compassion.' Jenna took a bite of cake and devoured it quickly. 'But I also told him that I've been feeling kinda down lately. And that some days I feel like I'm putting on a fake happy face when inside I feel like crying, and I don't know why.' Her last few words wavered and she paused, holding a hand to her chest and clamping her eyes shut for a moment.

Katy instinctively placed her hand on top of Jenna's. 'Oh, Jen. I know you haven't been yourself.'

'I know. I thought it was just an emotional phase, hormones or something, but it's been persisting and I think maybe... I need to do something about it?'

Katy nodded with relief. She had been wondering how to broach the subject further with her dear friend.

'Anyway, back to that later. So, he asked me what I loved doing, and I said being with my daughter, helping other people, and doing a few creative things.'

'We had a similar conversation recently too, if I recall,' Katy mentioned.

'Yes, I said I had a great friend who suggested art classes or something, and he said maybe I should do art while also listening to music that uplifts me.'

'Good idea. If you want me to come over once a month for an arty farty Sunday, just let me know and I'll be there with bells on.' Katy grinned.

'Like, literal bells?' She flashed a cheeky grin.

'If I must. Maybe some dangly, jingly earrings or something.' She fiddled with her plain stud earrings, as she never wore dangly, jingly earrings, but maybe she should start. Try something different, as Dan advised.

'Deal. We can both wear fancy earrings just because. Maybe silly fun things like that'll lift my spirits, you know? But,' she sighed, 'I'm also going to make an appointment with Doctor Sylvia too, and maybe Mark. Discuss whether I could try antidepressants, or even some natural options, make sure I'm getting enough of all the vitamins and minerals, and get a referral to a counsellor. It's been a while since I had any counselling after the... incident.'

'I think that all sounds fantastic. Jen, do you ever get any flashbacks or feel triggered by certain things that remind you of your ex?'

Jenna nodded and lowered her head as some tears escaped

her eyes. 'I thought I was free of him, but the memories live on. And the fear too. I know the court gave me a restraining order against him, but it's always in the back of my mind, you know?'

'I understand. You may have some post-traumatic stress, so it'd be good to get a psychologist's opinion, and some treatment.'

Jenna released a wobbly exhale. 'I will, hun, I will. It's time.'

'So, how did the date end?'

'Any kiss, you mean? Well, no. At the start of the night I was *really* hoping it would go that way – these lips of mine get nothing but strawberry-flavoured lip balm these days – but by the end of the night I felt differently, and I think he did too. I realised I had to put myself and Lexi first, and told him I thought it would be best if I take some more time to get help for my depressive symptoms and continue to rebuild myself up after all we've been through.'

'I'm proud of you, well done. How did he respond?'

'Really well. He agreed that it seemed like it was for the best, and that he would be happy to be a friend if I needed one, and maybe catch up for coffee and a chat or a gig occasionally, even in a group if you and Kane wanted to come too.'

'Could be fun. But only if it feels right for you.'

'I'll see how things go. Anyway, when we said goodbye, he gave me the best squishiest, most comforting and caring hug I've had in a long time. Even better than yours, sorry to say. Seriously, I think it healed me by at least seventy-nine per cent! Maybe I just needed some manly touch, I don't know.' She shrugged.

'It sounds to me like you needed manly touch *and* a good listener to share your story with, and he probably did too. I think you both probably helped each other.'

'It was a great night. I worried I might've overshared, but he sorta did too, and he didn't seem to mind.'

'It's nice to offload what's on your mind, isn't it?'

She nodded. 'Hey, tell me about your skateboarding yesterday, you young thing you.'

Katy chuckled. 'A whole lot more happened than just skateboarding.'

'Whaaat?' Jenna's eyes bulged. 'Do you mean, with *Dan?*'

Katy tilted her head. 'Well, sorta. I mean, we had a really fantastic day. I've missed him so much and we still get on so well even after all these years. We skated, laughed, had a *divine* lunch, wandered the Trees of Life gardens, got caught in a thunderstorm, and almost kissed at his cabin.'

Jenna's fork clanged against her plate. 'Don't tell me you two had another *almost-kiss* two decades after the first? Can you just *kiss* or *not kiss*? Geez, girl.' She laughed and shook her head. 'Nah seriously, what happened? Did he initiate like before?'

'This time, it was mutual. Our lips actually brushed together a little. It felt like slow motion. Maybe we were just caught up in the magic of the day, of the resort – it's a special place.'

'Hun, you don't almost kiss someone because you're in a special place, you almost kiss because you *feel something* for them.'

Katy shuffled on the chair and scratched her chin. 'We've known each other since we were born, it's just a familiarity, a comfort. I broke the kiss off as soon as it began, told him I'm not getting involved in any romance until after my divorce-a-versary.' She gave an affirmative nod.

'Okay, well that's not too far away. Wait till then, see if you feel anything more for him. If you do, tell him. I know he lives overseas and travels for work, but still, the guy is a love guru – he out of anyone would be more than likely to change his whole life for love.'

Katy raised her hands in the air. 'I don't know what I feel. I just know that since his return I've been feeling more connected to him. And I miss it when I'm not with him. But I don't want to ruin our friendship *again*. I don't want to mess him around, especially as he's about to lose his cousin at any time.'

'Katy McKenzie, you are very good at worrying about other people, but just this once, can you think about what *you* actually want?' Jenna leaned forward and held her gaze like a laser locked on its target.

Katy scratched her temple, unsure why she was suddenly itchy, and offered a half smile. 'Okay, I'll try.'

'And not only that, have you thought about the possibility that you might not be messing Dan about if you feel something for him? That you might actually be giving Dan the possibility of the one thing he's dreamed about for years?'

'But what if it all went wrong? Like my marriage did? What if I realised that it was just a close friendship after all, not romantic, and then it became all weird again and we lose what we had?'

'What if it all goes right? What if you learned lessons in your marriage that won't be repeated, and what if you realise that your friendship is actually the foundation for a fulfilling and successful romance?' Jenna's words spilled forth rapidly and she paused for a quick breath. 'You have the chance of something special, why not take it?'

'You sound like a bit of a love guru yourself.'

Jenna plumped her curls with her hands. 'Well. Just doing what comes naturally.' She smiled. 'A love guru I definitely am not, but a friend I am. And you two always had something special, whether you want to believe it or not. I know it was weird for you back then and you were just starting to discover the world of boys, but now, you've got life experience and maturity, and so does he.'

'True. Either way, I still think I need time. And he's about to take part in a reality show. The timing's off.'

'Will you reassess after your divorce-a-versary?'

'Guess so. I think he's heading back home in December.'

'Plenty of time to keep hanging out with him before then and see how it evolves. Whatever chemistry is there might fizzle out or you might realise that it is indeed only friendship, or you might realise that he is and always has been the true love of your life.'

'I've just thought of a business idea for you,' Katy digressed. 'Coffee, cake, and counselling with Jenna.'

'Ha, I don't know about that, but thanks. Actually, I've been thinking of looking into some business ideas, seriously. I don't know if I'll work at the clinic forever. I feel like there's something else for me out there but I don't know what yet.'

'Well, I'd miss you so much, but I'm here to support you in any business endeavour you wish to pursue. Keep me posted on your ideas!'

'Sure will. And you keep me posted on your... situation with Dan. Promise me you'll take a chance if you do end up feeling that way? Go with your heart, not your head.' She held her hand to her chest.

'Okay, I promise.' Katy breathed out a sigh and relaxed her shoulders. She wasn't convinced there could or would be anything between her and Dan, but one thing she was definitely curious about, was watching him on his upcoming television show. How bizarre, amazing, and exciting to see your best childhood friend on national TV as the actual guru people are looking up to. She was so proud of him. Whatever it was, and although she thought she'd pushed it down last night, that warm feeling was starting to rise and grow again within.

CHAPTER TWENTY

Dan adjusted his tie as he looked in the mirror in the dressing room of Channel Four studios, after having his make-up and hair done. He let out a quiet chuckle at his appearance: so... polished. He always felt strange doing TV, but it had proven the best way of reaching more people and gaining publicity for his books and his work. He'd always scoffed at reality television, but agreed to this opportunity when he saw it wasn't like the usual fare of botoxed, scantily-clad singles mingling on islands or at five-star resorts, or people never having met before being expected to fall in love and live happily ever after. *Love, Unfiltered* was authentic and, although they'd edit the show and add some music and drama, it was more aligned to his values, which is why he was excited to take part.

'Dan, on in five!' the production assistant called out through the slight gap in his open door.

Right. Time to go. He took a big, sharp breath then puffed out air and nerves from his lungs. He smiled at himself in the mirror and checked his teeth. Good to go. He closed his eyes a few moments and calmed himself, then exited the room and walked down the narrow hall towards the set. He'd done some pre-filming for the show – background segments about his life and work, and intros with the participants – but this was his first live component where the show would officially begin on air and the pre-recorded segments would be interspersed with the live follow-ups and coaching sessions.

He stood to the side with the assistant and her iPad, the anticipatory energy building within until the lights brightened and music played. The host, Brent Calder, who'd hosted similar reality shows in the past, stepped out onto the stage with a wave, smiling at the audience. Dan barely absorbed the introduction until it came to the important bit where he'd have to step onto the stage too.

'Who's ready to see some raw, unscripted, unfiltered luurve?!' Brent asked the audience, to which they cheered. 'We are beyond thrilled to have a special guest with us throughout this series, someone who is both highly qualified *and* experienced in helping singles and couples communicate better, be their best selves, *and* find success in the world of dating. Ladies and gentlemen, it is an honour to welcome, psychologist and dating guru, Dan Dexter!'

The audience clapped and cheered, and Dan stepped out onto the stage with energy, doing a cute but as dignified as possible little jig on the way, knowing that Katy would be watching and laughing at home. He waved and smiled, took in the expanse of audience that always appeared bigger when watching on TV but was actually fairly small – it was all about camera angles and the way they panned the audience in sweeping movements to add to the illusion that there were more people there. But the audience was full, which was a good sign. With live television, you'd never know how a show would be received because there were no advance screenings among industry professionals as there was with regular shows, and what would happen on air was anyone's guess. But he hoped it would shine a light on the challenges people faced when dating.

'Thanks, everyone, for the warm welcome, and thanks, Brent, I'm excited to be here!'

Someone wolf-whistled from the audience and others laughed. He smiled. 'Thanks, Mum,' he joked, and they laughed again.

He took a seat on one of the two armchairs that sat in a V-shape alongside a 'love couch', and Brent took the other. He tried not to look directly at the bright lights shining into his eyes, but instead he softened his gaze on the audience, although they were hard to see with the glare from the lights.

'Now, Dan, you've been helping people with dating for many years. What's the number one recurring theme you see in people who are having trouble?'

Dan had been presented earlier with a list of possible questions he'd be asked, so he'd mentally rehearsed each answer, while leaving room for spontaneity as well.

'I don't know about one singular theme, but the two most common issues are: having rigid expectations,' he touched one of his fingers, 'and not being authentic and honest.' He touched another finger as though counting.

'Okay, so how will you help the participants in the show to overcome those issues?'

'I'll be educating them on how to really tune in and ask themselves some tough questions about what they really want and how to express that, declare that, and ask for that. Dating success starts with self-success.' He smiled.

'Well, I for one can't wait to see how it all unfolds for our participants.' Brent rubbed his hands together. 'And who knows, maybe I'll learn a thing or two myself!' He air-nudged Dan who gave an assured nod.

'Now, let's get to know our participants a bit more before we bring them to the stage to start the fun and games. Sit back and relax and watch these compelling backstories and, as I'm sure you'll agree, you'll be rooting for each of them to find the love and happiness they're looking for.' Brent gestured to the large screen behind them where the pre-recorded segments began airing, which gave Dan a few moments to recoup after the adrenaline rush of the show's introduction.

'Can you chew any more quietly?' Katy asked Kane as they sat on the couch watching *Love, Unfiltered* while eating popcorn. Kane leaned forward and munched eagerly as though he hadn't eaten in days.

'These morning walks are giving me an appetite,' he said, continuing to chew loudly.

Katy had paused eating while watching Dan's intro as she didn't want to miss a thing. But now, she realised she was hungry too. As they watched the backstories she also munched away, slowing down when Dan and Brent came back on the screen.

Things had been slightly stilted between them after their second almost-kiss. But despite that, they'd been keeping in contact and Dan had been practising what he preached: trying something new. He'd been to two of Katy's Pilates classes so far, and the participants, of which nine out of ten were female, were loving it. The instructor commented that she had more bookings than ever for upcoming classes, and Katy noticed the regulars trying extra hard while Dan was there, which made her giggle. Dan was probably more concerned with how *he* did the exercises than with how anyone else did them. She admired him for giving it a go.

Brent stood. 'Let's welcome Carly and her friend Anna to the stage; ladies, take a seat on the love couch!'

Two women in their forties walked on stage, the first slightly wobbly in her high heels, the other seemingly a pro at it. Carly's name and occupation (vet nurse) flashed on the bottom of the screen as she waved and sat, followed by Anna (office assistant).

'Now, Carly, you must come across some eligible bachelors who love animals in your line of work?'

'Oh yes, but it's not appropriate to date clients, so that's where I struggle. My social life revolves around my job which is my life, and I don't know how to make a move on anyone without feeling like I shouldn't be.'

Dan nodded his understanding. 'Work places can be both positive and negative for dating; some places have rules against colleagues dating and of course clients, students, patients, or other such situations where it could become a legal issue if anything went wrong. But with your profession, I can't see any problem with connecting with a client outside of work if they agree, since they themselves are not the patient. But to make it easier to find like-minded people, I would suggest dog walking on the weekends, even walking other people's dogs, or joining an animal-related group. There are lots of ways to connect with fellow animal lovers.'

Carly nodded.

'And, Anna, you've been friends with Carly since she helped you through your cat's long illness. Would you say if two people can become friends through their workplace, a relationship could also be possible should someone she connects with come along?'

'Absolutely. And in my case, office romance is a no-no, so I have to look outside my workplace, but when I use online dating apps I get the usual "oh, right" response when I tell potential dates what I do. Like they think I'm a boring secretary or something. They have no idea the skill and dedication it takes to do what I do, so I'm looking at how I can better present myself to others to show them I'm a very interesting person!' She laughed.

Dan leaned forward. 'The issue might be with them not being inquisitive enough. If they're worth your time, they might say "tell me more about your work" or something similar, which gives you a chance to talk more about what your job involves. And this is something I encourage you to do too; ask the questions you want to be asked. Often questions become two-way, so if they haven't asked, you can try, and go from there.' Anna nodded and Dan continued. 'But you can also define your career purpose more specifically.'

Katy smiled as Dan explained to Anna how to do this, remembering their conversation about it at his clinic talk.

Anna scratched her head. 'Well, I do a lot of varying tasks, but maybe I could put it like this.' She cleared her throat. 'I manage the daily operations of an advertising agency to keep things running smoothly and allow the company to achieve its goals. Oh, and last year we increased turnover by twenty-seven per cent and my boss gave me a pay rise, so I'm pretty happy about that!'

The audience clapped, and Katy grinned.

'I don't have a career purpose,' Kane said. 'I need a career purpose.'

'You'll get there,' she said.

'I lift stuff and move stuff and unpack stuff,' he said with a laugh. 'Surely there's more to life than that for me?'

Katy missed Dan's response to Anna but she was glad it was also prompting Kane to think about his life.

She was glued to the screen as each participant divulged their fascinating stories, and Dan gave surface level guidance to help them. The diversity of people on the show made it interesting to watch: a widower in his sixties with health challenges, a young neurodivergent guy who'd never had a second date, two men who'd broken up and reunited multiple times, a thirty-year-old cancer survivor with limited dating experience, and a divorced mother of five worried that no man would want an instant large family. When it came to a deep dive with newly attached couple Rahna and Del, she ended up with tears streaming down her face as Dan guided them through their past hurts and barriers to love. He got them to declare their goals and intentions, their values and what was important to them, and what they liked about each other. She wondered if she and Erik had received guidance at the start of their relationship, would their divorce have been prevented? She sometimes missed him, but then she would remind herself of all that happened and she knew it was best they'd gone their separate ways.

'You okay?' Kane asked. 'Why the tears? It's not *Virgin River*, you know.'

She smiled. 'I'm okay. Just reminiscing. And wondering what if.'

'Ah, okay.' Kane finally put down his popcorn. 'You know, I liked Erik but to be honest, I think there's someone more worthy of you out there.' He patted her back.

'Thanks, bro.' She looked at him. 'And what about you? Interested in finding anyone at some stage?'

'After I get myself together. Again. Maybe I should have gone on the show, but then again, I don't want the whole country knowing what I've been through as then no one will want to date me.'

Katy hoped that one day her brother would start speaking more highly of himself. 'I don't know about that. It could have helped people understand and you might find someone proud of you, or even someone who's been through something similar.'

He shrugged. 'I get lonely sometimes. I've never been able to hold down a serious relationship, only one-night stands or brief flings – don't worry I'll spare you the details.'

'Phew, thanks. But yeah, focus on yourself. What did Dan say? Dating success starts with self-success.' She smiled at her recall. Dan's words always got in her head. Then again, she had always been good with rote memory, which had come in handy during her nursing degree and while taking patient histories.

When the show ended, Katy clapped, even though no one except Kane could hear. 'Dan did so well,' she said, and Kane agreed.

Dan was bound to be feeling relieved, first show done and dusted. She checked the Instagram feed for the show and all the comments coming in, many asking if Dan was single. Others saying they're going to try the tips, especially the career purpose one, and being more honest with their dates. There were also a few negative comments, which made Katy purse her lips. *Load of garbage! If he's such a guru, why is he still single? No one needs dating tips; they just need to wait for the right person! He shouldn't be wasting his degree on such trivial matters!*

She opened her text messages and texted him.

> Congratulations! You were amazing. Well done. Kane is rethinking his career purpose now. And what you said to that couple brought tears to my eyes. Looking forward to next week's show. PS: don't read the comments.

She smiled and put away her phone, not expecting a reply to come anytime soon as he'd probably have to debrief with the producer and remove all his make-up.

She and Kane watched two more *Virgin River* episodes (which didn't make her cry but gave her the warm fuzzies), and she was quite amused with Kane's attraction to the character of

Muriel. Personally, she liked Preacher, such a heart of gold and, well, the rest of him was pretty appealing too. It was nice to live in a fictional world for a while, and with these daydreams in her mind she got into bed and closed her eyes with a smile.

When she had just fallen asleep a chime woke her up. Fumbling with her phone and dropping it twice, she saw the text from Dan.

> Thanks so much. I was soooo nervous. Glad about Kane. And oh no! Is that a good thing, your tears? I hope the show will help people. And don't worry, I try not to read the comments after big publicity. My socials manager will delete any nasty ones and let me know of any I might like to reply to when I have a chance.

She laid back down and smiled herself back to sleep, honoured that with the hundreds of comments and messages he would receive, he'd replied to her as priority.

CHAPTER TWENTY-ONE

The following week, Dan's show got even more interesting, with an emotional deep dive for the single mother of five, giving her the confidence and self-worth to stand proud of who she was and what she had to offer. There was also a dating challenge presented for the on-again-off-again couple to try out and report back next week. It was just as enjoyable as fictional TV shows. She and Kane had designated it their TV and popcorn night.

By Friday that week, Katy found herself hearing Dan's words in her head more often. 'Speak the truth. What's the worst that can happen and is it really that bad?' and 'Life is short and precious, don't waste opportunities.' She sometimes wondered if these were things he'd told himself in moments of loneliness or dissatisfaction. It sure felt like he was speaking to her directly too.

She stepped out of the clinic – another week gone by so fast. Life seemed to be going faster and faster yet it always went by at the same speed. She hooked her backpack through her arms, having swapped it in place of her regular handbag as it was more convenient for her new choice of transportation.

She hopped on her skateboard and pushed herself along around the side of the building. When she'd first skated to work last week, a few people had glanced her way, some with big smiles on their faces, others with looks of confusion, and another skateboarder (albeit about eighteen) gave her the *Hunger Games* salute. She tried not to worry what people thought. She was good at it and she enjoyed it, and that's all that mattered. Okay, so she was wearing her scrubs with the clinic logo, but Joyce hadn't mentioned any problems with their professional image or anything, and Mark the naturopath as well as the part-time physiotherapist had applauded her for exercising her way to work.

Being the start of the weekend, and with spring warmth and the scent of jasmine and sea salt in the air, she decided to go skating around the harbour and then maybe for a quick walk along the beach nearby. She didn't worry about any tricks as she wasn't wearing protective gear, just a few basic moves to curve her way around people and obstacles; a bit like Dan's dating advice, really – just do your best to glide along and move past obstacles, don't let them stop you. If you fall, pick yourself up again and keep moving.

She saw a couple of patients and waved at them, and by the time she got to the beach she was ready to whip off her shoes, roll up her pants, and feel the ocean lap at her feet. *It might even be warm enough for a swim this weekend*, she thought. She took a moment to glance around, breathing in the salty air and feeling alive. Gratitude filled her heart with thoughts of how lucky she was, and how she was finally feeling more like herself after her relationship break-up.

She hung her lace-up shoes over her crooked elbow as she carried the board under her arm, and stepped onto the soft sand. It wasn't yet warm enough to need footwear. In summer, sometimes the sand was too hot to walk on and shoes were necessary until you got to where it was wet.

She headed towards the shore and paused a moment when she saw... *is that a wheelchair?* She narrowed her gaze and homed in on it. It was one of those beach wheelchairs with the special wider wheels made for sand transport. She knew some patients hired them to be able to visit the beach like able-bodied people, with the help of someone to push them. The person in the chair was pushed by a man of about sixty, and on one side was a woman about the same age, and on the other side a younger man who looked a lot like... *hang on, it was Dan!*

He leaned down and said something to the person in the wheelchair, who she now knew must be Harry. In that moment, she knew what was happening. They were helping Harry experience the beach again in whatever way possible before he could no more.

She resisted the urge to go up to them and ask if they needed help, opting to stay back, not wanting to interrupt them or get in the way of Dan's moment with his cousin. The trio helped Harry from his chair and the frail petite frame of what should be a young man in his prime, rose up and walked in slow clunky steps to the water's edge.

Katy's chin quivered and she blinked back tears. She could see Dan's face side on as he looked at Harry with a smile on his face and said something, then looked back in front of him where they met the water and paused, small waves lapping at their feet. Harry's head turned to the side to face his mother and Katy saw a brief flash of a smile, which made her smile. This was what life was about – the simple pleasures, helping those who needed it, and being surrounded by people you loved. She didn't have many people in her life, but those that were, mattered. She may not have her parents anymore but she had a brother, Jenna and a couple of other friends, her awesome colleagues, and Dan. It was like Dan was in his own category. She didn't know what to call him. A friend, yes, but different to other friends. And although they'd almost kissed, they weren't dating so it wasn't a romance either. It was just, and always had been, simply her and Dan.

The group walked a little, giving Harry a chance to experience it further, while his mum kept glancing back at the chair, obviously making sure it was nearby should he not be able to walk any further.

Katy continued on her way but from the back of the beach so as to not cross paths with them, until she was further away, and then walked closer to the shoreline, eventually meeting the same water that was washing the feet of a terminal man. It was a humbling thought. How many people over the years had walked along this beach and known it was their last time? Probably not many, as so many deaths were unexpected or doing things like this wasn't possible for some people. She was glad they'd been able to bring Harry, it must've taken a lot of planning and effort around his medication times, need for sleep, waiting till he was rested and had enough energy, and the transport of the wheelchair.

She looked at the tiny wheels on her skateboard and her feet easily walking along the wet and shifting sand. She would not take her life for granted. She would do as much as she could do while she still could. She stood and gazed out at the ocean for a while, breathing in its promise of renewal, of consistency, of healing. When she glanced back to the side, Harry was being helped back into his wheelchair. That was it. He'd had his last experience of being one with the ocean. A tear escaped her eye and she wiped it away. Should she tell Dan that she saw him? She didn't want him to think she'd been spying on them. But Dan was all about honesty, so she thought it'd probably be okay to tell him on Monday at Pilates class if she didn't speak to him before then. Dan was currently spending Tuesday to Thursdays in Sydney to focus on the show and the rest of the time in the Bay. It was probably best that he wasn't as available as he'd first been when he'd arrived. The more she saw him the more she found it difficult to withdraw, but her promise to herself stood strong and she would honour it. By the end of the first week of November, she'd reassess everything: her life, her relationships, and her dreams of having a family either with a man or on her own. Dan's life wasn't here anymore, she knew that. His parents were here, but his soul was not, it had settled into a happy and successful life in America and she didn't want to hold him back or confuse him. But like Jenna had said, she'd see how she felt when the time came.

Katy left the beach and washed her feet under a tap, dried them, then put her shoes back on and skated home.

When she got there, the sky was slowly fading to a deep, dusky pink and the garage door was open. Kane had the light on and was crouched down, doing something.

'Hey, was wondering when you'd get back.' He stood and she saw paint stains on the old shirt he was wearing.

With curious eyes she walked towards him, eyeing the small side table that he'd been sanding down. 'I hope that's not my furniture?'

'Don't worry, I brought it from work, they were throwing out some old things from the office storeroom and I said I'd take this off their hands. Carried it on the train home! Had an idea to paint it and make it like new.'

'Good idea.' She nodded, glad he was keeping busy.

'I've already tested some paint on these pieces of cardboard to get an idea of colours.' He held them up. 'Which one do you think?'

'Hmm. Where's it gonna go, is the question. My spare room where you're staying?'

'For now. But when I move out, I'll take it with me. I might look in the freebies Facebook group for more old finds and do them up, that's if I can store them here on this side of the garage?' he asked, eyebrows arched high.

'Sure, as long as I can get my car in and out and you don't accidentally paint my vehicle, all good!'

'Awesome.'

'And I like the silvery aqua colour. Or the dark burgundy. Oh geez, that's probably not much help, they're so different!'

'I'm thinking the silvery aqua, something different and not as "normal" as other furniture. Maybe I could even start a business restoring old furniture or doing up pieces all fancy and stuff.'

Katy smiled. 'It could be good. But my garage will only hold so many items so you'd need to hire a space or wait until you get your own to really give it a go. You'll have to look out for a place with a garage or big shed when the time comes.'

'Yep. Oh, this is going to be so much fun! I could even do some normal painting, like people's rooms and stuff, for ongoing work. If you want anything painted, let me know. Remember I used to love it as a kid?'

She eyed him sternly.

'Okay, so I was mostly into graffiti, but still, I was good at it.'

She watched him work and realised that he also needed a hobby, a passion, for the sake of his mental health, just like Jenna. Maybe she'd been so focused on helping him find a job and get settled that she'd forgotten to encourage him to do more of what brought him joy.

'When I'm painting, I don't overthink other stuff,' he said. 'I think it's good for me. It's also kinda symbolic, you know? Rehabilitating old worn-out things and making them like new, like I'm trying to do with myself.' Katy nodded in agreement. 'And,' he stood again, wiping his brow, 'there are a couple of dudes at work, I don't know if I want to be around them too much, long term and that. They talk about getting stoned on the weekends and it's setting off alarm bells in my head.'

Katy could feel the vibration from said alarm bells. 'Oh no. In that case, it isn't great to be around them. Can you talk to your boss, or avoid them as much as possible?'

'Not sure. I've been trying not to engage in conversation much with them, I don't want to get caught up or...'

Tempted.

'So I thought I'd start looking into my own business ideas for the future. Maybe one day I won't have to work for someone else and I can just do my own thing.'

She liked his enthusiasm, but she also knew starting a business would be a lot of work and he got bored easily. He hadn't always shown commitment to things either. But she'd give him the benefit of the doubt and encourage him. If something brought a smile to his face and was good for him, she was happy.

'Jenna's thinking of doing the same, looking into business opportunities. Maybe you two could bounce ideas off each other.'

'Maybe.'

'Anyway, I'll leave you to it.' She went inside and got out of her scrubs, had a shower, and sent texts to two of her occasional friends, asking if any were free that weekend. She didn't want to lose contact with any more people and wanted to make sure they were all okay. Seeing Harry today had brought it home to her that anyone could die at any time, which she'd already known all too well after her parents' accident, but still, sometimes an uncomfortable reminder would be shoved in her face.

After an hour, she had two replies and had arranged to meet with them both for lunch the next day. Life really was what you made it. Even if you had to sometimes take the initiative, it was worth it to have no regrets. She thought about Dan, and knew she didn't want any regrets when it came to him either. She looked forward to seeing him on Monday, as did every other member of their Pilates class. Good ol' Dan Dexter was a local celebrity. Katy laughed as she looked at the childhood photo she'd stuck on her fridge. Soon, not yet, but soon, she would need to think of her own 'dating purpose', and most importantly, whether Dan would be part of that purpose.

CHAPTER TWENTY-TWO

NOVEMBER

'I'm here! And I brought cake!' Jenna scurried over to the picnic table in Miracle Park where Katy sat waiting, a bundle of hot fish and chips in front of her. The sun was low but warm, with daylight saving allowing them to have an evening picnic. 'Happy divorce-a-versary!' She placed the cake down on the table. 'Oh wait, I've got something else.' She took it out of her pocket and blew on the small party whistle, making a funny high-pitched sound. 'Woohoo!'

Katy laughed. 'Oh my God, Jenna, I love you!' She held out her arms and embraced her friend. 'You're like an instant one-person party.'

She puffed up her curls. 'I do my best.' She sat and Katy unwrapped the dinner. 'Sorry I was late. Had to drop Lexi off at her friend's house and she was running late getting ready.'

'That's okay, that's motherhood. How are you feeling on the antidepressants?'

'A bit better. Still working on the art therapy classes and going to my psychologist. You were right about the PTSD. I booked Lexi in for an assessment too.'

'Good idea. You'll get through it all. I'm here anytime you need me.'

Jenna blew her a kiss. 'Right, let's dig in, I'm starving.' Jenna put a piece of fish on a paper plate Katy had brought and devoured it, along with the chips. Katy ate slowly, savouring every mouthful. She had opted against a fancy dinner at a restaurant, preferring to have a simple, casual celebration of this new phase of her life, with her best friend for company.

They sipped on bottles of lemonade and chatted and giggled like the teenagers they used to be. Neither Katy nor Jenna were overly keen on alcohol, especially as Jenna's ex used to get drunk and that often led to violence.

'How are those business ideas coming along?' Katy asked. 'Kane has been doing up old furniture and also repainted my hallway a fresh light lemon colour, looks fab. He wants to try doing it as a business eventually. Furniture Rehab he calls it!'

'Good for him! As for me, all I know is I still want to be around people every day and I want something creative. I thought of doing monthly market stalls, but I don't know if I can make enough selling mine and Lexi's art and craft creations.' She took another sip of lemonade. 'A shop could be good, but where? All the good spots in the street are taken.'

'Have you put in an expression of interest with the real estate agents? They can let you know if any shop spaces come up for lease.'

'Good idea. I'll do that tomorrow. Except, I have to save more money to be able to pay a bond and the rent until the shop makes enough to cover the bills. I could see if the bank will give me a loan, I guess, while I still have my job at the clinic.'

'There are lots of options. So what sort of shop would you love to own? Apart from selling your creations.'

Jenna's eyes brightened. 'Basically, everything I'd love to

own myself but can't afford or can't fit in my house!' She chuckled.

'So, like, homeware and stuff?'

'Yeah, but unique things. And from local artists and creators. A mixture of homeware and décor, photography, art, gifts, cushions, candles, crystals, a bit of everything!' The excitement in her friend's voice was palpable.

'The Bay does need something like that, it doesn't have a one-stop shop for all of those things.'

'True! Oh, I hope I can make it a reality one day.'

Katy's thoughts swirled, forming possibilities in her mind. She had some savings and equity in her home. She would never leave her job as a nurse, but... 'Hey, just a thought, if you like, we could meet with a lawyer and draw up a contract of sorts, and I could become a silent partner.'

Jenna's mouth gaped. 'Like an investor?'

'Guess so, yeah. I could help you get it started and depending on the percentage of joint ownership, share a small amount of the profits but leave all the business decisions to you.'

'Oh my God. If I had some help, I might not even need a loan. Katy, would you really? Can you afford it?'

'Yeah, and my house is close to being paid off anyway thanks to my inheritance. I'd love to invest in something like that! How about we set up a meeting with a lawyer and look at all the options?'

Jenna's lips tightened and her eyes became watery. 'You're the best friend anyone could ask for.'

'Aww, come here. Likewise.' They hugged and when Katy pulled back, her gaze was drawn to a man jogging through the park. He broke from the path and jogged across to a bubbler near their table, took a sip of water, then splashed his face. His very attractive and *familiar* face.

His eyes caught her gaze. 'Katy?'

'Jon?'

He strode over, all sweaty and tanned, his muscular arms bulging. 'Hey, how are you doing?'

'I'm great, thanks! How are you?'

'Awesome. What a beautiful evening, eh?'

'Gorgeous. This is my friend, Jenna.' She gestured with a flourish.

'Hi!' Jenna gave a little wave and by the sudden look of understanding on her face, she probably realised that he was the date Katy had back before the reunion, when Kane had turned up on her doorstep.

'Nice to meet you,' he said. 'Looks like you two are having a little celebration. Birthday?'

'Oh no, it's Katy's divorce-a-versary!' Jenna picked up the whistle and blew it, the shiny foil ribbons attached to it shimmering with her breath.

Oh God. Katy lowered her head. *How embarrassing.* But then again, she was more than grateful Jenna was here with her, bringing positive vibes to her new life.

Jon chuckled and his eyes widened. 'Well, happy divorce-a-versary to you.' He held out his hand and she shook it. A bit different to the kiss they'd shared back in August. His hand was warm and although the touch of a man's skin was still nice, she wasn't sure it sent the same spark through her body as it had before. Maybe all she had needed back then was to *feel* wanted, unlike the last couple of years of her marriage.

'You in town for anything?' she asked.

'Scouting some locations to run some outdoor fitness bootcamps. Apparently, there's a gap in the market around Tarrin's Bay.'

'Yeah, I think there's a women's over-forties one or something, but that's about it.'

'Yeah. Need something for men too, and everyone of all ages. Just an idea I'm considering.'

'Oh, well good luck. I'm sure it'd do well.' She smiled.

'Thanks. I'll leave you to it then.' He locked eyes with Katy. 'Hope to run into you again. Have a great night.' He jogged away.

Jenna watched him as though hypnotised.

'Earth to Jenna. Earth to Jenna.' Katy laughed.

'Man, he is hot. And he might be around town a lot more. What about giving it another go with him?' she asked, her eyes pleading. 'I would join his class.'

Katy's cheeks warmed. 'Oh, I dunno. He's great, yes, but it felt like a sign that our date got interrupted. Maybe it's not meant to be.'

'It was the wrong time then, but now? Seriously, it's literally your divorce-a-versary and we just happen to bump into him? Now *that's* a sign.'

Katy twisted her lips to the side. She had a point. Maybe she should go on one more date to see if there was anything there. She'd think about it. Dan would be leaving next month and Jon wasn't.

'Anyway, no pressure. Just enjoy your night.' Jenna blew the whistle again and Katy laughed.

'I think one thing I am ready for is cake!' Katy opened the box to find a marble cake with pink icing decorated with a tiara and silver sprinkles.

'For the queen of the night,' Jenna said.

'Oh, that reminds me of that song.' Katy cleared her throat. 'How does it go?' She hummed, then the lyrics came to her and she began singing. Jenna joined in and they belted out the chorus, not caring that people walking by were looking at them with big grins and shaking their heads.

For the next hour they ate cake, chatted more, laughed more, and Katy smiled with more happiness than she'd felt in a long time. Her new life was waiting for her, and she was ready.

CHAPTER TWENTY-THREE

Dan did his usual deep breath and smile in front of the mirror in the dressing room. Tonight was the second-last show of the series and he was hoping to hear some good results from the participants after the challenges he'd presented last week before they wrapped everything up. The ratings had been good, his social media following had increased by twenty per cent, and his latest book was now an Amazon bestseller.

All was going well, but all was also coming to an end, both for his time in the Bay and for Harry. He'd lasted longer than anyone thought he would and was still fighting. Dan was so proud of how his cousin was handling his prognosis. He'd been fulfilling his last few wishes: getting his feet in the ocean, writing letters to his loved ones with Dan's help, and tying up loose ends with old friends and old dreams, making peace with what was and what would no longer be. Uncle Robbie and Aunt Eliza had even given him an early Christmas – put the tree up and everything – in case he didn't make it to December. They'd sung Christmas carols, opened presents, and reminisced with photos of times gone by. Dan's mothers had taken part too, and it had also been nice for Dan as he wouldn't be here come

Christmas time and missed spending the season with his family in sunny Australia.

'Dan, on in five!'

Here we go. He walked along the hall and waited for the usual intro, then stepped confidently onto the stage. He was getting used to this weekly role bringing energy and enthusiasm and giving him an adrenaline boost. Apparently, Katy and Kane had deemed it their weekly TV night and she would text him her feedback after each show, as would his parents. He'd had a ball doing this gig and would miss it when it ended next week. He would miss Katy too. She had withdrawn slightly since their almost-kiss, but not to the extreme as she had when they were teenagers. They were still acting like good friends, going to occasional Pilates classes, skateboarding, texting, and having coffee catch-ups in the park. But there were no more visits to the resort or his cabin where temptation lay. At least for him. He wasn't sure if she had buried whatever feelings she might have had, or if she hadn't really felt them at all and it had just been a caught-up-in-the-moment thing. He knew she'd had her divorce-a-versary last week, but he hadn't heard anything more from her and he had held back from contacting her so she could have space to reassess what she wanted. Whatever it was that she did want would be okay with him. Her happiness was important, and like he taught others, he would only want her to get involved with him if she really, *genuinely* felt it. The ball was in her court and he would respect her choices.

Lights shone into his eyes and he glanced at the love couch where widower Gavin with his walking stick and neurodivergent Cam sat. They had both been dealing with issues of self-worth and feeling like they had unsurmountable obstacles to finding love.

'Gavin, you're looking a little brighter tonight, what's changed for you over the past week?' Dan asked.

The man cleared his throat and shifted his position. He lifted his walking stick slightly and used it as a pointing device to emphasise his words. Dan sat back slightly.

'Well, I'll tell ya, never before have I been inundated with so much support, even from people I've never met! This show has been a godsend for me, and I thank you, Dan, from the bottom of my wonky old ticker.' He held his other hand to his heart.

'Thanks, Gav, means a lot.'

'Even people I used to know from years ago have been getting in touch with me saying how brave I am for putting myself out there again. I've arranged to meet up with an old friend, and a stranger messaged me a link to a social group for widowers who are looking at dating again. I didn't know such a group existed! I went along to my first meeting, and,' he pointed the stick at the audience, 'I felt so supported and understood. If anyone out there is struggling or feeling alone, I want you to know there are people who are like you and who care.'

'I agree,' interjected Cam. 'I've avoided joining groups and being open about my autism until now but last week when I met up with some other autistic singles, I had an awesome time. We laughed a lot. They treated me like a celebrity. I can't wait to see them again.'

Dan smiled. 'That's great! And I heard you started an interesting new online project?'

'Yes. I'm making videos telling people what it's like to be autistic and how to support those who are. I was nervous at first but I've had four thousand one hundred and seventy-eight views so far on my latest video and lots of nice comments.' He looked at the audience and held up a sign with his social media username and smiled cheekily.

'Awesome, Cam. And how do you feel this will help you in your dating life?'

He fiddled with the watch on his left wrist. 'It's making me feel more proud of who I am and not like it's a problem. My brain sees and reacts to the world differently, that's all. I have trouble knowing how to interact well with people, but I really want to. So I think by embracing my differences and being proud of them, I'm being more authentic and confident, and I think others will appreciate that. And I don't have to try to pretend I'm someone I'm not.'

'Excellent. That's the way to go. I look forward to following you and seeing how things progress!' Dan held out his fist and Cam tapped it with his.

'Besides, Cam,' Gavin added, 'you're a handsome and articulate young chap, soon women will be lining up to meet you! What I'd give for your youth with a whole life ahead. But, as I've learned, I've been lucky to have the life I've had so far, and my obstacles are not obstacles but simply evidence of my life experience. I can't wait to meet more people and find out about their life experiences too.' He glanced at Dan. 'What you said last week about showing more interest in other people's feelings and experiences really made a difference. I've always been so caught up in my own stuff that I realised I've probably been too focused on it. I'm going to make it my mission on dates to discover more about the other person and show interest in *them* instead of being worried about how I come across myself.'

Cam held up a hand and Gavin high-fived it.

'Glad to hear that,' Dan replied. 'I'm so proud of both of you. You've shown that we all have unique circumstances affecting our lives as well as our love lives, and that it's really up to us to change our perspective from a negative view of ourselves to a positive one. And to take the initiative to reach out and connect with others in whatever way we feel comfortable with.'

The audience clapped as the pair left the stage and the show went to an ad break. Dan took a sip of water and Brent leaned closer to him. 'Just between us, I got myself a date for this Friday night.' He winked. 'I know that she'll know I'm using your tips, but I'm choosing to see that as a positive!'

'Way to go, man.' Dan fist-bumped him. 'Without naming her, why not share your experience here on the show? It'd really add to the authenticity I'm all for encouraging.'

Brent rubbed his chin. 'I'll think about it and chat to the producer. Don't want to scare off my date, but at the same time I love how raw and honest everyone's being here, and the feedback about the show tells us people are opening up more to their dates, which is refreshing.'

'Sure, no pressure. See how you feel after the date – maybe even ask her at the end if she'd mind you mentioning a bit about your experience – and let me know if you want me to lead a line of questioning towards you on the love couch!'

'Now I know how the participants feel! Geez, they're brave, eh? Oh, ads are almost done.' He waved at the director his readiness to resume.

After some pre-recorded content of the participants' challenges and experiences from last week was shown, Dan welcomed friends Carly and Anna to the love couch. Anna, the office-assistant-turned-advertising-agency-success-manager, explained the new 'system' she'd created for online dating to ensure she portrayed herself in the most authentic and positive light and put out what she really wanted. She'd made a checklist to go through when interacting with each date and a list of dealbreakers, as well as her long-term goals. 'I find it's keeping me from getting too caught up in short-term desire, and helps me to stay focused on what I want long term, so I don't waste time with anyone who doesn't feel right or who has completely different relationship goals to me.' She held up a printout of her system and checklist. 'I'm turning this into a free guide for my newsletter subscribers – Be Your Own Successful

Advertisement – that helps women over forty not to waste any time looking for love. There'll be self-care and self-love tips, organisational life tips, and how to fit dating into an already fulfilling life. And I've decided to do a life coaching course, and after that I hope to coach other women my age to feel confident in going after what they want in life and love.' She took a much-needed breath and looked at Dan. 'I promise, I'm not taking over your job!' She laughed.

'Ha, that's no problem. It sounds like you've found your niche and a new business opportunity that will utilise your organisational skills, marketing skills, and personal experience that a lot of women will really connect and resonate with. Well done!' He clapped along with the audience.

Dan noticed Carly wiping at the inner corner of her eye. 'Carly, how are you feeling?'

She sniffled. 'I'm so proud of her. And she helped me realise something.' She glanced up at the ceiling for a moment as though channelling insight. 'Part of the reason why I love animals so much is that they are so unconditionally loving. I love being with them all day. They are easier for me to handle than people.' She wiped at her other eye. 'I didn't have the best upbringing; I was always made to feel not good enough and anytime I'd try to speak up for myself I'd get criticised or put down. I would hang out with animals for comfort and peace. Not that that's a bad thing, but I've realised I shy away from close human connection for fear of being hurt like I was as a child.' Her voice quivered and Anna wrapped an arm around her. 'I'm going to get some therapy for my past experiences and learn ways to feel safe in myself and confident in dealing with... well, humans!'

Dan's heart always tugged on hearing people's challenging histories, but then the protective bubble he'd been taught to visualise to protect his own energy from being dragged down would appear, and he was able to be both empathetic and strong in himself. Many psychologists became burnt out because they were too affected by people's stories, so he learned early on how important these techniques were for his own well-being.

'That sounds like a real breakthrough, Carly. Good on you for becoming aware of this and taking steps to deal with it. And remember, also focus on your love of animals as a gift too, a way to express your caring nature. Often, people who care for others, animal or human, can have trouble caring for themselves; taking time to really look after their own needs because they feel others need help more.' He looked directly into the camera, hoping to reach whoever needed to hear it, and he thought of Katy. 'Remember, you are the most important person in your life. Treat yourself like that. Self-success before dating success, self-love before relationship love. That's how we create the life and love we truly deserve.'

Katy's eyes were glued to the screen, her body frozen to the couch. It was as though Dan's eyes were looking straight into hers. She cared a lot for others both in her job and her personal life, but over the past few months she had been gradually prioritising her own care and happiness more and more, and was reaping the benefits. She always knew it was important, but never fully practised it until Dan came back into her life. Whatever happened from this point on, she was grateful for that. But she also knew she couldn't let him go without getting a chance to express her feelings and see if acting on them was worth the risk to their lifelong friendship.

'You okay? Ready for *Virgin River*? One episode left of the season,' Kane asked, putting his popcorn bowl on the coffee table.

'Um, I just need to have a break and go shower. Don't start without me, 'kay?' She stood.

'Sis, what is it?'

She shifted from one foot to the other and scratched her arm even though it wasn't itchy.

'Something Dan said?'

There it was, that twin intuition. She nodded.

'You two were always like peas in a pod. Seriously, I don't know why you didn't just get married after school and have five kids together.'

She laughed. 'It was different back then. It wasn't, I wasn't...' She didn't know what she was trying to say.

'And now?'

'It's differently different.'

'You're making *a lot* of sense,' he said with a sarcastic tone. 'How different?'

'This time I feel the same.'

CHAPTER TWENTY-FOUR

After two days, nothing had changed, yet everything had changed. With the sun low on the horizon, Katy stood on the shore, right where Dan and his parents had helped Harry stand, and breathed in the salty air coming off the calm yet occasionally tumultuous ocean. Dan was still in Sydney filming and doing publicity, preparing for the final show next week. A couple walked past, each holding the hand of a smiling toddler who was trying to dash into the ocean, unaware of both the joy and danger it contained. She smiled as they passed and for a moment, felt alone. She stepped away from the water and got her phone from her backpack, and sent a text to Dan.

> Hey, great show on Tuesday. Any change with Harry?

She waited a while, walked further along the shoreline then heard the chime of his reply.

> Thanks. No word yet, he's in bed 24/7 now though. Nurse is there daily; he's on IV medication. Drowsy all the time and a bit incoherent. I'll be visiting tomorrow and probably every day until I'm needed back on set next Tuesday. Just got back to town and stopped by Café Lagoon, about to head back to the resort.

She smiled at his always detailed and informative texts. He often said more than was necessary or that she'd asked for. Unlike her ex-husband whose replies were usually limited to single words or abbreviations with the occasional emoji thrown in.

> I'm at the beach near the harbour if you're still around.

She sent the reply quickly, hoping to catch him.

> On my way! Can I get you anything?

> No thanks, had something just before. See you soon x

She took a deep breath, trying to compose her thoughts and her feelings, and her feelings about her thoughts and her feelings. It was time. Two decades of wasted opportunity would end here. Well, maybe it hadn't been wasted, she'd enjoyed many happy years with Erik and had a rewarding career, but time was getting on and the one person she'd always cared about immensely would be leaving again soon.

She sensed him before she saw him, almost like twin intuition. She turned and saw him taking off his shoes and leaving them by the junction where the grass gave way to the sand. He smiled and waved as he walked towards her. Her heart beat faster, knowing that with each step he took she was one step closer to being fully authentic, open, and honest with him – how could she be anything else after what she'd learned from his expertise?

She gulped and her heart fluttered. This was it. She wouldn't back down or allow past awkwardness to resurface. She wasn't a teenager anymore, but a grown woman with a full life still to live. And she wanted him to be part of it, somehow.

'Hey, stranger. Fancy seeing you here,' he said as he approached. He gave her a quick hug.

'Perfect timing.' She smiled.

'Ah, beautiful evening.' He took a loud deep breath, just as she'd done before, as he gazed at the ocean.

'I love the feeling of the ocean air filling my lungs, it's so enlivening,' she said.

'Indeed.' He turned to her.

'Hey, I didn't mention it before but I saw you here with Harry. I was just passing by and didn't want to intrude so I didn't come over.'

'Oh,' he said. 'I didn't realise. It would have been okay if you did, but thanks for giving us the space to have that moment with him.' He dropped his gaze a little.

'Must've been special.' Katy knew if he was on an IV at home and not totally coherent anymore, it wouldn't be much longer. They could only increase his meds so much before it would send him into a sleep from which he wouldn't return.

'Yeah. Bittersweet. I keep telling him if he gets scared, just remember the feeling of the water around his feet. Focus on the moments and memories that feel special.'

'I don't remember the last time my parents dipped their toes in the ocean, but I hope when they did, they felt the magic of it.'

They both took that moment to step towards the lapping waves, allowing the water to immerse them in the sensation that would only live in Harry's mind from now on.

She felt a gentle touch on her lower back and glanced to the side.

'How are you?' Dan asked. 'The anniversary of your divorce has been and gone I presume?'

She nodded. 'I'm good. I'm glad I took time to focus on myself a bit more, get back into what brings me joy and think about where I thought I'd be at this age and what I want both now and in the future.'

'Glad to hear. And where did you think you'd be?'

'I thought I'd still be happily married and with a couple of kids.' She shrugged and smiled feebly. 'Well, I did freeze some of my eggs anyway so at least there's no rush with that.'

'Ah, because of your mum's struggles to conceive?'

'Yeah, she educated me about these things from early on so I was well informed and prepared to do that.'

He looked her in the eye with genuine admiration, and a hint of... sadness? 'You'd make a great mum.'

Her heart warmed and softened. 'Thank you. And you'd make a great dad.' Her belly tingled with anticipation and the feeling that perhaps now it was all coming together the way it should.

Dan broke her gaze and shrugged. 'Oh, I don't know if I'm meant for that. I mean, I decided a long time ago that I didn't want to add having kids to my list of life goals.'

Her heart cooled and sunk to the pit of her belly.

No.

Why now? No.

She thought she hadn't been ready for another relationship, maybe with someone new, but it was different with Dan. Dan! Her childhood best friend, who she once rejected. Oh, how part of her wished she'd just kissed him back then at that dodgy old bus stop. But then again, she was right not to do something that didn't feel right at the time. Now, so many years later, it *finally* felt right.

But the reality was, it wasn't. They wanted different things.

She gulped and swallowed her desire to grab hold of him and kiss him passionately, declaring her feelings without fear. She couldn't betray her own needs and goals, and didn't want to mess around with his, especially knowing how he'd felt about her for so long. He himself taught people not to get caught up in a relationship with someone who didn't want the same things. She would honour them both and save what they had.

Katy glanced at her watch. 'I... I better get going,' she said shakily.

'Katy, are you okay?' He touched her arm.

She bit her lower lip to stop it from trembling, then took a steadying breath. She gently wrapped her arms around him and leaned her head on his chest below his right shoulder.

'Oh,' he whispered, as though not sure what to make of this moment. He caressed her hair and held her close. When it felt like the appropriate time to pull away, she didn't. She stayed, holding him and breathing in his comforting warmth and familiar scent.

After more time had passed, he asked tentatively, 'Why are you still holding on to me?'

Katy angled her head so her voice was closer to his ear. 'When you've lost people close to you, you hold on to those you love a little tighter, a little longer, and memorise the moment, in case it's the last time.' Her voice wavered.

Dan pulled back enough to look into her eyes. 'Are you saying you love me?'

Katy's breath caught in her upper chest and she stepped back. 'I've always loved you, Dan.' She gave him a soft but resigned smile then turned away. As the sand crumbled beneath her feet, she willed her heart not to do the same. And she avoided turning back because she knew if she did, she might not ever turn away from him again.

———

Dan stood on the wet sand, one arm reaching aimlessly out towards her fading figure as she walked off the beach.

In what way? In what way? he'd wanted to ask when she said she'd always loved him. But she was gone.

The lapping waves made his legs feel wobbly, or was it from this moment; a confusing swirl of emotions he didn't know what to make of?

He thought she would turn around, even just to give one more wave, but she didn't and that wasn't like Katy.

When the water drained away from around his feet, clarity and understanding set into his bones. She wanted a family, he didn't. It was as simple as that.

He realised then that she quite possibly *was* in love with him *in that way*, had finally been ready to share her feelings, and then he'd told her he didn't want the same thing she wanted.

He lowered his head and shook it, kicking a clump of wet sand, then whooshed out a frustrated breath, running a hand through his hair.

Sometimes being true to yourself sucked.

More than two decades of trying to move on and he'd had a brief, fleeting chance with the only woman he'd ever truly loved, and now it was gone.

CHAPTER TWENTY-FIVE

Dan had not heard from Katy and had decided to give her space. After some self-reflection, he also realised he was probably a little scared about being rejected again if he allowed himself to open up to the possibility of them being together after all these years. Even if she was feeling things now, what if it wasn't enough? What if what he'd always felt for her was stronger and they'd never be an equal match? Anyway, it didn't matter since him not wanting to have a family was obviously a dealbreaker for her, and he respected that. He needed to focus on Harry right now, and being there to support his uncle and aunt. Harry's comfort and peace was all that really mattered.

He arrived at Robbie and Eliza's house at the same time as his parents, and embraced them both with a long exhale.

'Long week?' Ellen asked.

He nodded.

'You're doing a great job on the show, we're so proud of you.' She smiled.

'Thanks. Can't believe it's coming to an end.'

'Do you have to go back to the States in December or can

you stay for Christmas?' Sandy asked, lifting a casserole dish from the back seat.

'Hmm, I did need to tie up some loose ends and get organised before the new book tour in January, but... I guess it depends. Harry's lasted longer than expected, and I don't want to not be here when...' He couldn't finish the sentence.

Ellen rubbed his arm. 'We know.'

It was a strange feeling to be awaiting someone's death, both dreading and anticipating it because you didn't want to lose them but you didn't want them to suffer for too long.

'Let's see how things are come December and go from there, huh?' Ellen offered another smile, which he knew took effort. They glanced at the mahogany-stained front door with the 'Welcome' sign on it. Anyone passing by would have no idea of the impending grief that lay behind it, of the sadness at the hopes and dreams of one young man that would never be fulfilled.

Dan swallowed the lump in his throat. Every time he arrived to visit Harry, he mentally prepared himself for the possibility that when he walked through the door, they'd tell him he was gone, or that he'd spend time with him but that would be it and it'd happen when he was there. That today would be the day.

When Eliza opened the door, she actually smiled. 'I can't believe it,' she said, holding up an envelope.

'What's this?' Dan asked.

'A letter. Harry, he actually wrote it. Himself. Bit by bit, day by day. We offered to write the words for him, but he refused, said he wanted his own handwriting.'

'Who's the letter for?' Sandy asked.

'No one in particular, and everyone.' She looked at Dan and handed him the letter. 'Can you keep this with you? He said it's for your next time capsule.'

Dan's heart lifted like a hot air balloon. There was no excuse now, if Harry wanted them to do a time capsule then they'd do a time capsule. He popped the letter into the zippered pocket of his knapsack.

'Also, it's not sealed and he said you can read it but not until,' she gulped, 'till after he's gone.' She held a hand over her mouth and sniffed, and Ellen rubbed her back. 'He wrote a separate one earlier too for me and Robbie, but they are sealed.'

'So amazing he was able to do that,' Sandy said.

'It was like he summoned whatever last bit of energy he has to write them.' Eliza welcomed them inside, hobbling slightly.

Sandy carried the casserole dish into the kitchen and placed it in the fridge. 'Pop it in the oven for about a half hour or so tonight,' she said to Eliza who hugged her thanks. 'We'll bring more food over the next few days so your freezer is well stocked and you don't have to worry about cooking.'

'You are all the best,' said Robbie, who had appeared at the entrance to the hallway. 'Just going to make coffee, who wants one?'

Everyone said yes, even Ellen who normally had tea.

It could be a long day.

Katy grabbed a quick sip of water while a patient was getting into a gown. She'd been run off her feet all day and couldn't remember when she'd last had a drink, not to mention food. Jenna was on her lunch break and when she got back, Katy didn't know if she would have time for a break. But it was Friday and the weekend would soon be here and she could relax. Or try to. Her mind swirled with regret, confusion, and unidentified emotions. But she had no time to process them.

An alarm went off and Katy checked the arms of an

eighteen-month-old who'd just had her vaccinations. 'All good to go. See? You're okay, sweetie!' The red-cheeked little girl had stopped crying and was clinging desperately to a bottle filled with water. The mother took her child down the hall and Katy was about to return to the patient in the treatment bay when Jenna bounded into the clinic, a wide smile on her face.

'Nice lunch?' Katy asked.

'Yes, though I had to eat a sandwich on the run as I stopped by the real estate agency.'

'Oh?'

Jenna gestured for Katy to come to the storage room.

'Be with you in a moment, Mrs Casters!' Katy called through the curtain of the treatment bay.

'Take your time!' the patient replied. 'I'm just having a little snooze.'

Katy smiled and sidled up to Jenna.

'Bayside is closing down, did you know?' Jenna said.

'Really? But they do the best buffet dinners.'

'I know, but I walked past and saw them closing up shop and a For Lease sign on the window. Apparently, business has been tough since Home restaurant opened and is doing so well, but I popped in to talk to the owners and they said it was about time they retired anyway. They're going travelling around Australia.'

'Oh, good for them! So they're not selling the restaurant itself?'

'No, selling off all their equipment and closing for good. I popped into the real estate agency and asked for details, so they've given me some info and I'm going in tomorrow for a meeting to discuss it.'

'Oh wow, so you might be able to use the premises for your new shop idea?'

'Yes, hopefully!' She nodded rapidly, her curls bouncing.

'Well, when you need the financial side of things sorted out for my share in it, just let me know. I'll start to get things ready.'

'Ooh! So excited, Thanks, my dear.' She gave Katy a kiss on the cheek. 'Anyway, for now we have patients to care for. Off you go! Oh, but when will you have lunch?'

Katy shrugged.

'After Mrs Casters you should go. Just a quick break. Don't worry about those coming in shortly, I'll keep them occupied and let them know their fabulous nurse needs to eat.'

'Thanks.' Katy smiled and returned to her patient, excited about Jenna's new opportunity. Kane had said if she found a place to open a shop that he'd help out with any painting for free, so he could build up experience and references for his future business.

After Jenna ushered her through the door so she could have lunch outside, Katy found a picnic table in the park and revelled in the sunshine warming the skin on her arms. She got out her phone to check her messages and found one from Jon.

> Hey, how are you? Was nice to see you recently. If you're up for catching up again sometime, let me know.

Katy smiled. He was still interested, despite multiple interruptions, but was she?

She ummed and ahhed, typed then deleted, then gave up for now and ate her food quickly.

Another text came in.

> No pressure and no rush to respond. Whenever you're ready.

She relaxed her shoulders and sent a thumbs-up reaction to his message. She would think about it. She was still in turmoil from her growing feelings towards Dan, and didn't want to mess anyone else around. But she also knew that things with Dan were futile if he didn't share her dreams, and she needed to expand her horizons.

Maybe bumping into Jon was fate, and though she couldn't shake her feelings for Dan, they would pass – they'd have to. Maybe she could start a friendship with Jon, slowly, and see where things went. Yes, she would think about it.

CHAPTER TWENTY-SIX

The weekend had been much the same as Friday, with Harry being occasionally coherent and able to talk, and other times sleeping or struggling with his breathing, drowsiness, or pain whenever the meds started wearing off. His ankles and lower legs had swollen up, and the nurse helped put compression stockings on him to assist with his comfort and circulation. He had also needed to have fluid drained regularly from his lungs through a tube. His organs were failing, but it was as though his stubbornness was winning. Sadly, the gaming had stopped a few weeks back as he simply didn't have the energy or inclination anymore. He had told Dan he wanted him to have the PlayStation when he died and that every time he played a game, he would be there in spirit helping him battle the bad guys.

As Dan stepped out of his cabin on Monday morning and onto the garden path, he stopped where Nathan the gardener was working, building a plant wall with a lattice structure. 'That will look good, what are those?' he asked, gesturing to the hanging plants Nathan was securing to various spots on the wall.

'Oh, hey there. Trailing ivy.' He untangled some of the vines and arranged it to hang naturally, then stepped back as though to get a look at the bigger picture. 'It can get overgrown so it needs appropriate positioning. He moved one of the pots to another spot nearby. 'That one was too close to the other one. Sometimes you've gotta step back a bit and see how things fit together.'

'Gotta get the right balance visually and practically, I guess.'

'Yep. Work with nature, not against it, and sometimes subtlety is better than going overboard and displaying too much. Though my boss said he did want the garden here to start resembling more of a secret magical garden type of space, with tangling vines, fairy lights in the trees, and colourful solar lights along the pathways in time for the Christmas season.'

Dan could visualise it all. 'I hope I get to see all that before I head back home,' he said, admiring Nathan's handiwork having never been able to keep even a houseplant alive.

'Oh, when do you leave?' Nathan asked.

'Supposed to be early December, but depends on a few uncertainties at the moment.'

Nathan took off his gloves for a moment and gulped water from his bottle, his wide-brimmed hat tipping backwards as he drank. 'Ahh, that's better. So, uncertainties... What is life without them, eh?'

'Too true, mate, too true.'

Nathan eyed him curiously. 'Do you have a special person waiting for you back home?'

'Me? No. I mean, friends, yes, but no wife or girlfriend or anything.'

Nathan nodded.

Dan could have said 'have a nice day' and kept walking, but even psychologists needed someone to talk to sometimes, and Nathan seemed laid-back and easy to chat to. 'There was someone, *is* someone. Here, actually. But it doesn't look like it's going to work.'

'Because you live there and she lives here?'

'Partly. She wants a family and I never factored that into my plans. I like my lifestyle the way it is.'

'Ah.' Nathan rubbed his chin stubble. 'So you told her it's not going to work out?'

'Didn't get a chance. She basically told me about her desire to have kids, and I told her about my desire not to, then she kinda said she'd always loved me then walked off. Haven't spoken to her since.'

Nathan's eyebrows rose. 'Sounds complicated, dude. But it also sounds special. You might have some thinking to do.'

'Hmm. We've been friends pretty much our whole lives, although we drifted apart after school. I don't want it to get weird, so I thought it best to give her space and try to let go. And I always teach people to not betray their own goals and dreams just to be with someone. Anyway, as you said, she's here and I'm there, definitely tricky and complicated.'

Nathan leaned on his shovel. 'Mate, I got involved with someone who was on the other side of the world *and* was having some other guy's baby. And I love them both to bits. You two have a fresh start while you're here. It can be anything you want it to be. The question is, would you be willing to have a family with her if it meant being with the one you love? Or is it a dealbreaker and you absolutely have to be with someone who shares your child-free goal? That's what you need to think about,' Nathan said, giving his shovel a prod in the ground. He chuckled. 'Here I am, giving the dating coach advice! Sorry, man, feel free to ignore anything I say. I just know how much I struggled and it took us over a year to get it together and just be with each other. Time is not to be wasted.'

Dan gave a slow nod. 'Time sure is precious. And thanks,

you're actually pretty good at the dating advice thing. I will definitely think over what you've said.'

'Oh, good. Let me know if you think I should give up my day job.' He grinned.

Dan eyed the plant wall that was half completed. 'Absolutely not. It looks like you take great pride in your job and I can see you love the creative side of it. Keep it up.'

'Don't worry, I will. Love being around plants all day when I'm not with my girls. Plants are good listeners.'

'So are you. Thanks, mate.' He held out his hand and Nathan shook it firmly.

'Nice chatting. I hope you get to hang around a bit and see the Christmas decorations. And good luck with everything else you're facing.'

'Thanks. Enjoy your day.' Dan waved and walked off down the path, a smile on his face and a spring in his step. He knew how his clients must feel having someone to talk to, and be listened to. It was a great way to relieve pressure that often built up in the mind, causing overthinking and worry. He still didn't know how anything could work with him and Katy, but it'd been nice to chat and hear another guy's perspective.

When he arrived at his aunt and uncle's house, his smile faded on seeing Sandy's solemn face at the front door, holding it open for him.

'Come in, quick. He's not doing great,' she said. 'Everyone's gathered around the bed. I don't think he has much longer.'

An anchor sunk inside him, securing him to a place of unwanted certainty, immobilising him and trapping him somewhere he didn't want to be. He dumped his knapsack on the entry table along with the muffins he'd picked up from the bakery, and went straight into Harry's room. He had to bite his lip to stop it quivering as he slowly approached Harry on the bed.

'I'm here, man,' he whispered. 'We're all here with you.' He placed a hand gently on the young man's forehead. It was cool to touch and had a mottled grey appearance. His chest rose inconsistently, sometimes slowly, sometimes sharply and suddenly, but each breath came with a rattle that was unmistakeable. He hadn't had that before. The fluid was building up in his airways despite regular draining. It was getting hard for him to swallow. Dan had to gulp three times before the lump in his throat would go down. He was glad the final episode of *Love, Unfiltered* wasn't on until tomorrow. Even so, he had been wondering what to do should he be needed here. He couldn't break his contract and live television couldn't always be rescheduled. He decided, if necessary, he would simply drive up for the show and come straight back, cancelling the wrap party the producer had organised. That way he'd only be gone a few hours.

Dan took a steadying breath. It was more important right now that he stay present in the moment. It was a normal human response in times of crisis or impending crisis to start making logistical plans or preparing the mind for something, to avoid having to organise things or make decisions later in a state of distress. But the reality was, Harry may not even last until tomorrow. Then again, he'd kept defying the odds up until now, so who knew what would happen.

By lunchtime, there'd been no change. Robbie played easy tunes on his guitar for Harry, and though he made no sign of being able to hear them, Dan was sure he could. He and Ellen went to the kitchen to make sandwiches for everyone, while Eliza went to the bathroom and Sandy stayed with Robbie, swaying to the music.

They layered sandwich ingredients and cut bread into triangles in silence, which was unlike his mum. He knew she was trying to hold it together for the sake of her brother and his wife, to be there for them as they lost their only son.

Eliza came back from the bathroom and joined them in the kitchen, picking up a sandwich. 'I didn't realise how hungry I was,' she said, taking a bite.

Ellen took a bite of one also. 'Me too.' She smiled.

Dan ate his quickly as they stood at the kitchen bench, then brought a tray into the bedroom for the others, along with the muffins. At least they'd all be well fed, which always helped when it came to coping with stress. Sometimes he'd treated clients who had major mood swings from blood sugar imbalances or malnutrition, and he often encouraged people to get back to basics sometimes to help regulate emotions: hydration, healthy food, sleep, exercise, and downtime. When that foundation was present, everything else was much easier to treat and manage. But there was nothing food could do to negate the grief from the loss of a loved one. Still, he felt some comfort at everyone having a full stomach, at least for a while.

Robbie decided to put on one of Harry's favourite movies, *Weekend at Bernie's*, and they watched and laughed, even though Harry's eyes were closed, much like Bernie's. Dan knew that if Harry were with it right now, he'd probably be laughing at the irony – a movie about a dead man and other people pretending he was still alive.

When Dan took a break after the film and went to the bathroom, he splashed water on his face and looked at his reflection. Tired eyes and a serious expression that belied the fact he'd just been laughing at the movie. He checked his phone for nothing in particular, as usual ignoring all the comment notifications on social media his manager would take care of, and flicked through some photos. He smiled at the skateboarding pictures of him and Katy, and the garden photos from Trees of Life. He thought of all the things Harry wouldn't get to do and his chest shook with impending tears. But he clamped his lips together. *Not now.*

'Dan?' A tap at the door sounded.

He opened it and Ellen grasped his arm gently. 'Any moment now, they think.'

He hurried back into the room, again letting Harry know he was there. Robbie played his guitar again, Eliza sang a little though her voice was shaky and weak, and Sandy and Ellen swayed together. Dan couldn't sit. He stood back and waited. And waited. The question of *when* hung constantly in the air, with no answer. Was he waiting for them to give him space? He had heard that sometimes people finally pass when others leave the room, and he was about to suggest that, but...

One rattling breath, in and out, and then...

All fell silent as they watched, but Harry did not draw another breath. His chest lay frozen in time, and Dan held his too, as though by taking a breath he might miss his cousin's last one. But he hadn't. Harry had breathed in, he'd breathed out, and that was it. No more. No more air, no more oxygen, no more life.

Eliza's hand flew to his cheek, shaking as she caressed it. Still, he did not breathe.

Robbie put down his guitar and held a hand in front of Harry's nose and mouth, feeling for air. He put his hand gently on his son's chest, but it didn't rise. Then something like a cross between a sigh and a howl came out of Eliza's mouth. The sound punctured Dan's heart like needles and his eyes stung. Robbie held one hand to his own forehead, rubbing it, the other on his wife's back as she shook with sobs.

Sandy and Ellen put their arms around Dan as he stood between them. Ellen sniffled; Sandy stayed quiet. Dan reached out a hand to Harry's and held it, lifeless and limp. 'Rest now, brother,' he whispered.

He didn't know how long they all stayed like that, but after a while something changed in the air, a shift in the energy and Eliza stood suddenly. 'Coffee, anyone?'

'I'll get it, love,' said Robbie.

'No, it's okay. I need to... do something.' She left the room and busied herself in the kitchen. Dan followed and hung about the entrance, to make sure she was okay. He knew it was best to let people grieve in their own way. She'd cried, she'd howled, and now she wanted coffee. Perfectly reasonable.

Robbie poked his head around the corner. 'She okay?' he whispered.

Dan nodded. '*You* okay?' Dan asked.

Robbie nodded. 'I will be.' He patted Dan's back and went back to the room.

Yes, he would be. They all would be, eventually. But for now, they weren't, and that was okay.

The air was thick with humidity and Katy tightened the elastic on her ponytail as escaped strands of hair stuck to her neck with sweat. She hooked her arms into her backpack and got on her skateboard, riding her way home. She stopped by the park to sip from the bubbler and stood with her hands on her hips, glancing out at the nearby ocean. She looked down and prodded her hips, feeling bone and muscle. She had only just noticed that she'd lost some weight and had become more sculpted from the extra exercise.

'Huh. Well, there you go,' she said to herself. Skateboarding was the new Pilates.

She watched a couple walk by hand in hand and smiled. *Ah, young love.*

She thought of Dan and decided she'd get in touch with him

after dinner, apologise for being distant but say she'd needed some space to sort through some things. He would understand, he probably needed space too after her declaration of love, which she'd only realised afterwards may have come across as ambiguous. She'd meant it in two ways. She *had* always loved him, as a childhood friend, a part of her life she couldn't imagine being without. But she also *loved* him loved him. As an adult, a part of her life she couldn't imagine being without. But she couldn't be with him in that way, it would be taking a step backward instead of forward. She needed to move to the future she wanted and deserved. Starting now. She got out her phone and started typing a reply to the text Jon had sent last week.

> Hi! Thanks for getting in touch. Appreciate your patience. So, um, I've been thinking… I would be keen to catch up sometime, if you'd still like to?

She nibbled her lip and reread the message, not ready to send it just yet.

Her phone chimed and she jumped, dropping it. Luckily only on the grass and it didn't break this time. She picked it up. A text from Dan.

> Katy, Harry passed away a couple of hours ago. Just wanted to let you know. xo

She gasped, almost dropping the phone again. 'Oh my.' She held a hand to her heart and stared at the text until the letters blurred together and looked like they had no meaning, except they did.

She'd lost patients, lost her parents, so she knew grief all too well. But what she felt now was different. Empathic grief, yes, for Dan and his family, but also a longing. A longing to be there, to support, to love. In whatever way she could. It was as though her heart had leapt from her chest and launched like a rocket to be with Dan's, and she had the urge to run, to follow her heart's lead and be there with him, *for* him.

Instead of texting a reply, she pressed his name and called him.

'Katy?'

'Dan. Oh, Dan, I'm so sorry.'

He sighed on the other end of the line. 'Thank you.'

'What can I do, do you want me to be there? To do anything... medical? To come over later? Or bring anything to help you and your family?'

'No, no, it's okay. But thanks. The nurse will be here shortly along with a doctor to confirm things. I'm going to stay here tonight and help my aunt and uncle get Harry organised for when the funeral director comes in the morning. Then I'll have to drive to Sydney and do the final show. God, I don't know how, it seems irrelevant now, but I'll just do it. Then I can focus on helping with the funeral arrangements.'

Katy's mind swirled. He was in action mode, not grief mode. She knew it well. When you focus on what you can do, it's somehow slightly less painful. 'I'll drive you,' she blurted. 'And don't say "no it's okay". I insist.'

There was a moment of silence. 'Are you sure?'

'Of course. Let me help you get through your last show. I can wait in the car, or...'

'Don't be silly, we'll be able to get you a seat in the audience. If you want to, that is.'

It did feel irrelevant, watching a show about dating when someone had just died. But it was Dan's job and had to be done. Harry would want him to finish his contract on the show. And he was helping people live the lives they wanted. If that wasn't important, she didn't know what was. 'Sure thing. Text me tomorrow when and where to pick you up.'

'Thanks, Katy, I appreciate it.'
'That's what friends are for,' she said softly.

Dan ended the phone call and ran a hand through his hair. He stepped outside and sat on the front step. The sky was turning a dusky pink and purple. Ellen was heating up some dinner, though he didn't have much of an appetite and the others probably didn't either. But he would eat. He had to keep going.

He needed to do something first though. He went back inside and opened his knapsack. He retrieved the envelope, his hand shaking slightly. He went back outside, sat on the step again, and opened the letter.

He took a sharp intake of breath and waited for the relief of the exhale before reading Harry's handwriting...

Hello!

This is Harry. And this is my final letter. I am dying. And although I am tired, I am determined to write, to get all this out. It feels liberating to actually write the truth down on paper. To not be afraid of it. Either way it's happening so I might as well come to terms with it.

This letter is both for my cousin Dan and also his next time capsule. He opened his first one a couple of decades too early! I'm glad. It inspired me to write to my family and to write this. And sometimes the future doesn't wait.

I guess that's what this letter is about. Whether Dan opens this again in the future or someone else finds it, if I can give any advice from my deathbed, it would be: don't wait for what you want to do. Do it now. And don't think that everything will be exactly as you plan it to be. Life has a way of surprising us, so roll with the punches, expect the unexpected, but don't let life weigh you down. If you're still breathing, you've still got life to live. Even if all you can do is immerse your mind in memories, remember those you're grateful for. Forget those so-called mistakes. We are all just apprentices in life and no one gets it perfectly right.

I hope I made my parents proud. I sometimes wish I'd done more, seen more, contributed more, but by the time I realised life was short, my time left was short. Illness is life's greatest teacher. It brings everything into perspective. Not only for the sick, but for their loved ones. I want those I love to know I'm okay. I'll be okay. Wherever I'm going. I was angry at my disease for a long time but then I realised I was also amazed at how my body fought it off for so long. Most people are stronger than they think. Don't ever think you're not, we have more strength inside of us than we ever realise.

If there's anything you've been wanting to do one day, don't put it off, get started now. Don't wait for a diagnosis to start rethinking your life. And don't wait for things to be perfect. Just take action and move forward. If you are lucky, you will get a longer life than I did, but duration is not the be all and end all. It's what you do and how you choose to live and love that matters. Live big, love big. I did my best, and I'm grateful for the awesome life I've had.

Harry.

Dan lowered the letter and looked up at the now mostly dark sky. It was as though by reading his words, the sky's transition had helped Harry with his. It had finally happened. A life cut short, but a life lived well. Heaviness hovered above Dan and he folded the letter, each crease closing in on his heart. His breath came faster, and with his next exhalation came a sob. And another. He buried his face in his hands and allowed the grief to overwhelm him.

A gentle hand eased onto his back, and he glanced sideways to see Ellen sitting next to him on the step. She didn't ask to see the letter, simply held her steady hand on him and breathed and sobbed with him. United in grief. And relief, for him, that he was still here with his parents. He wouldn't waste that gift.

CHAPTER TWENTY-SEVEN

It was only when Katy got into bed that night after shedding a few tears in the shower, that she realised she hadn't sent her message to Jon about meeting up. She opened it and reread the words that waited in the reply window. Her stomach twisted into a knot.

She couldn't bring herself to hit send.

She pressed backspace until all the words were gone.

Then she typed again.

> Hi Jon. Thanks for getting in touch. Appreciate your patience. I've been thinking… I don't want to mess you around. You're fantastic and I'm glad we met. But the truth is, I'm in love with my best friend. Not Jenna! My friend Dan. I don't think he and I will be able to be together, but I can't be with anyone else right now. I hope you understand. Just wanted to be honest. Thanks, and I wish you all the best.
> Katy.

Sent. She breathed slowly and relaxed into the bed. Oh well. It was what it was. At least she was being authentic and if that meant she'd be on her own, then so be it.

The next morning Katy had a text from Dan saying when and where to pick him up. She also had a text from Jon saying he appreciated her honesty and although he was disappointed he wouldn't get to know her better, he wished her well and hoped to see her around town if he went ahead with his new bootcamp business. She had told work after her call with Dan that she would need the day off, so one of the clinic's casual nurses would be filling in for her.

Katy took advantage of the day off and the time on her own while Kane was at work by doing some decluttering around the house. She stood with hands on hips, surveying her bedroom, and realised she still had a few items that were related to her marriage. A framed print of two love birds given to them on their wedding day, which she'd always liked so hadn't wanted to get rid of. But was it really appropriate to display artwork that resembled love in a marriage that had failed? She took it off the wall and placed it in a donation bag. She also added a decorative trinket tray that Erik's sister had given her. It was nice, but linked to him. It wasn't that she wanted to cut her ex out of her life completely, they were still on good terms, but she wanted to feel like she had a fresh start with no residue from her previous life and relationship.

She eyed the queen-sized bed that only had one pillow on it right in the middle, and chuckled. She'd read in one of Dan's books about preparing your living space to include a partner at some stage, if that was your intention, through simple things like having two pillows on the bed (easy enough), making room in the wardrobe (not as easy), and displaying pairs of things around the bedroom or house (so much for the two love birds print). By doing that you were apparently declaring your intention to the universe to find partnership or love. Well, she'd found it, but it wasn't hers to keep. She'd realised that love was part chemistry, part effort, part mutual goals, and part timing. All four had to be in place and aligned for both people for something to work. Like four legs of a table. Without one, it would topple. Her marriage had it all initially, but then began failing on the chemistry and effort parts. And now, this *thing* with Dan was all about timing and different goals. Back when they were young, he had felt the chemistry but she had not, and now she felt it and it seemed he still did too, and no doubt they'd make the effort if they thought it could work, but the timing was wrong – for him and for her. They were getting older and a family was not part of his plans, even though she was sure he'd wanted one years ago. He was getting ready to go back overseas to his successful life and she had spent the past year starting a new one in Tarrin's Bay.

The only solution was to continue doing what she'd been doing as though Dan hadn't even re-entered her life. She'd be there for him as his friend during this difficult time, absolutely, but she couldn't allow herself to get swept away in whatever it was. The chemistry part never lasted long term anyway, and they'd eventually be left with the stark contrast between his goals and hers with no mutual ground beneath them except their childhood history.

After some time had passed, she'd probably be able to move on again. Would she need a Dan-a-versary to get over him after a year like she'd had for her divorce? She shook her head at her absurd thoughts and went to the linen cupboard in the hallway. She took out a pillow, placed a new pillow case on it from her matching sheet set, and placed it on her bed. Two pillows, side by side, one for her and the other for no one. But that was as far as she was prepared to go in moving forward right now. At least she'd have somewhere to rest her arm when she slept.

Katy glanced around the room again. The pale lilac walls

felt musty and old, and the white furniture too stark. She got out her phone and texted her brother.

> If you have time, can you bring home some paint swatches from the hardware store? I'm thinking light yellows and pinks. Also, looking for a painter to help makeover my bedroom – know anyone? 😌

A fresh new room would help her feel better. Once she decided on a new colour scheme, she'd either get Kane to help revamp her furniture too, or maybe even buy a new bed and bedside tables. Maybe something with a plush velvet headboard in rich fuchsia, or burgundy, or even bright purple. She opened up the Pinterest app on her phone and searched for ideas. She continued decluttering, placing clothes she hadn't worn in a while into a donation bag, and throwing out old bits and pieces.

Kane replied.

> Sure. I might know someone. Hey, what time will you be getting back?

She'd told him earlier that he'd have to watch *Love, Unfiltered* and *Virgin River* on his own tonight as she'd be in Dan's audience.

> Fairly late I'd say, don't wait up. Dan said he wants to come straight back to town after the show instead of staying in Sydney for the wrap party. The crew are going to postpone it till after Harry's funeral so he can take some mental space.

> That's nice. Should we go to the funeral? It'll be kinda hard. Last funeral I went to was Mum and Dad's.

Katy had been to several others since then, with the nature of her job, plus when Erik's uncle had died.

I will. But it's up to you. I know you didn't really know Harry, but if you think it'd be supportive for Dan and his family, I'm sure he'd appreciate it.

I'll think about it.

Katy paused her decluttering and went to her wardrobe, checking that her funeral outfit was still suitable. It was different to what she'd worn to her own parents' funeral. After that, she hadn't been able to keep the outfit and had donated it immediately. She exhaled and slid clothes across the rod, looking for something to wear tonight. Something simple but stylish should do. It wasn't like she was a guest, and any footage of the audience was bound to be fleeting. She settled on a slim fitting pair of three-quarter black pants with a slight sheen, half-height peep toe heels, and a patterned top with loose sleeves and a few subtle embellishments, which she'd bought from the local markets on Jenna's insistence. She'd worn it to a birthday party once and received compliments. She would wear her only pair of dangly earrings. Jenna had made them for her recently at a jewellery making course she and Lexi had been attending, and as they weren't suitable to wear to work, she thought tonight would be more appropriate. Though it felt strange to be getting dressed up to go out when someone had just passed away. Did these things really even matter? She could just go to the show in her scrubs and no one would probably even notice. But in a way, looking nice *felt* nice. And no doubt Dan would be dressed up and she wanted to join in and help him feel as normal and as ready as possible to face his final show before his gig in Australia ended.

She hung the pants and top on the door handle and,

suddenly fatigued, collapsed eagerly onto the bed. Her head rested in between the two pillows and she laughed. Before too long, she had fallen into a much-needed sleep, immersed in bizarre dreams of skateboarding while dressed up in a ball gown and heels, and then blowing bubble gum in front of the patients' faces at work. When her alarm sounded to indicate it was time to begin getting ready for the journey to Sydney, she scrambled out of bed and texted Dan that she'd be there soon.

Sun streamed down through the trees as she parked at Trees of Life Resort, and she gazed around, admiring the natural sanctuary that it was, remembering the beautiful day she'd shared with Dan here. Her reminiscing was broken a few minutes later when he appeared at the bottom of the steps and waved with a small smile, clearly trying to put on a brave face to get through the day.

She got out of the car and held her arms out, wanting to give her condolences, but he held her at arm's length.

'No, not yet. If I feel your arms around me, I might crumple,' he confessed.

Katy stepped back, her arms tingling a little at the unmet need to embrace him. She clasped her hands together. 'Of course. I'm here to help you get through the night. Whatever you need. I'm here.'

'Thanks,' he said softly. 'I appreciate the support, I just... can't do... hugs right now.'

Just like how she had to stay focused and objective in her work while performing certain procedures, he had to as well. She also knew that he quite possibly *would* crumple later on, and if that happened, she was here to be a shoulder to cry on.

On the drive he told her how Harry's body had been

collected and taken to the funeral home, and that with everything having already been planned, unlike with an unexpected death, the funeral was all organised and would be early next week. She told him she would take another day off work for that and be there with him and his family.

They switched the topic of conversation to the participants on the show and what was planned for tonight. She told him how immersed she'd become in each person's journey, and that it took reality television to a whole new level. She knew, too, that at some stage they'd probably need to discuss their own journeys and what had transpired in Tarrin's Bay between them, so he could go back home with no regrets, no what ifs, and knowing that she was okay with everything. At least she thought she was.

When they arrived at the television studio, Dan took Katy through the cast and crew entrance and all thoughts of his own life dissipated as his heart beat a little faster at the now familiar excitement of being on a TV set. He noticed Katy's wide eyes taking it all in, and managed a smile. This was new to her. Crew members approached him with sombre expressions, a few went to hug him but he held them off or gave them a quick pat on the back and kept moving so as to not lose momentum. 'Let's do this,' he said, rubbing his hands together.

He introduced Katy to everyone, then showed her where she could sit in the audience and left her with Cassandra, one of the caterers, to give her some refreshments while he got ready in the dressing room and had his make-up put on.

Brent poked his head around the door. 'You've got this, mate,' he said with a thumbs up. Dan returned the gesture in gratitude for this simple offer of support. Yes, he had this. He could do this. He wasn't in the best emotional state, but this show was all about vulnerability, and although he would still put on his best television persona version of himself, he would still be himself and didn't have to hide anything. He was determined to give the show its happy ever after so the participants could have the best chance at their own.

He sent a quick text to Katy.

> All okay? Almost time.

She replied instantly.

> All good. Very exciting. The audience is filling up. Good luck!

He sent a smiley face then turned his phone to silent. A sense of relief flushed through him, knowing she was here. Her support and presence meant the world to him. He knew it would be time to part ways soon, though, which made this time even more bittersweet.

He waited in the wings until the show's intro was completed. Brent looked shiny and energetic on stage as he made the audience feel relaxed and excited for the show. Despite the bright lights Dan could see Katy sitting in an aisle seat in the middle of the crowd, she had probably not wanted to sit at the front and be right in his face, and in a way he was glad, so he could focus, but still know he had her supportive presence.

Dan plastered his best smile on his face, genuinely excited to finish up the series and do it justice and do both the producers, and Harry, proud. Harry had managed to watch some of the first few episodes and had even shared a laugh with him about it when he'd visited afterwards; Harry pretending he was a participant with an invisible date next to him in bed. Dan had jokingly advised he help his date be 'seen' and 'heard' so they felt validated, and Harry had said his date was a bit self-conscious of her appearance, or lack thereof. The memory made his lips twitch and he blew out a raspberry to relax his jaw and settle his nerves, then stepped out into the spotlight.

The audience clapped and cheered, and he took his seat next to Brent.

'It's been an honour, Brent, and I'm looking forward to hearing from our participants about what they're up to and how the show has impacted them.'

'Well, I for one have been impacted by your tips too,' Brent added. He cleared his throat and shuffled a little on his seat. 'I had myself a little date recently and let's just say... it was quite different to what I've normally experienced.'

'Oh? In what way?' Dan was glad Brent had opened things up for a line of questioning as he'd forgotten to check beforehand if it was okay to proceed.

'Obviously, my date knew I was the host of this show, and I assured her that her privacy was a priority and I would in no way share any details of our date. But then she said, "Why not? It could be good!"' He grinned. 'So, after enjoying a fabulous date being fully authentic and honest, I agreed to share the top three things we both found refreshing from the experience compared to other dates we've been on.'

'Awesome. And they are?' Dan asked.

'For me, it was feeling like I didn't have to be Brent the TV host, I could be Brent the regular guy who happens to work on a TV show – still me, but I didn't have to worry about not appearing as...' he circled his hands around, 'energetic or enthusiastic, if you know what I mean. In the past I always felt like I had to be who everyone expected me to be, but this time I felt like I could let my guard down a little, be more vulnerable. A bit more personal. And it was a relief.'

'That's great, it can be exhausting to feel like you have to keep up appearances between public and private life, but I'm glad you found a way to still be you without feeling like you're being watched by a camera.' He knew how that felt.

Brent nodded. 'And she said how nice it was to see a more personal version of me, that it also helped her relax, knowing she could be comfortable being herself too.'

'So number one for both of you, was feeling comfortable enough to be yourself?'

'Exactly. And number two for me was feeling more prepared, having some tips and guidelines in place to make the evening more intentional. Not in a structured and formal way, but I found it good to feel more *ready*. I think too often people just wing it and hope for the best, which is fine if they want to do that, but as a host I do like a bit of a structure and a plan for what's ahead!'

'I can understand that. Did your date appreciate this too?'

'She said she was a planner and had even written a list of questions to ask me if I didn't mind!'

'Did you mind?'

'Not at all! We had fun, I answered them, and then she answered them for me. I'd never done anything like that before.'

'So being yourself and feeling prepared.' Dan tapped two fingers and then a third. 'And the third thing you found refreshing?'

'Okay, this is a little awkward...' He shuffled again. 'But she said it was okay if I shared it, so...' He cleared his throat again. 'She said she felt comfortable to declare what she wanted, instead of waiting for the guy to initiate like she usually would.'

'And what did she want?'

His cheeks went pink and he smiled. 'Well, being the gentleman that I am, I would have said goodnight and called her the next day, but she straight up said, "Brent, that was such a great night, you are so cute and caring, and I would really love to kiss you right now".'

Dan's eyes widened and he grinned. This was the power of being open and taking a leap of faith. 'And...'

'And, well, let's just say I really wanted that too! I'm so glad she was upfront because I never know when to act and when to hold back.'

'I get the feeling things went quite well, eh?'

'They sure did. We've seen each other two more times and will be seeing each other again. We've made a pact to say whatever's on our minds, no holding back. Let's see how it goes!' He glanced to the camera and blew a kiss. 'For you, sweetie.' He winked and the audience laughed and clapped, and a few wolf-whistled.

Dan clapped too and said to the audience, 'What a great host Brent has been, wouldn't you agree? Getting into the true spirit of the show.'

Everyone cheered and clapped some more, and Brent's rosy face glowed under the lights.

He shrugged. 'Ah, just doing my part. And also doing their part are our wonderful participants. Here's some footage from the past week of what each has been up to, and we're going to chat more to some of them on the love couch shortly before we bring all of them onto the stage for the finale and for Dan's final speech.' He twisted and Dan followed suit to angle his gaze to the large screen behind them as the recorded footage was played.

As Katy turned her attention from Dan to the screen, she imagined Kane slouched on the couch at home eating popcorn, and giggled to herself. He was probably having a conversation with himself too. Despite her initial worries about a potential relapse, she'd enjoyed having him around again, especially now he had a job and was keeping himself busy. She hoped this period of stability would help him kickstart a new life where she could be confident in his ability to look after himself and stay clean. She still had plans for herself, still needed time to sort out her independent life, and she knew it would be easier once both Kane and Dan were gone. Kane would still be close, of course, but Dan would be far away. With him here now, however, it was like walking through low lying clouds, not able to see far in front of her or know where to step next.

She watched with interest the stories unfolding on the screen. The gay couple in their forties being filmed on one of their date nights where they'd decided to pick something to do out of a literal hat each week. Both had written a list of fun ideas to keep the spark alive and connect in a deeper way so as to not get stuck in a rut. They were clearly opposites, and the audience found it amusing how they responded to each different task. She smiled as they were shown doing stand-up paddleboarding one week (the more reserved of the pair with a worried expression the whole time), and a paint and sip class the next (the outgoing guy looking a little bored and fidgety while the other blissfully painted the rainbow-coloured tiger). She wondered if they had added skateboarding to their list of date ideas.

They shared a snippet of Cam's latest online video about autism and dating and what he had learned from Dan over the course of the show, which was quite emotional to see, along with the many positive comments and even a few from young women saying they'd love to go on a date with him.

Carly had created a new social group for animal-loving singles and thanks to the show had received a lot of interest for meet-ups at the park and off-leash beach. Her friend, Anna, with her newly refined career purpose was now being headhunted for new positions and considering all available offers. Turns out, working on your love life also had benefits for life in general, and Dan had explained in one of his pre-recorded segments how important it was to see dating as part of an overall fulfilling life, not the sole focus. 'When life falls into place, love often falls into place too,' he'd said.

When the footage went to single mother of five, Adriana, Katy felt a twinge in her heart. The woman balanced a toddler on one hip while preparing school lunches for the other kids, the eldest helping out by buttering bread for sandwiches. 'Every day is full on,' she said as she worked. 'For a man to be in my life again, he needs to be prepared for the fact that it's me *and* the kids,' she said proudly. 'I used to try and get babysitters, hide them away somewhat, but now, well, what you see is what you get. If that's not what they want, they can just tell me, no hard feelings.'

Katy felt a nudge from the elderly lady beside her who was sitting with another lady who looked similar, like they were sisters. 'I had five kids too,' she said into Katy's ear. 'Luckily my sister here helped me out when they were young while my husband worked. Got any kids?' she asked.

'Not yet.' Katy smiled. And she decided that once she was finished sorting out her own life and ready to consider dating again, she would be upfront and honest to any potential partner – she wanted to try for a baby before she got much older. She wanted to have that love that oozed from Adriana's eyes when she was surrounded by her children, and the love and joy they radiated when around her. Kane would be a great uncle and could do fun activities with them if she were to become a single mother, and no doubt Jenna and Lexi would dote on a new baby, so like the lady with the sister next to her, she wouldn't be fully alone.

After a commercial break, the cameras returned to Dan and Brent, and Katy's heart leapt with pride at how Dan was handling tonight, and how he had helped create such a life-affirming show with positive results. She only wished the same for him, that he would find someone one day who really saw him and appreciated him for who he was deep inside, and would want the same things he wanted. After all this time, he deserved that.

CHAPTER TWENTY-EIGHT

After a couple of chats on the love couch with some of the participants, Dan's jaw opened wide in surprise as Adriana came onto the stage with her five kids, and... a man. They squished themselves onto the couch, the toddler on her lap and the others perched in various spots on the sides.

'I see we have a special guest!' Brent stood and shook hands with the grey-haired man nearing fifty, a big smile on his face and looking like he just slotted right in with the instant family.

Dan did the same and took his seat again.

'This is Ricardo,' Adriana said. 'We've started dating and most of those dates so far have not been a table for two, but for seven!' She laughed.

'What a lovely surprise,' Dan said. 'Ricardo, how did you two meet?'

'It's a funny thing,' he said. 'Life. How it works out. I'd been watching the show and really admired Adriana, and of course, found her very attractive.' He shone a smiling glance her way. 'I thought to myself, I hope she finds someone special. And then I thought, hang on, *I'm* someone special! I knew it was a long shot but I messaged her on social media, and yes, it was a long shot, because I never got a reply!' He laughed.

'So how did you end up meeting then?'

'Good ol' fate,' he replied with a grateful smile, and Dan's curiosity was piqued. After all that had happened the past few months, he was actually starting to wonder if fate really did exist in some way. 'I figured she was probably being spammed by lots of messages,' Ricardo continued, 'so I tried to forget about it. Until one day, I was walking my dog through the park and as I passed the playground, I did a double take. And no, I didn't bump into Carly walking her dogs,' he laughed, 'there was Adriana, in real life, pushing little Harry on the swings.'

Dan jolted at the mention of his cousin's namesake. He didn't know how he had missed the child's name before, but then again, with all the other participants to remember, keeping track of the five kids as well was tricky.

'I saw this guy looking at me,' Adriana said, 'and a big smile just flashed on his face and for some reason, I couldn't help but smile too. "I found you," he said. And I thought, huh? He came over and said how well I was doing on the show and wished me all the best.'

'Yeah, silly me, I was about to walk away, I didn't want her to think I was a stalker or anything, but then I remembered Dan saying we should just be honest, so I said: I really admire you. You're a great person and mother. I know we don't know each other, but I would love to change that.'

'I was cautious, of course,' Adriana said. 'But also intrigued. He just seemed genuine. I don't know, maybe my authenticity radar was highly tuned and I could tell he was a decent guy. So I said to him, "Oh yeah? What's your dating purpose then?"'

Ricardo chuckled. 'Luckily, I had one I'd prepared earlier.'

'And what was it?' Dan asked, leaning forward in the chair.

'I showed it to her,' Ricardo said. 'I have it as my phone's lock screen.'

'I knew he wasn't just making things up on the spur of the moment when I saw it,' Adriana added. 'I thought, this man means business!'

'My dating purpose was: I'm ready to find the love of my life; a strong, vibrant woman with family in her heart and room for one more.'

'Beautiful,' Brent said. 'So you were basically saying you wanted a woman who had a family. That it wasn't an obstacle but a blessing?'

'Yes. Whether the woman I met wanted to have a family with me or already had one, I was ready for either, but with age getting on a bit I knew an instant family would be ideal and something I was wholeheartedly ready to embrace, no matter how challenging it would be initially.' The toddler reached out for Ricardo and he handed him a toy car, which the toddler began zooming along the love couch.

'And what made you decide you wanted an instant family?' Dan asked.

'I grew up with three siblings, lots of cousins, and when my ex-wife and I married, we started trying for a family but it never happened. Ten years later, it broke us up. She didn't want to consider other options and was ready to give up, but I wasn't. We just wanted different things and amicably went our separate ways.' He gave a nod. 'I always hoped I'd have the chance later on for a family, and now...' He glanced at all the children. 'I know it's early days, but I honestly feel like all my Christmases have come at once.' His eyes became watery and so did Adriana's. The toddler climbed back onto his mother's lap and one of the older kids held out a high-five for Ricardo.

'Adriana, how did that make you feel, knowing what you had was what Ricardo actually wanted?' Brent asked.

'Honestly, I couldn't believe it at first, and then I remembered all the work I'd done with Dan and realised I *could* believe it, because I had changed my perspective on what I, as a woman and a mother, had to offer. And I knew I was damn lucky either way to have my kids, whether single or not. I knew that if anyone was to enter our lives, they would be damn lucky too.' She wiped at the corner of her eye.

'Damn! Damn!' Harry the toddler echoed, and the audience laughed.

'At the end of the day,' Adriana continued, 'it's about finding that special person who fits into your own little jigsaw puzzle of life. I didn't think anyone would want five kids, but someone did.'

Dan's heart soared. This is what he loved about his work, seeing people go from a negative belief to a positive one – from believing her life held baggage to believing it was a blessing. And then finding someone who saw that truth.

Ricardo held a hand to his heart. 'I always thought I'd want my own biological kids one day. But as soon as I met Adriana and her kids, I knew I wanted her and them. Now it just feels like it was always meant to be.' The couple smiled and leaned in for a kiss amongst the bundle of arms, legs, and faces moving about on the seat. Cheers rang through the crowd and they went to another commercial break.

Crew dashed onto the set, preparing the stage for the group finale surprise, while inside, something tried to surface in Dan's mind. He couldn't quite grasp it in the flurry of the moment, but something about Adriana and Ricardo really hit home, and he felt... envious? He thought he was simply pleased for them, but there was something more. Anyway, he didn't have time to think about it, he had to get himself ready for what was next, and he hoped he could give his final speech without getting too emotional about Harry as he'd decided to bring some of Harry's words of wisdom into his wrap up of the show.

Within minutes, the set decorators had brought in a bamboo gazebo onto the stage decorated with flowers and heart-shaped fairy lights and a sign saying 'Love Shack' tacked onto the front.

Dan and Brent stood in front of it as the director counted them in.

'Welcome back, love birds,' Brent said. 'Are you ready to celebrate our graduating *Love, Unfiltered* participants?' The crowd cheered. 'I said, ARE YOU READY?!' They cheered more, music began playing, and the crowd clapped along.

They called each person onto the stage to shake hands (or hug) in front of the love shack and receive a heart-shaped wooden plaque with their name on it signed by Dan and Brent. The camera zoomed into each person holding up their plaque in victory – everyone was a winner on this show, there were no eliminations, no voting out, no last person standing. They were all there celebrating whatever progress each had made, and knowing they'd inspired many around the country to go out and live the life they wanted. When all had been congratulated, the song 'Love Shack' by the B52s played and everyone danced around the stage, singing along. Dan glanced at the audience, most of whom were standing and dancing too, Katy included – a big smile on her face as she swayed and clapped and sang along. His heart lifted on seeing her enjoy herself. He flashed her a smile and caught her gaze momentarily, the connection catching his heart and not letting go.

When the song ended, the camera zoomed into Brent who was waving a hand around his sweating face. 'I haven't had so much fun on a television show as I've had here,' he said. 'And don't go anywhere, folks, after the break we have some special final words from our dating coach, Dan, as well as an opportunity for one lucky viewer out there to win his complete set of signed books plus a private coaching session to kickstart your dating goals. You don't wanna miss it! See you soon!'

Dan welcomed a cold drink of water, handed to him by one of the crew members. The dancing had helped loosen his nerves and lighten his mood, relaxing him in preparation for the final part of the show. He went off to the side for a moment to gather himself, and the make-up artist dabbed blotting paper on his face and applied some powder.

When he returned, the lights were dim and battery-operated candles glowed on the table between him and the love couch. The prompts he'd given the producer for his speech were ready on the monitor in his line of sight so he could speak to the audience. He sat and took a steadying breath, the audience settling down and quietness descending.

'For those of you out there looking for love,' he began, 'or just wanting to get out into the dating world and meet new people, I hope the show has given you some valuable tips. And I'm sure the stories of our participants have inspired you as they have me.' He glanced back at the group gathered around the Love Shack. 'You can download the top tips fact sheet and printable dating worksheets on the website, and also enter for your chance to win a set of my books and a coaching session.' He pointed his finger downwards where the producer said the website address would flash on the screen. A grumbling rose in his belly, not from hunger, but from need, an unmet need that he wasn't expecting to feel. Shaken by Harry's death it was as though his insides were raw and exposed and any slight emotion was heightened, especially after the euphoria of the final show. He gulped a lump of raw grief and blinked his eyes.

'Folks... Yesterday, someone close to me passed away,' he revealed, and the audience gasped. 'I knew it was coming, but still, as those of you who've been through similar will know, you're never quite ready for it. I didn't know if I could get through tonight, but I did. And I want that to be something you remember, that whatever is happening in your life, you can get through it. With the support of a team behind you,' he gestured to the cast and crew, 'and with family and friends by your side.' He gestured towards Katy in the audience who held a hand to her heart.

'My cousin Harry had been enjoying the show, and I'm sad he couldn't see the finale, but I'm glad I got to be with him and witness *his*.' Dan gulped again and his bottom lip trembled. He closed his eyes a moment. 'Before he died, he reminded me that we're all just apprentices in life. So forget those so-called mistakes. Don't try to be perfect, just live. Live big and love big. And don't wait for what you want to do. Do it now. Whether that's travelling the world, starting a new hobby or a business, asking someone out on a date, or declaring your love – do it.' Dan stood, the power of those words and an irresistible rising energy fuelling him up off his chair. 'We don't know how long any of us have in this world, but what I do know is that what we choose to do today will create our tomorrow.'

He walked a few steps back and forth along the stage, the camera following his every move. He remembered his time capsule and how back then he had been imagining his possible future with Katy, not knowing that she wouldn't respond the way he'd hoped, and so he hadn't written his full dream in the time capsule: living in a top-floor apartment with his wife and shiny things everywhere, but also having a family together. Somehow, after her rejection and then moving forward with his own life and relationships, that dream had never felt the same. Had never felt right anymore. But now, realisation unravelled a long-knotted clump within his chest, and he knew exactly what he really wanted and needed from this moment on.

'Over the years I've been asked many times, am I single? Am I in a relationship? What does Dan the Dating Coach want from *his* dating life?' He raised his hands in the air as though the answers were elusive. But then he clasped them together, the answers gathering between them. 'I was always happy to live in the moment, to go from one experience to another, and to never settle for anything less than what I really wanted. Which, to be honest, is why I'm still single. Because what I always wanted, I wasn't able to have.' He stole a glance towards Katy, who sat frozen but mesmerised.

'You see, I've been in love with my best friend my whole life. And although I've been blessed to meet some wonderful women and have a few special relationships, they never lasted, because no person ever made me feel the way she did.' He held his hand to his heart. 'Nothing ever felt as right as she did. And I know that I may never get what I truly want, and that's okay. But tonight, here in front of you all, teaching you to be vulnerable and authentic... how can I teach that if I'm not prepared to do the same?'

He raised his hands again and stepped to the front of the stage. 'I thought I never wanted to have kids. But seeing Adriana and Ricardo's story unfold made me realise something. It's not that I didn't want kids, it's that I only wanted *one* particular person's kids.'

He looked straight at Katy, whose mouth had dropped open. He noticed some of the audience following his gaze and settling onto the woman he loved, realising he was speaking directly to her. He chuckled and tipped his head back at his own delayed understanding of the situation. How he had messed things up. They'd shared a beautiful moment back at his cabin, almost had the opportunity of a lifetime, and he'd put his foot in his mouth by declaring what he thought he didn't want. But he now knew it wasn't the complete truth.

'Katy,' he said, stepping right to the edge of the stage. A few people gasped as a spotlight shone on her. 'I know it wasn't the right time all those years ago. And I thought our life plans were too different now, but these past few months being back in town, being with you, has made me fall in love with you all over again.'

A few 'woo-hoos' and 'ohhhs' sounded through the crowd. Katy's hand flew to her heart and her eyes glistened under the light.

'Forget what I said about not wanting a family. Because I do. But *only* if it's with you. And if not, I'll move on and I'll be okay, just like I was back then. But if you love me the way I love you, then right here, right now, let's do this,' he said with determined urgency. 'Let's not wait another moment. It doesn't matter about the logistics of our lives in different countries, we'll figure it out. I'll make changes. I would do, and *will* do, anything to be with the love of my life. You.'

He held his open palm out towards her and offered her a gentle hopeful smile. Her chin wobbled and her chest rose rapidly up and down; he didn't know if she was laughing or crying. But what happened next surprised and delighted him. A grin spread across her face and she bit her bottom lip like an excited child. She stepped out from her seat, into the aisle, and instead of walking down the steps towards him, she did a little sway, a shuffle, and then a joyful jig, just like the ones he would always do. He laughed and held out his arms in waiting. She approached the edge of the stage and he grasped her hands, helping her up, and locked eyes with her.

'As I said, I've always loved you, Dan,' she said. And this time she didn't walk away. This time, she nodded as though to say 'yes, in *that* way' and he let her take the next step, not with her feet, but with her lips, as she pressed them against his in the most long-awaited, delicious explosion of bliss he had ever experienced. He allowed his eyes to close and in that moment, they weren't on television, they didn't have lights shining brightly on them, they didn't have thousands of people watching them and cheering loudly – it was just them, together, at last.

CHAPTER TWENTY-NINE

On the drive home, Katy's phone chimed with multiple messages, from Jenna and Kane mostly, but she'd respond to them all later. Dan had put his phone on silent. No doubt everyone had seen Dan's declaration of love on TV and were absolutely beside themselves. But tonight was about him and her. They held hands at traffic lights, gazed into each other's eyes, and giggled occasionally at the unexpected turn of events as the long road took them home to Tarrin's Bay. Her heart tingled and fluttered and flip-flopped the whole way.

After parking at Trees of Life Resort, they huddled close together and scurried up the steps, through the archway, around the garden path, and up to Dan's cabin in the hope of not being seen or recognised. The air was damp and dark clouds hovered, a light storm beckoning. Not unlike the other time she had been there, as though the weather was an atmospheric backdrop to the intensity of their connection.

They went inside and Dan exhaled loudly. 'I don't know whether I'm relieved, excited, exhausted, or a combination of all three.'

Katy felt the same, but she'd add surprised to the mix. She

had been fully ready to say goodbye to him and any possibility of a life together, but now? This changed everything. She slipped her arms around his waist. 'Let's be all those things together.'

He smiled and allowed his arms to envelop her. 'Who would've thought our first proper kiss would be on live television and not at a bus stop, huh?'

Katy giggled. 'Never in a million years.'

'And to be fair,' he continued, 'I never even thought I'd be lucky enough to *have* a proper kiss, let alone on TV.'

'Do you want an encore, just to make sure it really happened?' She eyed him with a cheeky tilt of her head.

He raised his eyebrows suggestively and she leaned in close, taking his lips with hers. It felt like home; albeit a brand-new, expertly decorated, very stylish, and luxurious home. She couldn't believe it had taken them so long to reconnect, let alone to connect in this way. In the fear of losing their friendship they had become distant anyway and whatever happened from now on, she knew there was no turning back, but there was also no need to turn back, or to turn away from him ever again. He was, always had been, and always would be, her best friend *and* her soulmate.

Warmth spread through her cheeks and travelled down her spine as their kiss intensified, his hands moving across her back eagerly. They shuffled backwards, finding his bed, kicked off their shoes and laid down together, tangling in the sheets, his body melding with hers like they were one. Thunder broke through the night with a roar and rain pattered on the roof. Time became warped, and she had no idea how long they lay there kissing, touching, exploring, but when he lifted her top off, she paused, her breath catching.

'You okay?' he whispered.

She nodded. 'It's just... different. New, for us.'

'I know,' he replied, drawing an arc along her cheek. 'It's been a big night, eh?'

'Are *you* okay?' she asked. 'After everything that's happened.'

He glanced to the side as though considering his answer. 'I feel like both the luckiest guy alive and also very, very sad.'

Katy snuggled in next to him, laying her arm across his chest. 'We can just lay here together for now. No need to rush. We have all the time in the world.' She wanted to make every moment, every next step between them, *really* count.

He smiled at her. 'We're really doing this, huh? Giving it a go?'

'Absolutely. It's time. I promise, I won't mess you around and I'm not going to disappear. Even though I thought we'd be saying goodbye, after the last few weeks, I honestly don't want to imagine you not being in my life. I know there'll be some things to sort out, but we can do this, step by step.'

'I love you so much,' he whispered and kissed her gently on the cheek.

Katy's heart melted and a tear slipped from her eye. 'I love you too.' Her voice quivered and she smiled. 'I really do.'

Dan lay on his back, smiling and staring at the ceiling. 'I was thinking, maybe I should finally try to get in contact with Mum's sperm donor. It never felt right before. But if we have a child in the future, maybe it might be helpful for them to know a bit more about their ancestry?'

Katy laughed. 'How have you had time to think about that with everything that's happened in the last few hours?'

He gave a small shrug. 'Just the way my brain works, I guess, always considering the possibilities, best choices, and consequences.'

'If it's something you want to do, I'll support you. But only if it feels right. I'm perfectly happy for our future child to know only what you've always known. And they'll have two wonderful grandmothers to spoil them as well.' She gulped, knowing they wouldn't get to meet their other set of grandparents though.

'I'll think more about it later. Just putting it out there. And with Harry gone, and Robbie and Eliza's grief...' He exhaled roughly. 'I don't know, I guess it got me thinking more about the bond between family.'

'I understand.' She rested her arm on his chest as it rose and fell slowly. Moonlight stained the room with patches of silvery light, accentuating the shadows and defining his jaw. Light glistened at the corner of his eye and like hers, a tear formed and dropped. She wiped her thumb against his cheek, knowing that after all the excitement of the evening, the emotions and grief would start to rise up and demand to be heard. Safe in her arms, his heart would need tending and she wasn't going anywhere.

His lips trembled and she gave him time and space to feel, to express, to release, her own heart aching alongside his.

He wiped his tears and rolled onto his side to face her, wrapping his arms around her like a blanket. 'I don't know why him and not me. Life is so random.'

'It's not for us to understand,' she said, their noses touching. 'Only for us to accept life as it happens and do what we can with what we've got.'

'I'm going to miss him. And I wish he'd had more time. Wish I had spent more time *with* him.'

'You were there at the end and that's what matters now. It would've brought him so much comfort.'

'I'll cherish those last moments. We actually had a few laughs, it was nice.'

She smiled. 'That's what's important to remember. And I'll be here to help you get through it all as time goes by.'

'Katy, I should have been there for you more after your parents died. I'm sorry.' He propped himself up on his elbow.

'You called me several times to check on me, you *were* there, just in a different way. And you're here now. Let's be here for each other.'

'I'm here.' He trailed a hand through her hair and kissed her lips softly. 'Forever.' They settled back onto the bed, wrapped the sheets around them, and Katy allowed her eyes to close. A deep, rewarding exhalation cleansed her lungs, and as rain fell and their slow breaths synchronised, all fear, confusion, and doubt left her body completely.

CHAPTER THIRTY

'Only a few slices left of this fairy bread, guys, get in quick if you want some because I can tell you, it ain't gonna last long around me!' Jenna popped a triangle of multicoloured sprinkle-coated bread into her mouth, then held the tray up in the air, her multicoloured dress competing for attention.

Katy smiled as Lexi reached up and Jenna held it out of reach, then lowered it with a chuckle and let her daughter take a slice. 'If anyone tells my friends I spent New Year's Eve with my mum and her friends eating fairy bread, I'll never live it down,' Lexi said.

'Some years you've just gotta do something out of the ordinary,' Jenna said, sliding an arm around Lexi.

'I'm honoured that you wanted to spend this special occasion with us, Lex,' Katy said, glancing at the sparkling diamond on her left ring finger that she still wasn't quite used to yet.

'How could I not. You're like a celebrity now along with Dan, so in a way maybe everyone will be jealous that I got to spend New Year's Eve with you guys.' Lexi grinned, her metallic eyeshadow shimmering. 'Anyways, I'm really looking forward to what we've got planned *after* the countdown.' She rubbed her hands together. 'And of course, I'm so grateful for your investment into mine and Mum's new business. Honestly, we haven't been able to stop talking about all the ideas we have for setting up the shop. She's probably getting sick of having me around so much.'

'Never, my darling.' Jenna kissed Lexi's cheek. 'But yes, we are so grateful, and so excited, and can't wait for you two to get back from your trip and, well, help us out with the set-up after Kane's finished all the painting and fixtures?'

'Of course,' Katy replied. 'The clinic will miss you, but it's going to be the most successful shop in town, I just know it.'

Jenna took the fairy bread tray into the lounge where everyone else was mingling by the floor-to-ceiling windows, ready to take in the fireworks that would be lit over the harbour at midnight. Lexi and Katy followed, and Katy slid her arms around Dan from behind, kissing him on the back of his neck, while Kane popped two triangles of fairy bread into his mouth.

'Are you sure you're all packed for tomorrow night's flight?' Ellen asked. 'We certainly are, aren't we, love?'

Sandy nodded.

'Katy was packed a week ago,' Dan said, 'and as for me, I only have what I came with back in August, so not much to organise!'

'It's so great you're all going to the States together,' Dan's Aunt Eliza said with a smile that Katy hadn't fully seen until now, her son's death still raw and all-consuming.

'Agreed,' added Uncle Robbie. 'Make every moment together count.'

Dan gave him a high-five. 'You bet. Here I was thinking I'd be doing my US book tour all on my own, but now I'll have an entourage of lovely women joining me. Okay, so my mothers and my fiancée, but still. I feel pretty special.' He accepted a side hug from Ellen. 'Just don't embarrass me on stage with stories from my childhood, okay?' he asked, and Ellen held a hand to her heart as if to say 'would I do that?'

'We'll leave the celebrity stuff to you, darling,' said Sandy. 'But as for packing up your life and bringing it back here, it'll be all hands on deck.'

'Thanks, everyone,' Dan said, his eyes glistening. 'I don't know how I'd do all this without you. I'll miss my friends over there, but I'd miss you all more. Tarrin's Bay, get ready, this little kid is coming back to where it all began!'

Katy smiled widely, looking forward to the day he would move in with her after their wedding in April, which was to be held in the gardens at Trees of Life Resort. He was buying half her house and they would share everything from this moment on. Kane was not far off the release of his term deposit and had been saving much of his wage too, building up a painting and furniture upcycling portfolio, and getting ready to look for a place of his own to live with the help of his rehab team who were supporting him every step of the way. Katy knew he would stay close now; the city was the past for him, small town life was his future, his stability. Surrounded by loved ones and a community that wanted to see him succeed.

'Mate, don't forget to bring me back a souvenir,' said Kane. 'The cheesiest thing you can find.'

'You got it.' Dan smiled.

'And, sis, don't worry about the house, I won't have any wild parties while you're gone and I promise the painting will be all finished and dry before you get back.'

'So exciting! Can't wait.' Katy and Dan had moved things into the centre of each room and covered most of the furniture, except for the main bedroom and the living room, which Kane would sort out after the new year with the help of Robbie. Robbie had taken a liking to Kane, and Katy knew it was partly his way of coping with the loss of Harry, helping another young guy in need to make the most of the life he had. In a way, they needed each other and she was glad there was someone looking out for him while she'd be gone. Kane had come to the funeral with her and something had shifted in him afterwards. He'd been more committed to his rehab and counselling appointments, and had even upcycled and gifted a special side table for Robbie and Eliza to display Harry's mementos on.

'So, bright pink for the bedroom, huh, guys?' Kane asked cheekily.

Dan's eyes widened and Katy gave him a reassuring shake of her head. She had opted for a pale lemon for the bedroom, which Dan had approved of, as it was like subtle morning sunlight instead of sunflower yellow, and the living room would be a muted aubergine with accents of silvery grey instead of the white and grey it currently was. Kane's current room, which they hoped would be a future baby's room, was simply going to be repainted a warm white, leaving the options open for the future. And the other spare room, which was currently a general office-slash-storage room, would become Dan's office – not to see clients face to face, but to coach them long distance and teach his online courses and programs via Zoom, as well as write his next bestseller, which was to be called *Re-Connection*. His office was to have a rich deep red feature wall behind his desk that he was going to call the Wall of Love, hanging his degrees and diplomas and most importantly, their upcoming wedding photo, and anything else that symbolised love to him. He was now a full personal and professional embodiment of everything he taught, and Katy couldn't be prouder.

Katy turned on the television to get ready for the countdown to the new year, the last singing act wrapping things up. They each picked up a glass from the dining table, ready to toast and cheer; Eliza had made alcohol-free fruit punch and they were drinking it out of wine glasses. They stood staring out at the ocean, moonlight casting shimmers across its surface, and there was a faint hum from the crowd who had gathered at the harbour. They could have gone down there to join in, but Katy was glad for a more intimate celebration with those she loved. The night had doubled as their engagement party, with Dan having proposed on Christmas Day at his parents' house. He jokingly said later that he'd thought of doing it on live television but figured they'd had enough of the limelight and had opted instead for 'Can you pass the gravy, please, and also, will you marry me?' She did not pass the gravy to him but did respond to his second question.

'Everyone ready to make their wish for the new year?' Jenna asked.

Lexi nodded, as did Kane, but Katy didn't have a wish. She had a purpose: Begin her new life with the man she loved and take steps to start a family, whether it would happen naturally or whether she would need her frozen eggs. She and Dan had decided to wait until about six months after the wedding to give themselves time to settle into their new life and home together, to find their stability, their foundation, before taking the next step. And she was looking forward to every part of the journey.

'It's time!' Kane called out. 'New year, here we come!'

'Ten, nine, eight, seven,' TV host Brent Calder said; his charming girlfriend by his side, having scored a new job in television along with him.

They all joined in to finish the countdown: 'Six, five, four, three, two... one! Happy New Year!' everyone said at the same time, cheering and sipping their drinks, hugging and kissing cheeks, laughing and smiling. Katy accepted a kiss from Dan as he mouthed 'I love you' and she mouthed 'I love you more'. Eliza and Robbie stood arm in arm gazing out at the ocean, holding up their glasses as though to Harry in the distance. Katy did the same, and the others followed; nine sparkling glasses reaching out to the flashing lights in the sky, toasting a life once lived and lives yet to live.

'To the future,' Jenna said.

'To the future,' they all chorused, then sipped their drinks and watched the light show unfold, partly outside and partly on the television screen; the Sydney Harbour Bridge showing all its glory.

When darkness and quiet descended, they placed their drinks down and Dan picked up a bag from under the coffee table. 'Did everyone bring their special items?'

They all nodded. He opened the bag and partly withdrew Harry's letter, as though to check it was still there. 'Shall we go?' His eyes sparkled as much as the fireworks.

'I'm ready if you are,' Katy said, excited for what they were doing.

Lexi pulled out a cylinder from her bag. 'I've got my letter to the future and an engraved pendant I made in jewellery class.'

'And I've got the adult version of our childhood funny photo,' Kane said. They had Jenna take a photo recently of the three of them in the same spot and with the same funny faces as the photo from when they were four or five years old. They'd also printed it with the original alongside it, and given it to Dan's parents in a frame as a Christmas present.

'And I've got the biscuit tin!' said Eliza, scurrying over to the side table where they'd left a big box.

'Now, if we're not alive to open the time capsule when you two love birds are sixty-five,' said Ellen, 'promise us you'll do what the letter says, yeah?'

'Whatever you say, Mum,' Dan replied. 'Though if it's skateboarding, I really don't know if my body will be able to handle it at that age.' He nudged Katy.

'Hey, speak for yourself. I'm going to skateboard *to* the time capsule to open it when I'm sixty-five.' She nudged him back.

'I wouldn't be surprised,' he said, and Katy's heart warmed. She couldn't wait to teach her own child or children how to skate, among other things. Her heart buzzed with excitement for the opportunities that lay ahead.

'Let's go!' Dan said, grabbing car keys and sorting out who would go in whose car. They would be burying it in the exact same spot as the one they'd buried as teenagers, only this time with more memories, more mementos, and more love. And Katy just knew that when the time came for them to unearth it again, it would not only be Dan and hopefully some of the others by her side, but their future child or children, all grown up, and she would tell them about this night, where they had planted their dreams together and love had reunited them – finally.

THE END

ACKNOWLEDGEMENTS

Thank you to my loyal readers for continuing with the Tarrin's Bay series, I hope you fall in love with Katy and Dan and the cast of secondary characters who've become like family to me as I write. If you're a new reader, I thank you too for choosing this book, and I hope it inspires you to return to Tarrin's Bay through the other books in the series.

To my editor, Abbie Rutherford, thank you for your thorough and helpful editing to help bring out the best in this book, and to Tara and the proofreading team for your attention to detail. Thanks also to Betsy, Fred, and the amazing Bloodhound Books team for supporting my work and this series.

A special mention to dating coach Matthew Hussey who many years ago inspired the character of Dan Dexter for this book, which I finally got to write! And to my partner, Zeynel, who inspires a little of each of my male characters, and sometimes gives me plot suggestions which although very interesting, I don't usually use!

And to my family, friends, and supporters of my writing life and books, thank you.

ABOUT THE AUTHOR

Juliet Madison is a bestselling and award-nominated author of books with humour, heart, and serendipity. Writing both fiction and self-help, she is also an artist and colouring book illustrator, and an intuitive life coach who loves creating online courses for writers and those wanting to live an empowered life.

With her background as a naturopath and a dancer, Juliet is passionate about living a healthy and positive life. She likes to combine her love of words, art, and self-empowerment to create books that entertain and inspire readers to find the magic in everyday life.

Juliet lives on the picturesque south coast of NSW, Australia, where she spends as much time as possible dreaming up new stories, following her passions, being with her family, and as little time as possible doing housework.

You can find out more about Juliet, her books, and her courses at http://www.julietmadison.com and connect with her on social media at Facebook http://www.facebook.com/julietmadisonauthor and Instagram http://www.instagram.com/julietmadisonauthorartist

A NOTE FROM THE PUBLISHER

Thank you for reading this book. If you enjoyed it please do consider leaving a review on Amazon to help others find it too.

We hate typos. All of our books have been rigorously edited and proofread, but sometimes mistakes do slip through. If you have spotted a typo, please do let us know and we can get it amended within hours.

info@bloodhoundbooks.com

www.ingramcontent.com/pod-product-compliance
Lightning Source LLC
Chambersburg PA
CBHW050608190726
48283CB00007B/2334